RAKES OF THE CARIBBEAN

Sun, sand and sizzling seduction

Notorious rogues Ren Dryden and Kitt Sherard used to cut a swathe through the *ton*, but they were too wild to be satisfied with London seasons and prim debutantes.

Now they've ventured to the sultry Caribbean to seek their fortunes…and women strong enough to tame them!

Ren meets his match in spirited Emma Ward. Relish their seductive battle of wits in PLAYING THE RAKE'S GAME Available January 2015

Kitt has never met a woman as unconventional as Bryn Rutherford. Enjoy their scorching chemistry in BREAKING THE RAKE'S RULES Available February 2015

And look out for the Mills & Boon® Historical *Undone!* eBook CRAVING THE RAKE'S TOUCH Already available

You won't want to miss this sizzling new series from Bronwyn Scott!

AUTHOR NOTE

I hope you enjoy the new locale for this mini-series: the sunny Caribbean! There was plenty of British activity in the Caribbean not just in the eighteenth century, when Britain tamed the waters against piracy, but in the nineteenth century too.

Ren's story is set against the backdrop of Barbados entering into its era of emancipation. His story comes right after the abolition of slavery—which had some significant anticipated *and* unanticipated repercussions.

One of the big issues which *was* anticipated dealt with wages and labour. Would it ruin the plantations' abilities to make a profit if labourers had to be paid? To offset this, the British parliament gave the planters what we might today call a 'financial incentive package'. They also set up the apprentice system. One historian notes that the system was meant to instruct newly freed slaves in the management of wages while helping planters access a 'stable labour force'. Needless to say what worked well in theory was soon abused by the planters, who were bemoaning the loss of their power.

Another concern was political: the Plantocracy feared that freed slaves would want to vote and, of course, those votes would outnumber the white vote. And the final, perhaps somewhat unlooked-for consequence of emancipation was the finite availability of land. Freed slaves who wanted to be landowners and farm their own land simply didn't have access to it. On an island, land is finite.

This is the scenario Ren Dryden enters when his story opens. He thinks a plantation in the Caribbean will be the answer to his family's own financial problems, only to realise he's inherited far more than he bargained for. I hope you enjoy Ren's story, and learning a little about the context in which it is set.

PLAYING THE RAKE'S GAME

Bronwyn Scott

Published in Great Britain 2015
by Mills & Boon, an imprint of Harlequin (UK) Limited,
Eton House, 18-24 Paradise Road, Richmond, Surrey, TW9 1SR

© 2015 Nikki Poppen

ISBN: 978-0-263-24755-8

Harlequin (UK) Limited's policy is to use papers that are natural,
renewable and recyclable products and made from wood grown in
sustainable forests. The logging and manufacturing processes conform
to the legal environmental regulations of the country of origin.

Printed and bound in
by CPI, Barcelona

Bronwyn Scott is a communications instructor at Pierce College in the United States, and is the proud mother of three wonderful children (one boy and two girls). When she's not teaching or writing she enjoys playing the piano, travelling—especially to Florence, Italy—and studying history and foreign languages.

Readers can stay in touch on Bronwyn's website, www.bronwynnscott.com, or at her blog, www.bronwynswriting.blogspot.com—she loves to hear from readers.

For my awesome staff on the Disney Fantasy:
Gabriella and Nicolas, who kept us fed,
and Puhl, who had to clean my kid's stateroom
every day and still greeted me happily every morning.

Chapter One

∽∾∽∾∽∾∽

Bridgetown, Barbados—early May, 1835

Ren Dryden believed two things about the nature of men: first, a wise man didn't run from his troubles and, second, only a foolish man ran from his opportunities. Ren considered himself in league with the former, which was why he'd spent two weeks aboard a mail packet aptly named the *Fury*, braving the Atlantic and sailing away from all he knew. In truth, a large part of himself had revelled in the danger of the adventure; revelled in pitting his strength against the sea. He even revelled in the unknown challenges that lay before him on land. At last, he could take action.

Ren levered himself out of the bumboat that had rowed him ashore, tossed the boatman a coin and stood on the Bridgetown dock, feeling a kindred spirit with the bustle of commerce about him. His blood hummed with the excitement of it. Ah, the Caribbean! Land of rum and risk.

Ren surveyed the activity with an appreciative eye, taking in the vibrant colours of people, of fruits, sky and sea, the scents of citrus and sweat, the feel of heat against his face. It was a veritable feast for the senses and he engaged the feast wholeheartedly. Life began today, more specifically *his* life, a life of his choosing and his making, not a life predestined for him based on the caprices of earlier generations of Drydens.

There were plenty of people in London who would say he was avoiding his problems. The list was long and distinguished, ranging from his family, who'd found the 'perfect solution' to their little problem of 'dynastic debt' in the form of a weak-eyed, sallow-cheeked heiress from York, to the creditors who hounded him through the grey streets of London, even being so bold as to lie in wait for him outside his exclusive clubs.

There were also plenty of men of his acquaintance who would have bowed to the inevitable, married the heiress, paid the debt and spent their lives blindly acquiring new debt until *their* sons had to make the same sacrifices a generation later. He had promised himself years ago when he'd come of age he would not be a slave to the past.

Ren found it rather frightening that not only would those men have bowed to the inevitable, but they would have *preferred* to bow instead of breaking free. After all, there was a certain comfort to be found in the known. He understood the penchant for the familiar and he pitied the men who craved it. Ren had never counted himself among that number.

On the outside, perhaps he resembled his peers in clothing, clubs and mannerisms, but inside, he'd always been different, always railed against the things and people that kept him leashed, his hopes restrained by the narrow parameters that defined a gentleman's potential.

All that railing had paid off, all that hope was now fulfilled. He was here and he'd broken free, although it came with a price, as freedom always did. If he failed in this venture, his family failed with him; his mother, who had wilted after his father's death; his two sisters, one waiting for a debut, the other waiting to wed; and thirteen-year-old Teddy who would be the earl of debt-ridden lands should Ren not return.

Ren's hand curled tightly around the valise he'd brought with him from the boat. He'd not trusted it to remain with his trunks to be brought ashore separately. His future was in the valise: the letter of introduction and a copy of Cousin Merrimore's will bequeathing him fifty-one per cent interest in a sugar plantation—*majority interest* in a profitable business.

There would be shareholders to deal with, but technically the entire place was his to control. He would not fail. As unseemly as it was for a gentleman of his birth, he'd made it a point to know the dynamics of trade—he'd quietly made investments on the Exchange, invested in an occasional cargo. He'd listened to discussions in Parliament and taken an active interest in political circles when he was in London.

As a result, he did not come to Barbados without at least some knowledge of Britain's colonial gem. Nor did he come without his opinions. He would make an honest profit and he would pay an honest wage to see it done. He would not raise his family up by abusing the sweat of other men. Even a desperate man had ethics.

'Ahoy there, Dryden, is that you?' A tall, bronzed man with sun-bleached hair cut through the crowd, taking Ren by momentary surprise. Ren might not have recognised the man, but he'd know the voice of his one-time best friend anywhere in the world, case in point. London would have an apoplexy if it could see its one-time ballroom favourite now. The Caribbean had bleached his dark-blond hair and tanned his pale skin.

'Kitt Sherard!' Ren felt his face break into wide grin. 'I wasn't sure if you'd make it.' He'd sent a letter on the mail packet preceding him telling Kitt of his arrival, but there'd been no chance to receive a response.

'Of course I made it. I wouldn't leave you stranded at the docks.' Kitt pulled him into a strong embrace. 'What has it been, Ren? Five years?'

'Five *long* years. Look at you, Kitt. Barbados agrees with you,' Ren exclaimed. He couldn't get over the completeness of his friend's transformation. Kitt had always been wild at heart, but now the wildness had entirely taken over. His hair was not only bleached, but long, and his dress more closely resembled the loose clothing of those swarming the docks than the traditional breeches and coats Ren had on. They looked more comfortable too. But the eyes were the same: a sharp, shrewd sea-blue. It was Kitt all right and it felt good to see a friendly face.

'It does indeed.' Kitt laughed as a pretty, coffee-skinned fruit seller approached, swinging her hips.

'Fresh fruit, me loves, de best on de island. Is this handsome fellow a friend of yours, Mr Kitt?' She wafted a firm round orange under Ren's nose, teasing him with its citrusy scent. The persuasion was effective. After two weeks without anything resembling 'fresh', the orange was a temptation nonpareil. She might as well have been Eve with the apple, and if Eve had been wearing a scoop-necked blouse like this island beauty, Ren completely understood why Adam had eaten it.

'He's come all the way from London, Liddie. You be good to him.' Kitt gave her two coins and took the fruit, tossing it to Ren.

'Are all your friends this handsome?' Liddie flirted with Ren, the loose neck of her blouse gaping open to offer a quick glimpse of firm, round fruit of a more erotic sort. She flashed him an inviting smile.

Kitt feigned wounded pride, a hand on his heart. 'More handsome than me, Liddie?'

Liddie laughed. 'You're too much for a poor girl like me, Mr Kitt. Are you going to introduce me?'

'Liddie, this is Ren Dryden, Albert Merrimore's cousin. He's going to be taking over Sugarland plantation.'

Ren thought he saw Liddie take the slightest step backwards. Her next words confirmed it wasn't his imagination. 'There's trouble out there.' She shot a warning glance at Kitt. 'You better tell him about the spirits and the witch woman, Mr Kitt.' She fumbled with a string about her neck and pulled a necklace over her head. A chunk of black coral hung from a strip of leather. She handed it to Ren. 'You're going to need protection. This will keep the bad spirits away.'

Ren took the charm, unsure of what to say. The idea there was trouble at his plantation was more than a little unsettling. That the trouble involved spirits and a witch woman seemed to portend the ominous. He looked a hasty question at Kitt, who merely shrugged at the mention.

'My friend and I are good Anglicans, Liddie. We don't believe in spirits.' Kitt dismissed Liddie's worries with an easy smile

Good Anglicans? Ren fought back a laugh at the notion. He didn't think Kitt had ever been a good anything except a good amount of trouble. Decent simply wasn't in Sherard's vocabulary.

Ren tucked the amulet inside his shirt and Kitt

went back to flirting with Liddie. 'I am a bit jealous though, Liddie. What about me? Don't I get an amulet, too, just in case?'

Liddie's face broke into a pretty smile. 'Mr Kitt, I pity the poor spirits that mess with you, Anglican or not.' It was a good note to leave on. Liddie sauntered away, hips swaying.

'She likes you.' Kitt elbowed Ren. 'Do you want me to arrange something?'

'No. I think women will need to wait until I can get my bearings at the plantation.' Ren laughed. 'You're the same old Kitt Sherard, women falling all over you wherever you go.'

Kitt seemed to sober at that. 'Well, not quite the same, I hope. I didn't come here to be what I was in London and I'm guessing neither did you.'

Ren nodded in understanding. For them both, Barbados was a place for new lives. Kitt had left London five years ago rather suddenly and without warning. He'd shown up one night on Ren's doorstep needing sanctuary but unable to explain. He'd left the next day, slinking out of town towards the ports, leaving everything behind including his real name. Ren had been the last to see him. After that, Kitt had cut all ties with the exception of random letter to him and the third of their trio, Benedict DeBreed.

Ren had no idea what Kitt had been up to since then. A silence had sprung up between them, a reminder of the profundity of their choices. Ren steered the conversation back to the practical. 'Were you able to bring a wagon?' It was easier not to think about the larger scope of his decisions, but to take it all step by step. The next step was to get out to the plantation.

'It's right over here. I think they've just brought your trunks ashore.' Kitt gestured to the returning bumboat. Ren's questions had to wait while they loaded his trunks, but his nerves were rising. What had Cousin Merrimore done? What was wrong at Sugarland? He'd expected a bit of unease. There'd been four months between his cousin's passing and his arrival, but surely there was enough sense in the group of investors to manage things in the short term.

In fact, he'd assumed there would be very little to handle. Most plantation owners were absentee landlords who left the running of the estate to an overseer while they lived in England. But if that was the case, none of them had contacted him. It would have been simple enough to meet if they had been in England.

Since no one had come forward, Ren was starting to believe the landlords were in residence on the island. Even so, with or without his cousin's presence or the presence of any other shareholders, the overseer would keep the plantation going just as he always had. Ren ran a finger beneath his collar, the heat starting to make his garments uncomfortable. He shot an envied glance Kitt's direction.

'Take off the damn coats, Ren. We aren't in England any more.' Kitt laughed at his discomfort. 'Even the heat's different here, but you'll learn how to cope. You'll get used to it.' He winked. 'If you're anything like me, you'll even like it.'

Ren grinned and shrugged out of his jacket. 'I love the heat and I don't think London ever had a sky this blue. This is paradise.' Just minutes off the boat and he could see the allure of this place. Everything was different: the sky, the heat, the fruit, the people.

The talk of spirits and witches didn't bother him so much as did the fact that they were connected to his property. He'd risked everything to come here. Hell, he'd left the earldom unprotected, having turned the day-to-day affairs entirely over to his steward and solicitors. He could trust them, of course, and if he was wrong on that account he'd left his close friend, Benedict

DeBreed, in charge to ensure he wasn't. He had protections in place, but still, if he'd been Trojan Horsed…well, the consequences didn't bear thinking about. He'd find a way to make it work.

Ren climbed up on to the wagon and squeezed in next to Kitt. He decided to ease into the conversation. 'Thanks again for coming to get me.'

'I'm glad to do it, although I'm sure someone from the plantation would have been happy to come out.' Kitt chirped to the horse and caught his eye when Ren said nothing. 'They do know you're coming, don't they?' He paused, interpreting the silence correctly. 'Oh, hell, they don't know.'

'Not exactly,' Ren said slowly. 'I wasn't sure there would be a "they" out there. I assumed Cousin Merrimore was the only one in residence.' By the time he'd rethought that hypothesis it had been too late to send a letter.

Kitt shifted on the seat next to him and Ren's sense of foreboding grew. 'Well, out with it, Kitt. Tell me what's wrong at Sugarland. Are there really witches and spirits?' Ren absently fingered the chunk of coral beneath his shirt. Bridgetown was behind them now and there was an overwhelming sense of isolation knowing that they'd just left the only town on the island behind. For a city man used to having entertainments, food and anything else he needed at his fingertips or at least within a few streets, it was a daunting prospect indeed, a reminder of the enormity of what he'd chosen to do. He would be relying on himself and himself alone. It would be a true test of his strength and knowledge.

Kitt shook his head. 'It's a bad business out there—of course, I don't know the half of it. I'm gone most weeks.' Ren didn't believe that for a moment. Kitt was the sort who knew everyone and knew everything.

'You don't have to sugar-coat anything for me,' Ren said sternly. 'I want to know what I'm up against.' Had he taken on more than he could manage? Assumptions were dangerous things and he'd made a few about Cousin Merrimore's property, but he'd had no choice. It was either marry the heiress or gamble on the inheritance.

Kitt gave another of his shrugs. 'It's the apprenticeship programme. It's a great source of controversy in the parish.'

Ren nodded. 'I am familiar with it.' Slavery in the British Caribbean had been abolished a couple of years ago. It had been replaced with the notion of apprenticeship. The idea was decent in theory: pay the former slaves who were willing to work the land they'd once worked for free. In practice, the situation was not far different than slavery.

Kitt went on. 'Finding enough labour has been difficult. The plantation owners feel they're losing too much money so they work the labourers to the bone, to death actually. As you can imagine, no one wants to work for those wages. Death doesn't really recommend itself.'

Great, his fields were rotting and there was no one to hire. But Kitt's next words riveted his attention. 'Except at Sugarland and that's what has all the neighbours angry.'

Ren let the thought settle. He tried to dissect the comment and couldn't make sense of it. 'You'll have to explain, I'm afraid.'

Kitt did. 'The plantation owners refuse to use the apprentice system fairly, except Sugarland. Anyone who wants field work, wants to work there where they are assured of a wage and safe conditions. As a result, Sugarland is the only place producing a significant profit right now.' That was good news. Ren breathed a little easier, but just for a moment. Kitt wasn't done.

'Someone put it about a few months ago, at the time of your cousin's death, that spirits were luring workers to Sugarland, that the woman running the place was in league with practitioners of black magic and that's why the plantation was successful. Since then, the rumours have multiplied: she's cursed the neighbouring crops, she's put a growing spell on her own.'

'Wait. Hold on.' Ren grasped the information one idea at a time. Spells? Witchcraft? A woman?

Kitt took pity on him, misunderstanding the source of his agitation. 'I know, the whole concept of black magic takes a bit of getting used to. The islands are full of it. The islands have their own names for it: voodoo, obeah. It's from Africa. It's full of superstitions and ghosts and spells.'

Ren thought of the chunk of coral beneath his shirt. Black magic was the least of his concerns. 'No, it's not that. Back up to the part about a woman. There's a *woman* at the plantation?' Cousin Merrimore's will hadn't said a thing about anyone, certainly not a woman.

Kitt nodded and said with the most seriousness Ren had ever heard him use. 'Her name is Emma Ward.'

A pit opened in his stomach and Ren knew with gut-clenching clarity there was no 'they'. There was no absentee landlord syndicate to write monthly updates to. There was only a 'she'. The other forty-nine per cent belonged to a crazy woman rumoured to be casting spells on her neighbours' crops.

Ren was starting to rethink the merits of surprise, especially when those merits were reversed. It was one thing to *be* the surprise as he'd planned to be. It was another to be the one who was surprised. Ren definitely preferred the former. A more cautious man would have waited in town until he could have notified the plantation. But he'd never been one to wait and he'd never been one to shy away from a challenge. He made a habit of meeting those head on, whether those challenges were notorious females or not.

Ren leaned back on the wagon seat, letting the sun bathe his face. Ah, the Caribbean. Land of rum, risk and apparently a little insanity, too.

Chapter Two

Waiting was driving her insane! Emma Ward took yet another long look at the clock on the corner of her desk. He should be here by now, Mr Fifty-One Per Cent. *If* he was coming. Emma idly shuffled the papers in front of her. They could have been written in Arabic for all she'd been able to focus on them today. Emma left the desk and began to pace, a far better use of her energies than staring at a paper.

Was she technically even waiting? Waiting assumed he was actually coming. What she really wanted to know was at what point could she *stop* waiting and be confident in the knowledge that he *wasn't* coming at all?

Her nerves were a wreck and they had been every mail day since Albert Merrimore's death. That meant she'd gone through this uncertainty for four months. Was this the day she got the letter saying Merrimore's cousin was coming? Or worse, would it be the day he actually showed up? Anything could happen. His ship could have been delayed, *he* could have been personally delayed and that was if he'd decided to come at all. It was just as likely he could have rethought the notion of coming halfway around the world simply to see his property when his profits didn't depend on whether he saw the place or not. Most gentlemen wouldn't bestir themselves if it wasn't required, especially since there was some risk involved. Who was she fooling? Not *some* risk. A *lot* of risk, starting with an ocean voyage. Ships went down even in the modern age of steam.

Emma scolded herself for such a morbid thought. It wasn't that she wished he was dead, merely marooned, her conscience clarified. It was possible his ship could founder and he could float to safety on an overturned table. For four months, she'd got her wish. How much longer before she could safely assume her wish had been granted on a more permanent basis? She didn't wish Mr Fifty-One Per Cent dead, she just wished he weren't here.

She had to stop calling him that. He had a name. It had been in the will and a terribly stuffy name at that. *Renford Dryden*. An old man's name. But of course, what sort of relations did dear old Merry have if not old ones? Merry had been in his late eighties. A cousin couldn't be expected to be much younger. Even twenty years younger would put him in his sixties. Which perplexed her further—why a man of advanced years would want to make such a dangerous trip that would only serve to disrupt both of their lives? Perhaps he wouldn't come at all. Perhaps she would be safe on that front at least.

Emma wanted nothing more than to grow her sugar cane in peace and independence without the interference of men. After everything she'd been through, it wasn't too much to ask. Men had never gone well for her, starting with her father and ending with a debacle of a marriage. The only man who'd done well by her had been old Merry and now she had his relative to contend with. She couldn't stop him from coming, but she didn't have to make it easy should that be his choice.

She'd already begun the campaign. She'd not written to him when she could have, explaining the situation when the solicitor had sent word to England. She'd feared a letter would be viewed as a personal invitation, as encouragement to come when that was the last thing she wanted. She hadn't sent the wagon into town on mail day these past months to see if anyone had arrived.

Guilt began to gnaw again. If he had arrived on this packet, she'd left an ageing man to fend for himself in the foreign heat. It was poorly done of her. She should have sent someone into town just to check. That was her conscience talking. She should tell Samuel to get the wagon ready and go to enquire about the mail. Emma glanced again at the clock, the knot in her stomach starting to ease. It was getting late. The threat had almost passed for another two weeks. If he was coming, he would be here by...

'Miss! Miss!' Hattie, one of the downstairs maids, rushed into the office, hardly attempting any pretence of decorum in her excitement. 'It's him, it's our Mr Dryden! I'm sure of it. He is coming and that rascal Mr Kitt is with him!'

'Kitt Sherard? Are you certain?' What would the local scoundrel of a rum runner have to do with a man in his dotage? Sherard was the last person she'd want Renford Dryden to meet. Emma stopped before the mirror hung over the side table to check her appearance. Sherard was only one step above a pirate. 'I hope he hasn't got our guest drunk already.' Emma muttered, tucking up a few errant stands of hair.

She wanted to make a good impression on all accounts. She had plans for that good impression and Kitt Sherard did not qualify as part of it. Emma was counting on that impression to convince Mr Dryden to sell his interest to her or, at the very least, to sail back to England secure in the knowledge that his money was in good hands, which was mostly true, she was just a bit short on funds right now. The harvest would change that.

She would gladly trade some profits for independence. The autonomy of the last four months had given her a taste of what it would be like to be on her own, to be free. She was loath to relinquish even an iota of that liberty or responsibility.

'Do I look all right, Hattie?' Emma smoothed the skirts of her aquamarine gown, one of her favourites. 'Are they out front?'

'They're pulling up just now, miss. You look fine.' Hattie gave her a saucy wink. 'After two weeks on a ship, I think anything would look fine to a gent like him.'

Emma gave a dry chuckle. 'I'm not sure that's a compliment, Hattie.' Satisfied with her appearance, Emma set out to meet Dryden with a brisk step as if her presence could undo any damage that had already been done. The sooner Dryden was free of Sherard, the better.

She was a little breathless in her eagerness and anxiety by the time she reached the covered porch. This was the moment she both feared and welcomed. At last, the future could begin now that Dryden was here. Perhaps, she thought optimistically, that future would be better than the limbo she'd been living in. If she could manage an entire plantation, she could certainly manage one old man.

The wagon pulled to a halt in front of the steps and she saw the flaw in her hypothesis immediately. Renford Dryden wasn't an old man, not even a middle-aged one, but an astonishingly handsome young one. The man who jumped down from the wagon seat was certainly able bodied if those wide shoulders and long legs were anything to go on. So much for trying to caution him about the rigours of island life. He certainly looked as if he was up for it and much more.

Emma shot Hattie a sharp look that said: *Why didn't you tell me?* But she supposed Hattie had warned her in her own way. She should have

known something was amiss the moment Kitt
Sherard's name entered the conversation. Now
she saw what it was. Up close, Renford Dryden
was six feet plus of muscle topped with thick
honey-blond hair and sharp blue eyes set above
a strong, straight nose. He mounted the steps,
oozing confidence and growing taller with each
step he took. Still, he was a man and men could
be managed, *must* be managed.

Emma took a deep breath. She needed to
begin as she meant to go on. Men who weren't
managed had run roughshod over her life to
date and she was done with them. Emma held
out her hand to greet him as if he was precisely
what she'd expected. 'Welcome to Sugarland, Mr
Dryden. We are so glad to see you.' She hoped
he couldn't hear the lie.

His grip was firm as his hand curled around
hers, sending a jolt of awareness through her.
His eyes riveted on her, making her aware of the
male presence of him. Never had a simple hand-
clasp seemed so intimate. 'I am so very glad to
be here, Miss Ward.' Was that a touch of irony
she heard? Did he suspect she hadn't been entirely truthful?

There was no chance to verify the impression. In the next moment she was very nearly

lost. Renford Dryden smiled, dimple and all. It was a most wicked smile that invited the mind to imagine all sorts of pleasantly sinful things without even meaning to. He was that type of man, all charisma. But there was more to him than a charming facade. There was self-assurance and intelligence, too. Those blue eyes were assessing eyes, eyes that took nothing at face value and when they looked at her, they were shrewd and wary. It occurred to her that in these initial moments they were both doing the same thing: measuring the opponent, selecting and discarding strategies.

It didn't take much guesswork to divine what his strategy would be. It was the strategy of all men when faced with a woman who had something they wanted. Emma stiffened her spine with a stern mental admonition to herself. She would not be wooed into giving up her independence. She had strategies of her own. It was time to teach Mr Dryden it wasn't easy to run a sugar-cane plantation, time to lead him to the conclusion that his best choice was to leave all this in her capable hands and go back to the life he knew.

She flicked her gaze down the length of him, taking in the cut of his clothes, the expense of the materials. Here was a man of quality, a man used to luxury. Perhaps she could use that against him. Luxuries here were hard won, something men of charisma and charm weren't used to. Those sorts usually didn't have to work too hard to get what they wanted, especially when they were endowed with a heavy dose of self-confidence like Mr Dryden. They just smiled. But smiles didn't harvest crops or pay the bills. Hard work was at the core of everything Sugarland had.

Emma gave him her hostess smile. 'I have lemonade waiting on the back veranda. We can sit and talk and become acquainted, Mr Dryden.' And he would learn how different they were and how he didn't have to be here to reap the benefits Sugarland had to offer.

'Call me Ren, please. No more of this Mr Dryden business,' he insisted, stepping aside as two servants came up the stairs with his trunks.

Emma looked past him to the wagon, using the disruption to ignore the request for informality. For now she would resist the temptation. First names were usually the first step in any seduction. 'Mr Sherard, would you care to join us?' Politeness required she ask. She hoped Sherard understood politeness also required he refused.

Sherard shook his head. 'No, thank you. I

leave tonight on business and there's much to be done before I sail. Now that the wagon's unloaded, I'll return to town.' He gave her a strong look that reminded her Sherard was a man with a well-warranted reputation for fierceness. 'I expect you'll take good care of my friend, Miss Ward.' He nodded to Dryden. 'Ren, I'll look in on you when I'm back in port.'

Great. The notorious Sherard was on a first-name basis with her guest and now felt he could use that familiarity as a reason to call regularly at her house. Her conscience prodded at her again. The bloody nuisance had been busy today. It probably served her right for stranding Dryden at the docks. She'd left him to his own devices and this was what she got.

Having the new partner befriend Sherard was not what she needed, considering the other rumours swirling about her. Never mind most people didn't believe the rumours wholesale about her, the mere presence of those rumours was enough to still cast a certain cloud on her reputation. It called attention to her, something no decently bred woman deliberately sought. Nor did Sherard's presence help her disposition towards her new house guest. Sherard already acted as if Dryden were in charge with his damnable fifty-one per cent, no matter that he technically was. *She* was the one who'd been here. She'd seen to the planting and nurturing of the crop. If Dryden had been a few days later he would have missed the harvest too. How dare he swoop in here, *unannounced*, at the last and claim any sort of credit for *her* labour.

Emma tamped down her roiling emotions and led her guest through the house to the back veranda. She liked that word, 'guest'. It was precisely how she should think of Dryden. It was a far nicer term than 'Mr Fifty-One Per Cent' and, better yet, guests were temporary. She would make sure of it.

He could stay forever! Ren let the lemonade slide down his throat, cool and wet. He didn't think anything had ever tasted as welcome, or any breeze had felt as pleasant. Things were definitely looking up. When Kitt had pulled up to Sugarland, Ren had been more than pleasantly surprised with the white-stucco manor house, threats of witches and magic receding. He'd felt an immediate sense of affinity for the place. This was somewhere he could belong, somewhere he could thrive.

Such an intuition was an odd sensation for

a man who prided himself on logic, yet Ren couldn't deny it was there. Possession, pure and primal, had hummed through his blood; *his*, *his*, *his*, it had sung. Then *she* had appeared at the top of the steps and his blood had hummed a more familiar tune of possession, a lustier tune. It was hard to mind being Trojan Horsed when it looked like Emma Ward. 'She doesn't *look* like a witch,' he'd murmured to Kitt.

'They never do.' Kitt had laughed as he leapt down from the wagon. 'Witches wouldn't be nearly as effective if they did.'

But Emma Ward did look like something else just as worrisome and perhaps more real, Ren thought as they sipped their lemonade. Trouble. She had a natural sensuality to her. It was there in the sway of her hips as she led him through the airy halls to the veranda, it was there in her dark hair, in the exotic, catlike tilt of her deep brown eyes. It emanated from her, raw and elemental; a sensuality that coaxed a man to overstep himself if he wasn't careful.

This woman was no virginal English rose. She was something much better and much worse. Maybe she was a witch, after all. He would have to reserve judgement. Ren raised his glass and stretched out an arm to clink his glass against hers. 'Here's to the future, Miss Ward.'

For someone who'd wanted to talk, she was awfully quiet, however. Perhaps he had misunderstood. He took the opportunity to learn a bit more about her. 'It is *Miss* Ward, isn't it?'

'Yes, Miss Ward is fine.' She supplied the bare basics of an answer and the briefest of smiles. Ren noted that smile didn't leave her mouth. Her eyes remained politely impassive. Perhaps her coolness was a result of his surprise arrival. She hadn't known he was coming and she was wary. A stranger had just arrived on her doorstep and announced his intention to live there.

'I am sure all of this comes as quite a shock…' Ren began congenially. He fully believed in the old adage that one caught more flies with sugar. It wouldn't do to put Miss Ward on the defensive without cause. 'It's a shock to me as well. Cousin Merrimore didn't mention anything about you in his papers and here we are, two strangers thrown together by circumstance.' He gave her a warm smile, the one he reserved for the *ton*'s stiff-necked matrons, the one that made them melt and relax their standards. It didn't work.

'In all fairness, Mr Dryden, I believe I have

the upper hand. I knew of you by name. Merry did mention you in the will quite specifically.'

Intriguing. Ren's critical mind couldn't overlook the self-incriminating evidence. She'd known of him. She could have contacted him, something his lack of details had prevented him from doing on his end. He could be forgiven for a surprise arrival having no information about who to contact in advance, but she'd known. She'd had the ability to send a letter with the copy of the will. She'd *chosen* not to.

Ren gave her a wry smile. What would she do if he confronted her? 'There is that, Miss Ward. You had my name. You were quite aware of my existence and yet you left me to find my own way here in my own time.' He would have to tread carefully here. It seemed Miss Ward was already on the defensive, a very interesting position for a woman. Given her circumstances, he would have thought she'd be quite glad to see him, to have him remove the burden of running the place alone. The past four months must have been daunting for a woman alone.

She flushed at having been called out. Good. She understood precisely what he was implying, a further sign Miss Ward was an astute opponent. 'It's nearly harvest season, Mr Dryden.

There's hardly time for someone to sit for hours at the docks waiting for a ship to come in when it might possibly not and even if it did, it might not carry what you're waiting for.'

Touché. She had him there. 'Even for a relative?' Ren probed. It was a shot in the dark, but he was curious to know how Emma Ward clung to the family tree. Undoubtedly she was more familiar with 'Merry' than he was. Where did that familiarity come from? Was she a lover? A mistress? Or merely a distant cousin like himself? Ren had met Cousin Merrimore, as *his* family called the old man, perhaps three times in his entire life, the last time being eight years ago when he'd finished his studies at Oxford.

Emma Ward gave a short laugh at the reference, but it was not warm. Ren had the distinct impression things were not getting off on the right foot. 'You and I are *not* family, Mr Dryden. Merry was my guardian for several years until I attained my majority. After that, he was my friend.' There was no help for him there. In his experience, 'friends' came in multiple varieties, bedfellows included. But if Merrimore had been her guardian, he could assume nothing untoward had followed.

'Ren, please,' he suggested again, making the

most of the opening the conversation provided. 'I should like for us to be friends as well.' If there was any naughty innuendo in his response, he would let her relationship with Merrimore be the measuring stick.

'*We* are business partners at present,' she replied firmly, moving the conversation away from the personal, although there were a host of questions he wanted to ask—how had a confirmed bachelor like his ancient cousin ended up as someone's guardian? Why hadn't she left the island? Surely Merrimore would have sent her to London when she came of age?

Those questions would have to wait until she liked him better. It was an unsettling, but not displeasing, discovery to make. In London he was accustomed to making a favourable first impression on women when he had to make one at all. Usually it was the other way around. Women sought to make a good impression on *him*. Not Emma Ward, however.

Then again, his title didn't precede him in Barbados. The York heiress had made it abundantly clear his antecedents were all she wanted. Her father would pay an outrageous sum for those antecedents to bed his daughter and give him a blue-blooded grandson. Ren had an aversion to being used as an aristocratic stud. A woman who didn't want him for his antecedents would be quite an adventure.

Ren grinned and set down his glass, ready to try out his theory. Emma Ward had been attempting to disconcert him from the first moment, now it was his turn. 'Miss Ward, I think you have not been entirely truthful with me.' He was gratified to see a flash of caution pass through her dark eyes.

'Whatever about, Mr Dryden?' she replied coolly.

'Contrary to your words earlier, you are *not* glad to see me. Since we've never met, I find that highly irregular.' It was not a gentleman's path he trod with that comment. But as she'd noted, *this* was business. More importantly, it was *his* business and quite a lot was at stake.

Miss Ward fixed him with the entirety of her dark gaze. 'I apologise if you find your reception lacking.'

'Really? I find that hard to believe when you don't sound the least bit penitent.' Ren pressed his advantage. If she meant to defy him, she would have to do it outright. Defiance he could deal with, it was open and honest. He would not tolerate passive aggression, not even from a pretty woman.

Her eyes flared with a dark flame, her mouth started to form a cutting rejoinder that never got past her lips. *Boom!* The air around them reverberated with sound that shook the windows and rattled the glasses on the table. Emma shrieked, bolting out of her chair, her eyes rapidly scanning the horizon for signs of the explosion.

Ren saw it first, his stomach clenching at the sight of uncontained flame. 'Over there!' He pointed in the distance to the telltale stream of smoke, clamping down on the wave of panic that threatened.

Emma had no such compunction for restraint. 'Oh goodness, no, not the home farm!' She pushed past him, racing down the steps, calling for her horse.

Ren bellowed behind her, 'Forget the saddles, there's no time!' But no one was listening. The stable was in chaos, people running everywhere trying to calm the horses after the explosion. Ren managed to pull a strong-looking horse out of a stall. 'Emma, give me your foot!' Emma leapt into his cupped hand and vaulted up on the horse's back. Ren swung up behind and grabbed the reins, kicking the horse into a canter as they sped out of the barnyard.

In other circumstances he might have taken a moment to appreciate the press of female flesh against him, the breasts that heaved against his arm where it crossed her and the excellent horse-flesh beneath him. As it was, all he could focus on was the explosion. He'd been here a handful of hours and his fifty-one per cent was already on fire.

Chapter Three

The home farm was all disorder and confusion when they arrived. Ren leapt off the horse, hauling Emma down behind him, letting his senses take in the scene. Smoke was everywhere, creating the illusion or the reality that the fire was worse than it initially appeared, It was hard to say which it was in the haze. Panicked workers raced about without any true direction futilely attempting to fight the flames. A lesser man might have panicked along with them, but Ren's instincts for command took over.

Ren grabbed the first man who ran past him. 'You, get a bucket brigade going.' He shoved the man towards the rain barrel and started funnelling people that direction, calling orders. 'Take a bucket, get in line, a single-file line. We have to contain the fire, we can't let it spread to other buildings.' That would be disastrous.

Ren turned to Emma, but she was already gone, issuing orders of her own. He scanned the crowd, catching sight of her dark hair and light-coloured dress as she set people to the task of gathering the livestock away from the flames. Clearly, there was no need to worry about her. She had things well in hand on her end. He just needed to see to his. Ren shrugged out of his coat and positioned himself at the front of the bucket brigade, placing himself closest to the flames.

Reach and throw, reach and throw. Ren settled into the rhythm of firefighting.

After a solid half hour of dousing, his shoulders ached and his back hurt from the repeated effort of lifting heavy buckets, but they were gaining on the flames.

Confident the line could handle the remainder, Ren stepped aside and looked for Emma. He found her in the centre of the farmyard talking with a large, muscled African and another man dressed in tall boots and riding clothes, holding the reins of his horse. He was obviously a new arrival, having missed all the 'fun' of fighting the fire. His clothes were clean and lacked the soot Emma had acquired. Even from here,

Ren could see Emma's gown wouldn't survive the afternoon. At a distance, too, he could tell this wasn't a friendly conversation on Emma's part. Emma waved her hand and shook her head almost vehemently at something the man said. Whoever he was, he was not welcome.

Ren strode towards the little group not so much for Emma's protection—she'd given every indication she could handle herself today and in fact preferred to work alone—as he did for his. Anyone who was a threat to Emma might very well be a threat to Sugarland. At the moment that was recommendation enough to intervene. Ren didn't hesitate to insert himself into the conversation. 'Do we know what happened?' he asked, his question directed towards Emma. Up close, she was a worried mess. Her hem had torn in places and a seam at the side had ripped, the white of her chemise playing peekaboo. Her hair fell loose over one shoulder. She looked both dirty and delicious at once, a concept his body seemed to find very arousing in the aftermath. All of his unspent adrenaline needed to find an alternate outlet.

The big African spoke. 'Dunno. One minute we were working and the next, there was a bang.' He snapped his fingers. 'The shed just went up. There was no warning, no time.' He shook his head.

'The building was a chicken coop.' Emma explained to Ren, filling him in. 'Some of the chickens were outside, but we likely lost at least twelve.'

Ren nodded. It could have been worse. As fires and damages went, this was minor; Just chickens and a shed. The loss would be an inconvenience, but they would recover from it. It could have been the hay, the cows, the food staples, human lives even. Fires were dangerous to a farm's prosperity.

The business of the fire satisfied for the moment, Ren turned his attention to the newcomer. Ren stuck out his hand when it became apparent Emma wasn't going to make introductions. 'I'm Ren Dryden, Merrimore's cousin.'

The stranger shook his hand, smiling. He was a strong man, tall, probably in his early forties. 'I'm Sir Arthur Gridley, your neighbour to the south. It looks like you've come just in time.' He gave Emma a sideways glance of friendly condescension that perhaps explained her reluctance to make introductions.

'Our Emma's had a struggle of it since Merrimore passed away. It has been one thing after the other for the poor girl. She's had quite the run of bad luck: a sick horse the other day, the broken wagon wheel last week, trouble with the equipment at the mill. We've all tried to pitch in, but Emma's stubborn and won't take a bit of help.'

Emma's mouth hardened into a grim line. Ren wondered what she disliked most, being talked about as if she weren't here or having her weaknesses exposed to an outsider. Or maybe, on second consideration, it was Gridley she was most opposed to.

The man seemed nice enough, certainly eager to be neighbourly but Ren noticed Emma had stepped closer to him during the exchange. Closer to himself or away from Gridley? Perhaps there was more there than met the eye. He'd have to follow that up later. Right now he had an explosion to solve. 'I'm going to walk through the ruins and see if I can't unearth any signs of what might have started the fire. I'd welcome any assistance.' He'd let Gridley prove himself. After all, Emma didn't much like him at the moment either. She might have an aversion to men in general or just to men who posed a threat to her authority.

Ren moved towards the remains of the chicken coop, Gridley on one side, Emma on the other.

'Look for anything that might have triggered an explosion: a wire, a fuse, a match. I don't think the fire had time to get too hot, clues have likely survived.'

He'd meant the instructions for Gridley, but Emma moved forward, ready to brave the ashes. Ren stuck out an arm, barring the way. 'Not you, Miss Ward. What's left of your slippers won't last. Hot or not, any residual ash could burn right through those flimsy soles. I need you to talk to people, they know you. Perhaps someone might remember some strange activity around the coop before the explosion.'

She shot him an angry glare. He wasn't scoring any points in his favour with this latest directive, but she went. Did she go out of acquiescence to his request or as a chance to be away from Gridley? His curiosity would liked to have seen what she'd have done if Gridley hadn't been there.

Digging through the rubble was more difficult than expected. Ren had thought it would be fairly easy to determine the cause of the fire—after all, the coop hadn't been that big to begin with once the smoke had cleared and there wasn't that much debris.

Ren pushed back his hair with a dirty, sweaty

hand and looked around him. They were nearly done and nothing had shown up. Gridley waved at him a few feet away and strode over.

'I think I've found something,' he called out loudly enough to draw attention. He held up a small bundle of grey cloth. The people working near him gasped and moved out of the away with anxious steps. Out of the corner of his eye, Ren saw Emma hurry towards him.

Ren took the item from Arthur Gridley and turned it over in study. 'What is it? It looks like a child's doll.' A poorly made one. It was nothing more than cloth sewn into a crude resemblance of a human form.

Gridley and Emma exchanged glances laced with challenge. Emma's voice conveyed a quiet anger when she spoke. 'It's obeah magic. This is a bad-luck charm.' She shot an accusing glare at Gridley.

Gridley blew out a breath, sounding genuinely aggrieved. 'I'm sorry, Emma. It's the last thing you need.' He stepped forward to put a consoling hand on Emma's arm. This time Ren didn't imagine her response. She moved out of reach, stepping on the toes of his boots as she backed up. Gridley's eyes narrowed, but he said nothing, opting instead to pretend he didn't notice the slight.

'This doll didn't start the fire,' Ren put in, drawing them away from whatever private war waged between them. He fingered the doll. Something wasn't right, but his mind couldn't grasp it.

Gridley gave a harsh laugh. 'I'm not sure it matters what started the fire. I'm not even sure it matters only a chicken coop burnt down. It's not the fire that's damaging.' He nodded to the huddle of people forming behind the big African. 'Emma's likely not to have any workers in the morning. Obeah magic is powerful and they believe in it.'

The tension between Emma and Gridley ratcheted up a notch. Gridley shifted on his feet and Ren flicked a covert glance over his person, noting the telltale beginnings of tightening trousers. Gridley tugged at his coat front in the age-old effort to disguise a growing arousal. For all of Gridley's bonhomie, Ren would wager his last guinea Emma didn't care for her neighbour as much as the neighbour cared for her, if caring was the right word. He wasn't convinced yet that it was. There were other less flattering, less worthy words that recommended themselves.

The big African approached tentatively. 'Miss Emma, no one wants to go back to work today. The healers need time to purify the farmyard, to make it safe again.'

Gridley spat on the ground and prepared to respond. 'Now you listen here, you're making a working wage—'

Emma interrupted firmly, her anger directed openly at Gridley. 'This is my place. *I* will handle any business that needs handling.' Ren had to give Emma Ward credit. Even in a tattered gown, she commanded authority. She'd acquitted herself well today in the face of a crisis.

Emma stepped forward towards the foreman, distancing herself from him and Gridley. 'Peter, tell everyone they can have the rest of the day off. They may do whatever they need to do. But make it clear, they are to be back at work tomorrow. If the harvest fails, we all fail and failure doesn't pay the bills.'

'You are too generous with them,' Gridley warned in low tones. The man was treading on dangerous ground. Couldn't he see Emma was spoiling for a fight? Maybe a fight was what he wanted. Perhaps it was the presence of conflict that fuelled his desire. Some men were like that.

Emma's chin went up in defiance and Ren

didn't think much of Gridley's chances. 'It is my mistake to make then. The last time I checked, it was my name on the deed, not yours. If you'll excuse me, I'd like to go home and clean up.'

Ren laughed to himself as he gave Emma a leg up on the horse. She'd neatly dismissed Sir Arthur Gridley and Gridley had been furious over it. Perhaps he'd been expecting an invitation to tea? Or perhaps not, given Emma's overt dislike of him. There probably hadn't been invitations to tea for quite a while. Such dislike didn't grow up overnight or without cause.

Ren wasn't laughing when she did the same thing to him back at the house, the sun starting to set in the sky. She wanted a bath and would it be all right, given the excitement of the day, if she took dinner in her rooms? She didn't think she was up for company.

He'd granted her request. He had little choice otherwise. She'd prettily made her excuses, playing the delicate maiden to the hilt, which had been entertaining to watch but hardly believable. He'd seen her in action today. Anyone who handled herself the way Emma had wasn't going to be put off by company for dinner. Still, he played the gentleman and gave her the reprieve. He allowed himself to be handed over to her house servants and hustled off to his quarters.

Ren stepped inside his rooms and immediately understood what she'd done. The minx had not only dismissed him, she'd relegated him to the care of servants *and* tucked him into the far reaches of the house. Even worse, Ren could find little to complain about. It wasn't as if she'd put him in the attics or that the house was so large it needed a map to navigate. It was the principle of the matter and what it signified.

The *garçonnière* was a novel idea borrowed from the French, a large spacious set of rooms put aside for a family's bachelor sons. On the surface, the rooms were the practical answer for housing a male guest. It was what lay beneath that surface Ren took issue with. He could indeed come and go as he pleased through a separate entrance without tramping through the main house. In fact, he need not even interact with anyone in the main house if he chose or vice versa; the main house need not interact with him, which he suspected was more the case.

The footman, Michael, offered to stay and unpack, but Ren excused him. He wanted time to think and sort through what had happened that day. Ren pulled off his cravat and undid his waistcoat. There was no sense in standing on ceremony for oneself. He was alone.

The impact of it hit him hard as he stacked his linen and filled the drawers. For the first time in his life, he was entirely alone without his family, his friends and without his title; it meant nothing here at the moment. Even the institutions that had filled the backdrop of his life to date were absent. What he wouldn't give for a quiet evening at his club, laughing over brandy with Benedict. Ren set out the personal effects he'd brought; his game board, his writing kit. He would need to pen a letter to his family and let them know he had arrived safely. He even rearranged a few pieces of furniture to better suit himself. He'd put his stamp on this place yet whether Emma Ward liked it or not, starting with these rooms.

The welcome he had received today was not what he'd expected. The element of surprise had served him well. Emma had not been able to hide behind the pomp and ceremony of a planned reception. She'd been forced into an impromptu situation which had left her exposed. Surprise worked both ways, though, and there'd been surprise for him as well. He'd not expected a single shareholder. He'd been prepared for a consortium of businessmen. He'd expected people would be glad, even relieved to see him. The burden of running a plantation would be lifted from their shoulders. The reality had proven a bit different. Emma Ward was clearly not eager to be relieved of her duties or to share them.

It did make him wonder what Emma Ward had to hide. Ren set out his shaving gear, a plan of attack starting to form. With another woman, he would have chosen a strategy of overwhelming kindness and politeness. He knew already that gambit would have disastrous outcomes with Emma Ward.

Emma would need to be handled directly and firmly. He'd seen how she'd treated Arthur Gridley, with unabridged disdain. She'd eat a 'nice' man alive, the sort of man who made the mistake of thinking she was a delicate flower. Ren chuckled at the thought, another image taking shape in his mind. If she was a flower, she would be the sort that lured their prey with their beauty and then shut their petals tight until there was no escape for the poor unsuspecting soul.

She would learn soon enough he was no fool to be played with. It would take more than bad manners to deter him. If Emma Ward thought a cold welcome would send him packing, she was in for another surprise. Of course, she had no idea of what he had faced in England—not even Kitt knew. Emma's bad-mannered welcome couldn't begin to compete against the consequences of genteel poverty awaiting him if he failed here; of watching his sisters become spinsters for lack of attractive dowries, or watching them settle for questionable matches simply because only men of dubious character would take them; of watching the estates dwindle into disrepair for lack of funds to fix roofs and replace failing furniture; of watching the tenants move off the land one by one looking for more lucrative fields.

Genteel poverty was a slow social death sentence. He would not go easily down that road. He would fight it with every resource he had for the sake of his family. Even if he could afford to leave Sugarland, which he couldn't, even if his family wasn't depending on his success here, which they were, this was his fifty-one per cent and more—this was his future. He was here to stay. Both practice and principle demanded it.

Ren Dryden couldn't stay! Emma slid deep into the soapy bubbles of her bath. Watching him manage the fire today had been proof enough of that. He'd done a good job, stepping in at a moment's notice. Too good of a job. He'd been a natural leader the way he'd formed the bucket brigade and then joined in, working alongside the others. Perhaps he'd been afraid it was his fifty-one per cent on fire, Emma thought uncharitably, soaping her arms. The men had respected him, too. She'd seen it in their faces when he'd given orders. He was *not* what she needed—a man with enough charisma to usurp her years of hard work.

That was exactly what would happen if he knew the truth of things. She'd desperately wanted to paint a picture of idyllic prosperity, that all was well in the hopes of convincing Ren Dryden there nothing to do here. He might as well go home. Then the chicken coop had exploded, the obeah doll had shown up and Gridley had nearly let the rest of the cat out of the bag with his 'poor Emma' remark. If Dryden thought his investment was in danger, she'd never dislodge him. He'd shown today that he was a protector by nature and protectors were warriors by necessity. They would fight for the things they cared about.

Heat that had nothing to do with the bath water began to simmer low at her core. Such a man was intoxicating, his strength a potent attractant and how she'd been attracted! She'd been poignantly aware of him today even amid the crisis. Her eye had followed him throughout the afternoon, her gaze drawn to the rolled-up sleeves and the flex of his arms hauling the buckets, to the ash smearing his jaw, the blaze of his eyes as he barked orders. There'd been the feel of him behind her on the horse, all muscle as his power surrounded her.

There was an intimacy about riding astride with a man, about being captured between the power of his thighs, nestled against his groin, home to more intimate items. It was a position Dryden had been comfortable with. He'd not thought twice about the potential indelicacy of drawing her close against him. It suggested he was a man comfortable and confident with his body, a man who would be good at a great many things, bed included.

Oh, it was poorly done of her to harbour such thoughts about her guest, especially when she wanted that guest to leave. She suspected she wasn't the only woman who'd entertained the idea of bed with Ren Dryden. He was the sort who could conjure up all sorts of hot thoughts with a single look, a single touch.

That makes him dangerous! her more logical side asserted. He was particularly dangerous to a woman like herself, who valued her independence, who didn't want to be protected. Protection meant sheltering, shielding. She wanted neither. If she wasn't careful, Ren Dryden would undermine all she was simply because it was in his nature to do so. Her best interests required she stay the course—ignore him when possible and when it wasn't, resist.

In the meanwhile, she needed to continue life as usual. That meant praying her workers showed up and firing the fields tomorrow as planned in preparation for the harvest.

Firing the fields! Emma shot up in her bath, sending water and suds splashing on the tile floor. She should have told Ren. It was too late. She'd already effectively said goodnight with her dismissal and going to him now would require getting dressed. She wasn't about to traipse through the house in her dressing robe. Ren might believe she'd rethought her welcome and that certainly wasn't what she wanted. Ren Dryden was a spark she couldn't risk igniting.

Chapter Four

Fire! Ren came awake in a rush of awareness, his senses bombarded on all fronts: the heat, the overpowering stench of smoke and the blinding darkness. His brain raced. Teddy! The girls! He had to get to them. Panic engulfed him, adrenaline propelled him.

He lurched out of bed, stumbling in the darkness. His foot tripped on the corner of the bed and he swore. Outside the slats of his blinds orange flames flickered. His senses registered the scent of smoke more thoroughly now. It smelled of burning leaves. The panic receded infinitesimally. This was not England. Teddy and the girls were safe. But his fields...

Ren pulled up the blinds and stared in horrified amazement. This was not even the fire from yesterday. It wasn't a chicken coop this morning, it was the cane fields. *His cane fields!* Talk about money going up in literal smoke. The panic returned momentarily before his brain caught up with his senses. He remembered his research. The fire was deliberate, a prelude to the harvest, burning off the leaves and the cane's waxy outer layer to make reaping and milling more efficient.

Ren braced his arms against the window sill, breathing deeply, letting the shock pass. His family was safe half a world away. His fields were secure. All was well. But his panic was understandable. Knowing didn't make the fire appear any less harmless or smell any better. The dawn sky was black with smoke and the orange flames looked menacing. It would have been easy to misinterpret the fire for something more sinister, especially when one was groggy with the fog of a sudden awakening.

Perhaps that had been the intent? In his more alert state, it occurred to Ren that Emma could have warned him, just like she could have written, informing him of the business situation. Again, she'd elected not to, choosing instead to let him find his own level.

Ren looked down at himself. He was stark naked and in his standard, early morning, state of arousal. He usually slept nude and he'd seen no reason not to continue the practice last night. If he had misunderstood the fire, and if he had let his initial panic drive him out the door, Miss Ward might have been in for quite the surprise. As it was, she might still be in for one, although this one would be clothed. If she thought she could burn his fields without his presence or permission, or if she thought she could force him into the role of the silly, uninformed newcomer, she would be wrong on all accounts.

Ren dressed in trousers and a clean shirt. He pulled on his boots and took time to put on a jacket. He didn't want to give any ounce of credence to the idea that he'd rolled straight out of bed and raced to the fields. He wanted Emma convinced he'd not panicked.

Once outside, he spied a group of men gathered at the edge of the field and strode towards them. They were standing a safe distance from the flames, monitoring the fire's progress with a nonchalance that affirmed his conclusion: the firing was deliberate. All three heads turned towards him as he approached, but not all were male. Of course she'd be there.

Emma Ward stood between two men, dressed in trousers, tall boots and a man's cut-down shirt, her hair tucked into a tight, dark braid that fell over one shoulder; a look that emphasised long legs, high firm breasts and did absolutely nothing for taming his morning arousal.

Emma met his gaze with a cool stare of her own. 'We are firing the fields today.' Firing the fields, firing his blood, his temper. There was fire aplenty today.

Ren chose to ignore the obvious quality of the statement and went straight to the pronoun. 'We? That seems an odd choice of words considering you left me in bed.'

Emma coloured, his innuendo not lost. 'I did *not* leave you in bed the way you suggest. You'd had a long journey. I let you sleep.' She turned towards the other two men with her. 'Mr Paulson and Peter, allow me to introduce Albert Merrimore's relative, Mr Renford Dryden. He arrived yesterday afternoon. Mr Dryden, this is my overseer, Mr Paulsen, and my field foreman, Peter, whom you met yesterday.'

Paulsen was a tall, slender man with leathery skin, a man who'd seen years under a hot sun. Peter was the thick-muscled African from the home farm. Ren offered his hand to the two men and took the opportunity to establish his ground. 'I'm pleased to meet you. I will want to discuss the plantation with each of you over the next few days.'

That brought a shuffling of feet from Peter, who hastily looked away, and a hesitant nod from Mr Paulsen. Ren was pleased to see they were loyal and not wanting to betray their allegiance to Emma, but resistance was resistance. As such, it was only a step away from outward defiance. Ren decided to address it head on with a smile. 'I am the primary shareholder now. I will, of course, be ably assisted by Miss Ward, but you should accustom yourselves to a new line of authority.' Ren shot a stern look at Emma. 'This is a partnership now.'

Partnership, her foot! This was a slippery slope to dictatorship if it was anything at all. Emma glared out over the smoky fields, arms crossed. If he was going to begin as he meant to go on, she should, too. His 'partnership' would have to be nipped in the bud, but that nipping would have to wait until they could return to the house. She was not petty enough to argue in front of Mr Paulsen and Peter.

Nor was she naive enough to think she was going to get away with nothing more than the veiled scolding of Ren's last remark. That remark had been a warning and now he was making her wait for the other proverbial shoe to fall. She was not a patient person by nature and he'd already tried what little patience she possessed over the past four months *waiting* for him to arrive or not. Apparently, she was not done waiting.

She waited until the burning was nearly complete and could be left in Mr Paulsen's capable hands. She waited through the walk back to the house. She waited while they filled their plates with a late breakfast and sat down at the table. She waited as he took a few bites of his eggs and buttered his toast.

Ren took a bite of that well-buttered toast and looked a question at her with an arch of his brows. 'Yes? Do you have something you want to say?'

'No, do you?' Emma sipped at her coffee in hopes of disguising her agitation. She wanted him to engage first.

'I have nothing to say that you do not already know.' His eyes held hers, blue fire simmering in them. 'You tried to play me for a fool this morning.' His tone was even, neutral. 'We both know it. You deliberately didn't tell me about firing the fields.'

Emma gathered her practised defence. 'By the

time I remembered, I had already undressed for the evening.' It had sounded better in her head. Out loud, it only proved to be provocative and Ren had indicated already he wasn't above innuendo. He would not let such a reference pass.

'Were you now?' His gaze was steady but the faintest ribbon of a smile played across his mouth, bringing to mind images that were entirely too intimate for the breakfast table, images that left her stripped bare beneath his gaze and not the least bit protected from the direction of his thoughts and hers.

Emma looked down at her eggs. 'I couldn't very well traipse around the house in my nightgown.' That was even worse. She was making a mess of this. Usually, she was considered quite the wit. Not today. Not with this man.

'I, too, had retired for the evening,' Ren said drily. 'In fact, I was wearing far less than a nightshirt. Had you come, you would have been overdressed.' The last comment brought her eyes up, her cheeks starting to heat. 'I sleep in the nude, Emma. In case you were wondering.'

'I wasn't,' Emma snapped in mortification. It was absolutely a lie, however. She *had* been wondering, her mind filling rather quickly with images of a naked Ren Dryden.

'More to the point, I awoke naked and nearly ran out to the fields in my altogether. I wonder who would have looked foolish then—me, for running out naked in concern for my crops, or you for having overlooked the simple courtesy of notifying me?'

Emma's cheeks were twin ovens now, her mind a riot of inappropriate images of her guest. She tried to sound oblivious to the implications of his words. 'I think we're being a little dramatic about a harmless episode.' Hot cheeks or not, she positively *refused* to let him turn this into an inquisition. Nor would she let him turn this into a favour he'd done her in which *he'd* saved *her* from embarrassment.

Ren's eyes were shrewd when they met hers. 'A harmless episode, but not an isolated one. In the past…' he stopped here and flipped open a pocket watch, doing a quick calculation '…eighteen hours since my arrival, you've made it clear you don't want me here. But I *am* here and this *will* be a partnership. There will be no more of these attempts to dissuade me.'

'My apologies if you feel that way,' Emma replied, but her tone was unrepentant. He'd proven to be a worthy opponent at present, catching on far too quickly to her strategy. That didn't mean she had to admit to it. It did mean, however, she would need another. Simply ignoring Ren Dryden wasn't going to work.

Her brain began to recalibrate. The new gambit would have to be something more subtle, something that would bind him to her without arousing his suspicions. After all, if he was going to stay, how could she best use him? Could she make him an ally against Gridley? He'd been quick enough to support her yesterday.

Emma studied Ren, well aware that he was watching her, waiting for her to cede the terms of their partnerships. *Watch me all you like.* He was not entirely immune to her. He knew very well what he was doing with his innuendo and his eyes. A man didn't play such games with a woman he wasn't attracted to. She was used to men watching her, men like Arthur Gridley and Thompson Hunt. Men who were always wondering about her, thinking they knew how best to manipulate her for their own gains.

Like them, perhaps Dryden's own confidence could be played against him. But how to do it? Perhaps a temporary show of agreement was in order until she sorted things out.

Emma stuck her hand out across the table, evincing appropriate reluctance. Her about-turn would have to be convincing. Ren Dryden would not find complete, immediate capitulation compelling. 'Very well, since it seems I have no choice, I agree. A partnership it is.' She would honour that partnership until it was no longer judicious for her to pursue a course of assumed equality. Her next gambit, whatever it was, needed to be something *more*. Her first gambit had not worked, based as it was on faulty assumptions about who Ren would be. She needed time to think the next one through. Agreement bought her time and this time she had to succeed. She wouldn't get another second chance.

Ren relinquished her hand, but his eyes didn't stray from hers. 'Perhaps we should seal our partnership with a tour of the property. I would like to start learning about the plantation immediately.'

A little spark of excitement travelled down her spine, a most unwanted reaction. She had the distinct impression he wasn't necessarily referencing the plantation. Her pulse raced, oblivious to what her mind already knew: it was only a game. Ren could flirt all he liked, but in the end, she needed to be the one in charge. If this was to be a game, she preferred it to be one played neutrally, at least on her part.

'I can arrange to have Peter or Mr Paulsen show you around.' After a morning of sharpening wits with him, a little distance was in order. She needed time to plan. Emma rose to make her departure, but Ren was ready for her. He rose with her, blocking her access to the door.

'I'm sure they're capable, but I'd prefer you. We can go right now.' He held his arms wide, showing off his riding attire with a laugh. 'Fortunately, I am dressed for it and so are you.' He gave her a conspiratorial grin at the inside joke. 'You're not in your nightgown and I'm not in my altogether, so there's no excuse.'

Emma recognised defeat. She'd been flanked. She would not be able to dismiss him as easily as she had yesterday by pawning him off on her servants. She smiled tightly. She *had* to capitulate, there was no way out of it and he knew it, he'd orchestrated it that way. 'Very well, I'll call for the horses.'

His grin widened. 'No need, I've already done that. I told the groom to have them ready at half past.' Not *your* groom, but *the* groom. Beneath his casual manner there was a sharp reminder that while Sugarland was her place, it was also his. *Theirs. Together.*

Emma let the comment pass and led the way

out to the drive. Sharing would take some getting used to. It would demand she reshape the way she viewed him entirely. At least temporarily, she had to move away from seeing him as the interloper, someone who was here only on Merry's posthumous good grace. Still, she had to be strong. Otherwise, Ren would think she was soft. Men exploited softness.

Horses were indeed waiting outside and Ren gave her a leg up, tossing her into the saddle with ease as he had done yesterday. He adjusted her stirrup and checked her girth one last time. It was either quite gallant of him, or quite patronising. Emma shot him a wry look, assuming the latter. 'You should know, Ren Dryden, I don't like high-handed men.'

Ren gave her stirrup a final tug and looked up, blue eyes sparking with amusement. '*You* should know I don't like scheming females. I think that makes us even.'

He swung up into his saddle with athletic grace, the heels of his boots automatically going down in the irons, his thighs naturally gripping the stallion, a bay Merry had bought from an officer who was returning to England. She felt a sharp stab of heat at the memory from yesterday of those thighs gripping her.

'You're a horseman,' Emma said as they turned their mounts out behind the house to begin the tour.

'I love to ride. My family prides themselves on their stable. We all grew up in the saddle.' Ren drew his horse alongside hers, his tone easy, inviting conversation as the path widened to easily accommodate two riders abreast.

'Do you have a large family?' The way he'd said 'all' implied that he did. She'd not imagined him having siblings. She'd spent her time planning for the arrival of an old man with few ties.

'Big enough. Not as large as some,' Ren answered. 'I have two younger sisters and a younger brother. How about yourself, do you have siblings?'

She shook her head. 'I barely had parents, let alone brothers and sisters. It was mostly my father and me. He was in the military and we travelled.'

'That must have been exciting.' Ren was studying her, giving her the full attention of his gaze. It was warming and unnerving all at once. This was supposed to have been a safe conversation but it was proving contrary to her intentions. Was it real or was it merely his brand of superficial politeness? Worse, was it the beginning of a seduction? Was he being nice to capitalise on the truce they'd established over breakfast? She'd seen such niceness often enough from those who had something to gain. If he thought to kiss the plantation out of her, he wouldn't be the first to try and he wouldn't be the last to fail.

This was where seduction, if that was what he was up to, became tricky. One had to be careful not to forget the game, no matter how appealing the fantasy. She wouldn't make it easy for him or for herself. Neither could she appear to be entirely resistant. Resistance would not convince him she'd rethought her position on his presence. Still, things didn't have to go too far.

Emma decided to put a halt to the moment before she had herself imagining he cared about something other than his fifty-one per cent. 'It was lonely. My father's career was all consuming. He lived for it and the adventure of always moving can be something of a burden when one is craving the stability of a normal home and friends. There was no one to fall back on when my father died.' They reached a fork in the rough trail. She gestured they should go right.

'There was my cousin,' Ren answered, swiftly coming to Merry's defence.

'Yes, there was Merry and I will always be

grateful. He was all that was generous and kind
to a lonely sixteen-year-old girl.' The trail narrowed and Emma pushed ahead of him. They
were climbing now. Emma was glad for a reason
to proceed single file. Even after four months,
her grief over Merry remained raw. Too much
sincerity, feigned or not from Ren Dryden, and
she'd be a gusher.

They reached the top of the incline and dis-
mounted. Emma went to stand at the edge, using
the time to gather her emotions. But Ren did not
give her long. He came up behind her, his boots
giving fair warning as they rustled the grass.
He was close, close enough for her to smell the
scent of honest sweat mixed with the scents of
horse and morning soap. The combination was
decidedly male and not at all unpleasing. There
was power to it and strength.

'This is the highest point on Sugarland, from
here you can see everything.' It was one of her
favourite places to visit. She and Merry had
come up often when he was well. The last time
had been two days before he died. The trip had
taken all of his strength. She remembered worrying that he *would* die on the hilltop, that it
had been his reason for coming; he'd wanted to
depart the earth where he could see his legacy

spread before him. It was the day he'd warned her of his suspicions about Gridley. She wished he'd warned her about Ren Dryden, too.

Ren let out a low whistle of appreciation. 'That's an amazing view. I can see why you'd want to come. A man could be a king here, surveying his domain.'

'Or a queen surveying hers,' Emma amended. This was her kingdom, a reminder of all she fought for, of all she defended. A reminder, too, of what she stood to lose if she was not a vigilant guardian. Gridley would wrest this place from her if she gave him half a chance. Perhaps Ren Dryden would, too.

'Tell me about it, tell me everything we see.' Ren's voice was quiet, intimate at her ear. It sent an unlooked-for trill of awareness down her spine, so unlike the prickles of hatred, even fear, that Gridley's presence roused.

Ren pointed in the distance. 'What's that building over there?'

'That's our sugar mill. Once we harvest the cane, it will be refined there. We're big enough to support our own mill. We're lucky. We mill the cane for some of the smaller plantations, too, who don't have their own,' Emma explained.

She moved their gaze to the east. 'That's

the main house. Then there's the cane fields.'
They were black beneath the sky, the recent firing causing them to stand out stark and naked against the lush background. 'There are the vegetable fields and the home farm.' She paused to glance over her shoulder, taking in Ren's expression. 'You're surprised. We're self-sufficient here. The trick is to balance the land between what we need to feed ourselves and what we can afford to grow for cane. Sugar cane is our money crop, but it won't do us any good if we starve or if we have to spend our profits on food. Already, so much of what we need has to be imported from England. It would be a shame to have to import food, too.'

Ren nodded slowly. She could almost see the wheels of his mind turning behind those eyes of his. He was interested in the plantation. Well, she'd see how interested he was in the middle of a sweltering summer when there was work to be done, although he'd done well yesterday with the fire. He hadn't hesitated.

'Is cane difficult to grow?' he asked, his gaze going back to the charred fields. 'From my reading, it doesn't seem to be.'

'Not too difficult. The cane regenerates itself.' She started to explain the process, acutely aware of the potent male presence behind her. Ren was making it difficult to talk about ratoon crops and he wasn't even touching her. He was just standing there. Only he wasn't. He was flirting silently with his body.

No, flirting was too superficial of a word. Flirting required witty banter and gay repartee, not an agricultural discussion. This wasn't flirting, this was *sampling*. He was letting her sample his physicality—the smell of him, the heat, the sensuality of him as he turned even the most mundane comment erotic by murmuring it near her ear.

There was no doubt he was a man who understood precisely how to use the nuances of space and touch to create a certain appeal. The bigger question was why? She had yet to meet a man who didn't have ulterior motives when it came to women or when it came to her. She didn't need to be a genius to figure out what Dryden was after. She'd been alert to that potential ever since he'd climbed down from Sherard's wagon in all his broad-shouldered, blue-eyed glory.

His subtle flirtation here on the bluff confirmed what she'd suspected. Even being alert for such a move from him, it was disappointing. Perhaps a small part of her had hoped the man she'd seen at the fire would be different. Not that knowledge of his likely game was enough apparently to stop her pulse from racing, or a little *frisson* of excitement from running down her spine as he abstrusely put his body on invitation. But it needed to be.

She was a smart woman and experience had made her smarter than most when it came to the nature of men. Those experiences would need to be her armour now. Emma stepped forward, away from the heat of his body. 'We should be getting back. I have work to do.' Anything would be better than being near Ren and his intoxicating presence without a plan of her own. Too much of him and she'd forget her resolve and his agenda.

Emma filled the ride back with business. She talked about the native flora and fauna, the seasonal changes on the island, even the hurricane of 1831 which had left much of the island devastated and claimed fifteen hundred lives. All of it done in an attempt to create distance and a reminder they were business partners and would be nothing more. She couldn't afford to be *more* with him.

The house came into view and Emma felt a

surge of relief. Sanctuary! She would not have to deal with Ren again until dinner. She could bury herself away in the office behind closed doors. That relief was short-lived. As they approached the drive, it was evident she had company. A rider was dismounting from a tall sorrel stallion. Damn and double damn. Hadn't yesterday been enough for him?

Ren drew his horse alongside. 'Expecting guests?'

Emma grimaced. 'Sir Arthur Gridley isn't exactly a guest.' He'd probably seen the smoke from the crops and wanted to poke his nose into Sugarland's business, something he'd made a habit of doing since Merry's death.

'A nuisance then?' Ren joked wryly.

'Something like that,' Emma responded tersely. Gridley was more than a nuisance. He was insidious. He liked to portray himself as the nosy neighbour who had her best interests at heart. Only she knew better.

'If he's not a nuisance or a guest, what is he, then?' The protectiveness she sensed in him yesterday gave an edge to Ren's voice.

'Nothing for you to worry about. I've got him under control.' She hoped she did anyway. She wasn't about to admit otherwise to Ren and alert him to the possibility that not all was perfect at Sugarland. Neither did she want to give Ren a possible weapon to use against her.

Arthur Gridley strode down the steps towards them, smiling pleasantly, playing the good neighbour to the hilt, definitely a bad sign. It seemed she was about to trade Ren Dryden for something worse, a classic case of out of the frying pan and into the fire.

Chapter Five

'Emma, my dear, you've been busy!' Arthur Gridley effused his usual charm and was dressed in the height of luxury. The packet was always bringing him expensive clothes. If the island had a dandy, he was it.

Emma smiled tightly, aware of how dirty she was again compared to Gridley's pristine neatness. He most certainly hadn't spent the morning firing fields and touring his land. Gridley wasn't exactly a hands-on manager when it came to his plantation. 'Sir Arthur, it's good to see you. Did we have an appointment?' She would not give him an inch. She would show no fear in his presence. It would only give him one more weapon.

Sir Arthur grinned, showing even, white teeth. Many women on the island found that smile attractive, including the governor's wife.

Emma did not count herself among their number.
Gridley's appeal had worn out ages ago for her.
'Since when do old friends need appointments
to call on one another?' He gave her a friendly
wink. 'I came to talk to Dryden. We didn't have
a chance to become acquainted yesterday with
all the chaos.' He said 'chaos' as if she'd planned
the fire deliberately. 'It was not the most ideal of
circumstances for introductions.'

Emma saw Gridley's intentions immediately.
He'd come to be the serpent in the garden, to
woo Ren with a false show of friendship. She
should have warned Ren when she'd had the
chance. Gridley had the devil's own tongue and
she could easily imagine the tales he would spin
now that Merry's heir was here, a new uninformed target for Gridley's ambitions to acquire
interest in Sugarland. Gridley was not a man to
face without forewarning.

'Albert and I were close. He was a good
friend,' Sir Arthur supplied with a sad smile
when she offered nothing to qualify the nature
of his relationship. What she said or didn't say
hardly mattered. He was never above a little self-
promotion.

Gridley's smile softened and fixed on her just
long enough to create an impression of caring

before turning back to Ren. 'I'm not just a friend to Merrimore, but to his dear Emma too, I hope?'

'You must forgive my manners, it's been a long morning,' Emma ground out with the barest of civility. It was the only demur he was going to get from her. Proper etiquette required she say something like 'I did not mean to imply otherwise' when she really did. She would not play the politeness game with him and avow him publicly in any form.

'Yes, I see you fired the fields.' Gridley raised a scolding eyebrow at Emma but he directed his next comment to Ren. 'Not all of us fire the fields, Dryden. It's too risky for some of us veteran planters, but Emma has a penchant for all the latest novelties.'

'You make it sound as if I fired the fields on a whim,' Emma cut in crisply. She would not let him reduce her farming methods to a female foible in front of the man she was desperately trying to impress with her capability. It was a sound decision to burn the fields and when she had her crop in first, she'd prove it to the others.

'I am confident Emma knows what she is doing.' She felt Ren move up behind her, the heat of his body echoing against her back. He was proprietarily close. Something dark flitted through Gridley's eyes, but his ever-present grin was benevolent when he spoke.

'Nonetheless, I'm glad you're here, Dryden. You can take things in hand now and let Emma focus on running the house.' Goodness, he was in full form today! He'd all but chucked her under the chin like a doting uncle, an identity which was a complete misnomer when it came to their dubious relationship. Gridley had no intentions of being a father figure to her. He had far lustier aspirations.

'I'd invite you in, but I'm busy today,' Emma said sharply, making apology for her breach in social manners.

'Never mind about me, you go on with your business. As I said, I'm not really here for you.' He gave another of his winks to indicate a friendly joke. 'I'm here to see Dryden and give him the lay of the land. We'll stay out of your way, just send a pitcher of falernum to the back porch where we can have a nice long visit.' He slapped Ren on the back. 'I'll give him a proper welcome to the neighbourhood.'

'A *proper* welcome?' Ren shot her a discreet glance and she could almost hear the private laughter in Ren's voice, laughter that was there just for her, some inside humour only the two of them shared. 'I think I'd like that very much.' The inside joke made Arthur Gridley a momentary outsider and in a subtle way let her know she had an ally.

Emma could feel the beginnings of a smile play on her lips. It could just be part of a larger strategy Ren was playing, but for now it felt good to know he had her back. It was certainly a new way to view Ren's presence and it just might provide the new gambit she was looking for. *The enemy of my enemy is my friend. For now.*

Enemy? Friend? Concerned neighbour or ambitious interloper? It was hard to know how to classify Sir Arthur Gridley. Ren took a seat in one of the twin rockers on the veranda, gathering his thoughts. Emma certainly didn't care for the man. But was that dislike or fear she felt? What was she hiding that Gridley might expose? All in all, Ren thought it would make a rather insightful afternoon.

'What do you think of our little piece of the world so far?' Gridley stretched out his legs, settling into his chair and looking quite comfortable at a home not his own. He'd said he was Merrimore's close friend. In all fairness, he was probably used to being here, but the action struck Ren as overtly territorial, the tactic of a man who wants to remind everyone of his superior claim to ownership.

'It's hot,' Ren replied affably. It couldn't hurt to be nice. Knowledge was power and Gridley would want to demonstrate his. If Ren played this right, Gridley would talk all afternoon, thinking he was establishing his ground, when in reality Ren would get precisely what he wanted—information.

Ren had learned years ago it was the listener who held the upper hand when navigating the social waters of the *ton*. He had to start making friends in this new place. He wanted those friends to be the right ones. He had a hunch there might be wrong ones and he still had to figure out where Emma fit into the balance. Who to trust? The supposedly crazy woman running Sugarland or the well-dressed, seemingly well-intentioned neighbour?

'It *is* hot, in an entirely different way than London,' Gridley agreed. 'You'll get used to it. We have our rainy seasons and our fever seasons, but it's not a bad way to live. There's no cold, no ice, no grey skies that go on for months.' Gridley was all friendly assurance.

A servant brought a tray carrying a pitcher

full of an amber liquid and two glasses. She set it down on the little table between them and poured. 'You'll like falernum,' Gridley said. 'It's sweet, full of spices and a hint of vanilla.'

Ren sipped tentatively, relieved Gridley was right. He could pick out the hints of ginger and almond, even a bit of lime. 'It *is* good.'

Gridley chuckled. 'You sound surprised. Don't be. Emma has the best falernum on the island, there's something about how her cook mixes it.' Gridley sighed and dropped his voice. 'Emma has the best of everything. The best cook, the best field manager, the best overseer, the best household staff. It's made her some enemies and I'm worried for her. I'm glad you're here. Perhaps you can talk sense into her.'

Gridley slid him a sideways glance, no doubt looking for compliance. But Ren was more astute than that. He needed information before he made any decisions about his support. Ren decided to play the 'fresh off the boat' card. 'I'm afraid I don't quite understand what you mean?'

'Of course not, no one expects you to. We'll show you the ropes around here. You'll get the hang of how we do things in no time at all.' Gridley gave him another friendly smile, but Ren was cautious.

'I'd appreciate that,' he said neutrally. Ren was starting to wonder if Gridley had come of his own accord or if the neighbours had elected him to be the one to call and sound out the newcomer. He was used to this discreet vetting process. It wasn't all that different from the way the gentlemen's clubs tested a member's viability in London.

'It's not Emma's fault.' Gridley was quick to establish. 'It's the damn apprentice system. It looks good on paper, but it's costing the planters a small fortune in profits and there's hardly enough labour to go around.'

Ren raised an eyebrow in query, hoping Gridley would take it as a sign to elaborate on the process. Gridley took the hint and continued. 'Under the new system, former slaves can choose if they wish to work on the plantations and they can choose *which* plantations. We can't compel them to do it. Naturally, they want to work for the places that pay more and demand they do less.' The complaint against Emma was implied in the comment. 'She might as well tuck them all in with quilts and feed them meat three times a day.' Gridley chuckled, but Ren heard the contempt beneath the humour. 'You saw such a display yesterday with the afternoon off over the obeah doll.'

'You disapprove of such equity?' Ren asked, eyeing Gridley carefully. Something more was at work here in his social call. Was his ulterior agenda political? Economic? Social?

'I disapprove when those choices jeopardise one's neighbours' ability to make a decent living,' Gridley answered squarely. Ren shot a quick glance at Gridley's expensive boots. He didn't think Emma's choices were hurting Gridley too much.

Gridley dismissed the harshness of his comment with a wave of his hand. 'Emma doesn't know better. She's too kind-hearted and impulsive as well, not the best combination for business. She doesn't see the big picture the consequences her actions have for all of us.' There was anger and heat in the man's words.

Ren felt himself bristle at the cut to Emma's character. It was a strangely protective reaction to have towards a woman who had made it clear she was intent on disliking him. Still, what sort of neighbour maligned another in her own home? 'Perhaps you judge her too harshly,' Ren offered in Emma's defence. 'She believes she's doing the best she can to sustain the property.'

Gridley's demeanour became intensely serious. 'She doesn't quite grasp the larger implications. It is *us* against *them* and *they* have us vastly outnumbered. If we don't stick together, they'll be asking for seats in the assembly next or taking them outright.' The voracity of his comment was almost disturbing.

Ren understood the reference. The white plantocracy was outflanked by the ex-slave population by nearly ten to one. The sheer numbers created a certain unrelieved tension between the two groups. The plantocracy minority held all the legitimate power, but the ex-slave faction held the overwhelming majority of force should they attempt to exercise it.

Rebellion, *successful* rebellion, was possible, even likely. He knew from talk in London that other islands in the West Indies had experienced such rebellions. There were people like Gridley who believed such rebellion against the legitimate power was inevitable, their only weapon being the ability to legislate punitive codes to keep rebellion at bay.

Even though Ren understood the motivation for the plantocracy's logic, he could not condone it. His position was something he apparently had in common with Emma. It was also something that would not endear him to Arthur Gridley and his other neighbours if his position were known. Caution suggested he wait to reveal his feelings on the subject.

'Perhaps if people work together they might find a middle ground.' Ren put the unformed idea forward. He didn't want to lie to Gridley or profess to hold an opinion he heartily disagreed with. However, he had navigated the shoals of London society long enough to know there were bridges one couldn't afford to burn. If Emma had already burned hers, he needed to maintain his for Sugarland's sake. He was staunchly in favour of the decision to abolish slavery and even of reallocating seats in the assembly to more accurately reflect the population.

Gridley's response was curt and immediate. 'I don't know that there's any middle ground to be had, or any ground at all. I mean that quite literally. Once you've seen the island in its fullness, you'll understand. We don't have any unowned land. It's all claimed. The freemen want to work their own land, but where would that be? There's no land for them to buy, no land to give them, without breaking up the existing plantations.' There was a defensive gleam in his eye that belied the intensity of his convictions.

Ah, illumination. Land was the real threat, the real fear, that somehow Britain would legislate land be taken from the planters. Ren nodded thoughtfully, allowing Gridley to pour him another glass of falernum. Ren had no doubt if that came to pass, Arthur Gridley would meet people at the door with a gun.

'But enough of politics, you'll learn all that,' Gridley said, his earlier bonhomie returning in a sudden wave of good humour. The man definitely possessed a mercurial range of emotions. One moment he was serious, almost fanatical in his commitment to his positions, the next he was easygoing. 'As for Emma doing the best she can, that's another issue. We all understand she has a huge responsibility. It doesn't have to be that way. She needn't shoulder the burden of Sugarland alone, but she refuses to listen to reason.'

By 'we' Ren supposed Gridley referred to the neighbours, all of them male. 'What sort of reason?' Ren asked, although he could already guess how their brand of reason had gone over with Emma. Even on short acquaintance he knew she would see the solutions as infringements on her independence.

'The usual,' Gridley said sobering. 'I was close with Albert Merrimore, especially during his last year. He was worried for Emma and what would become of her. He knew his time was limited. I promised him I would be there for her. If she wanted to go to London, I'd see it done. If she wanted to stay here, I promised him I'd make it possible. We were neighbours, our plantations abut one another, of course I'd watch over his charge.'

'And the options you put to Emma?' Ren steered the conversation back towards his original question. 'What did she want?'

'She wanted to stay.' Gridley gave a sad smile. 'A woman cannot be out here alone trying to run a plantation without all nature of hardship, so I offered her marriage and she refused.' His eyes met Ren's, convincingly full of a man's regret that something he valued had slipped through his fingers. 'I shall ask again once she has found her centre. In my eagerness to fulfil my promise to Albert, I rushed my fences. I see that now. She was grieving, she was sorting through the estate and the will.' He shot Ren a wry look. 'She was adjusting to the news that a relative was coming who'd been given the majority of the shares. She was in no state to appreciate what a proposal would mean to her.'

This was what Gridley had really come to discuss. He was staking his claim to Emma. Ren assessed Arthur Gridley with new eyes. This was a man who was more than a neighbour, even more than a random suitor who fancied Emma. He'd been a family intimate with Cousin Merry. He had attempted to wed Merry's ward and meant to try his luck again, regardless of Emma's rather obvious feelings on the subject.

Even if Emma professed undying love for Gridley, allowing such a thing to happen was not in Ren's best interests as long as Emma held the other portion of ownership. It provoked the question of what drove Gridley's persistence. It was an academic question only. Ren could not allow Gridley's persistence to win out.

His protective streak rose, coupled this time with a competitive urge. This wasn't only about protecting Emma, but about protecting himself and his family. If Emma married Gridley, Ren would have to share the estate with *him*. It was not an idea he liked. It was one thing to drink a casual glass of falernum with the man, but it was another to make him a business partner and tie his family's interests to Gridley's. The prospect sat ill with Ren. His sixth sense told him that was not what his cousin had intended. He supposed he could buy out her share. He wondered if Gridley would still want her if she was without property...

'That's where you come in, Dryden,' Gridley was saying as Ren dragged his thoughts back to the conversation. He must have missed the beginning.

'How is that, exactly?' Ren asked obliquely.

Gridley have a short chuckle. *'You're* to help her see reason, show her the best options for Sugarland. She can't go it alone forever without risking the plantation's viability.' There was a dark glint in Gridley's eye and Ren wondered if he referred to a risk that had less to do with Emma's ability to make agricultural decisions and more to do with what might be termed her 'personal welfare'.

'I will do my best to live up to my cousin's faith in me,' Ren said honestly, although his best might not lead to the decisions Gridley was hoping for. Ren took the opportunity to rise, signalling their conversation had come to a close. He had quite enough to digest. Gridley had discharged his duty to the so-far-anonymous neighbours quite well. All that needed to be shared had been shared and any necessary warnings had been given. Perhaps even more than was necessary. Were the neighbours astute enough to know that Gridley would advocate for himself as well as them? Gridley's measure was clear. He was a man who did what benefited him.

Gridley shook his hand. 'It's good to meet you, Dryden. I want to have a dinner for you, give you a chance to meet everyone. I'll set it up and let Emma know.'

'I will look forward to it.' Ren showed Gridley out, understanding that the next move was up to him. Gridley had initiated, had laid out the rules of the game. Gridley and the neighbours would wait to see what his response would be. They could be in for a surprise. He might not know much about sugar cane, but he knew a little something about navigating society, especially when a game was afoot. If Emma Ward thought she had everything under control, she needed to think again.

Chapter Six

She had everything under control. Emma took a deep breath and moved her pip on the backgammon board, embracing the silent mantra that had sustained her throughout the evening. *Everything was going to be fine.* Not just the game but *everything*: the harvest, Arthur Gridley's unwanted attention, the plantation. She was balancing a rather precarious load just now, not counting the arrival of Ren Dryden.

One false step and it would all come tumbling down. But it wouldn't. It simply couldn't. To lose Sugarland was unthinkable. To allow Gridley to triumph, even more so. She told herself it was a good sign Ren hadn't run to her immediately after Gridley had left. It meant there was no need to worry. Right? Ren had said nothing during dinner. They'd talked about the plantation and adjourned here to the library for back-gammon.

Across from her, Ren critically surveyed the board, jiggling the dice in his dice cup. 'Double would be useful about now. I won't get off the bar without at least one five.' It was the only open point he could move to. She'd completely blocked out her field.

'You'll never get it.' Emma laughed, feeling confident she would have the advantage for another turn. She was starting to relax and enjoy the novelty of having someone to share the evening with. Surely, if something had alarmed Ren he would have brought it up by now.

'You're a very cocky minx, Emma Ward.' Ren grinned, looking devastating in the lamplight. He'd dressed for dinner, but he'd shed his coat when they'd begun to play. She'd thought he'd been handsome in his evening attire. He was far more attractive in his shirt and waistcoat, his cufflinks set aside, his sleeves rolled up.

The gesture had created a sense of domestic intimacy and a domestic fantasy, too; a glimpse of what life might be like for a husband and wife spending a quiet evening at home after a busy day with the plantation. He was a master indeed if he could conjure such images for her with the simple gesture of removing a coat.

If there wasn't so much on the line, the plantation, her own future; if she didn't have to be vigilant regarding any covert game Ren might be playing with her, she would have allowed herself to fall for him. It had been a long time since she'd let herself fall. Surely, she'd learned enough in the interim to fall safely, to enjoy the fantasy.

Without the trappings of her present circumstances, an affair with Ren Dryden would be a delightful diversion. As it was, at this point it could only be a dangerous diversion, a delusion. 'Are you going to roll?' Emma prompted with a sly smile. 'Staring at the board won't change anything.'

Ren sat back in his chair, his eyes on her. 'You are so sure I won't roll double fives. Why don't we wager on it? If I get double fives, I claim a forfeit. If I don't, you claim the forfeit.' He shook the cup and then halted, his eyes dancing with mischief. 'The forfeit should be something little, Emma. No property, no crazy requests that either of us abdicate our percentage of the plantation. I don't imagine you'd be terribly good at cards, my dear. Your thoughts are written all your pretty face.'

Emma feigned indignation over the teasing. 'Very well, I'll take your bet. I'm already thinking of all the "little" things you can do for me. It's just so hard to choose one.' The banter was almost enough to take her mind off her real worries: what had Gridley told him this afternoon? What was Ren thinking about her now? What sort of poison had Gridley added to the proverbial well?

Ren rolled his dice and let out a whoop. Emma stared in disbelief as double fives tumbled out. Emma shook her head. 'You have the devil's own luck. I'd thought to have you trapped on the bar a little longer.'

Ren gave a confident grin and moved his marker off the bar. 'Now I have a chance to catch up, I might make a match of this yet.' There was a warm twinkle in his eye and Emma realised he was having a good time. Whatever Gridley had imparted, it hadn't dampened his spirits.

'And your forfeit?' Emma asked, bearing off her first pips.

'I think I'll hold on to it a while.' Ren's voice was low and mysterious, conjuring up images of a decadent forfeit. 'It will give you something to worry about besides Gridley's visit.'

Emma gave him a sharp look. 'I'm not worried about Gridley's visit.'

Ren took his turn. 'Yes, you are. You've been worried all night.'

'As I told you, I have Arthur Gridley under control.' Emma rolled a disappointing two-three combination that slowed her march towards victory. She reached out to move her pieces.

Ren grabbed her wrist over the board, his eyes boring into hers, the sudden ferocity of his move startling her. 'No, you don't have him under control. You have a rejected suitor who isn't taking your refusal as final. It makes me wonder what motivates his perseverance.'

Emma swallowed, her heart sinking. Gridley had told him! Goodness knew how Gridley had cased *that* particular story. 'That's private business. He should not have told you.' She pulled her wrist from Ren's grasp.

'Probably not. Nonetheless, I was glad for the information. It adds a certain layer of understanding to the local dynamic.' There was an accusatory edge to his response. He'd asked what Gridley was to her and she'd prevaricated. But Gridley had not. Gridley had seized the advantage and told the story first, no doubt to his advantage.

Ren played, rolling another set of doubles and neatly evening out the game. 'The way I see it, a man would only share such personal information with a stranger because he was still wounded over the rejection and not thinking clearly, or because he has another agenda to advance. What do *you* think Gridley's reason is?' He was more serious now, the fun-loving Ren from a few moments ago had disappeared.

She tossed the dice. Another disappointment. 'I think Gridley has overreached his ambitions.' It was a non-answer, but she wasn't about to voice her suspicions of what Gridley really wanted or what he'd done to get it. She hadn't any proof of it. Even so, she didn't know if she could trust Ren Dryden to side with her. He had done so briefly today because it had suited him. Gridley's revelations might have changed that.

Ren made his last play, claiming victory with another miraculous roll. Emma shook her head. She'd had that game right up until the end. 'You play like Merry. He was always coming from behind for spectacular finishes. Whenever I thought I had him, he'd surprise me. The dice never failed him. If he needed doubles, he got them.'

Ren laughed. 'I'm glad to hear it. I have to

confess I didn't know my cousin all that well. He was here, I was in London. There was an ocean between us in distance and in age. I enjoyed his company the few times he visited, though. The last time was when I'd completed my studies at Oxford, about ten years ago.'

Emma gave a soft smile. 'Merry was a good man, one of the best people I've ever met. He was always thinking of others.' Ten years seemed a lifetime. She'd have been fifteen, her father still alive, their own arrival to the island new.

She hesitated and then took the plunge while the moment was poignant and they were both feeling charitable. There was unfinished business between them. She didn't want to put it off any longer. 'I hope Arthur Gridley said nothing today that would undermine Merry's memory.'

Ren began stacking his pips. 'It seems Gridley and Cousin Merrimore were close friends, especially at the end. I must confess to finding it an odd friendship. Gridley is younger by several decades. I would not think they'd be natural companions, but perhaps one cannot be choosy about who one's friends are out here?' It was a question, not a commentary. He was the one probing now, daring her to confirm or deny Gridley's assertion.

Her probe had not resulted in a direct answer. Emma opted for a different tack. She wanted to know where Gridley stood in Ren's estimation before she committed. 'And you? How did you find our neighbour? Will he be your friend?' They were both dancing around the conversation gingerly.

'I suppose he could be,' Ren answered vaguely, closing the case. 'I can't say I know him well enough after one visit. I think in large part that decision depends on you.' Ren paused 'Do you want me to be his friend? Is there something useful we might cultivate there for Sugarland?'

She noted the reference to *we. Something useful we might cultivate?* It was a reminder he meant to be an active participant in the plantation. Still the question remained: did he mean to partner her or usurp her? In that regard, what made him different from Gridley? She'd had indications of both today.

'I fear I have upset Gridley,' Emma ventured cautiously. 'My choices are not his choices and it has become a contention between us, one that has created irreconcilable differences.' She was sure Ren would press her for more. Her answer was both descriptive and oblique.

Ren seemed to ponder her words. He moved towards the open French doors, his back to her. Without his coat, he presented a nice view of his backside, evening trousers pulled tight over firm buttocks, the tailoring of his waistcoat delineating the outline of broad shoulders before tapering to a trim waist. Not only did he possess a handsome presence but a commanding one, one that inspired confidence, even trust if she dared. She had to admit, it was easier to dare such a thing in the intimacy of the evening.

'I suspect Gridley is not a complacent loser,' he said at last.

She stood and went to join him at the doors, hoping the pleasant evening breeze would dispel the hot images in her mind. She needed to focus on the conversation, not on undressing her guest. He was fishing for something with his questions and she might inadvertently give it up. 'Yes,' Emma said carefully, 'Gridley likes to win.'

'Do *you* like to win, Emma?' His voice was quiet in the darkness.

'I like to protect what is mine. I think that's a fundamental difference between men and women.'

'You're very direct. Such directness has wounded Gridley's ego a bit.'

Emma let out a sigh. They were back to that dratted proposal. 'How much did Gridley tell you?'

'He explained he'd felt moved to act swiftly out of loyalty to Cousin Merrimore, but that you were in no state to properly assess the benefits of that proposal.' He turned his blue gaze on her in full force, his voice low and private, moving a business conversation into something more intimate, just as the removal of his jacket had turned a simple backgammon game into a domestic fantasy. 'Gridley indicated he meant to ask you again. Would his suit be welcome now that you've had time to settle and reconsider your situation?'

'That is a bold question,' Emma prevaricated. Her answer would be no. Gridley's suit would never be welcome, but telling Ren Dryden that on the acquaintance of a day would be giving away too much. It might even be encouraging him to pursue his flirtation. She did not know if she could trust Ren any more than she'd been able to trust Gridley. But who to play off against whom? If she said yes, would the gentleman in Ren feel compelled to back off? If she said no, would the seducer in him pursue and could she could use his interest as a buffer against Gridley?

'It's meant as a business question,' Ren answered. 'Who you marry affects me greatly. I'll have to work with them, trust them with forty-nine per cent of my livelihood.'

'Perhaps I'll never marry for exactly that reason. I, too, have to trust them with my forty-nine per cent.' At some point in the conversation, Ren had picked up her hand and was tracing circles on the back of it with his finger. It was idly done, but the gesture was doing warm, tingling things to her arm.

'Then Gridley will be refused?' Ren brought the conversation full circle. 'I sensed there was some tension between you this afternoon and yesterday.' It was all she needed to be reminded of the favour he'd done her, taking her part without being asked. For literally stepping up. Now, she owed him and he wanted payment in the form of an answer.

'Yes. Gridley will always be refused.' She did not offer the reasons why. She'd paid her debt. Ren would have to judge the rest on his own.

Ren nodded. 'The neighbourhood might not take kindly to that.'

'I know,' she said simply. There were advantages for everyone if she married Gridley, not the least being the cessation of her version of the apprenticeship programme. 'Your presence should appease them for now. They want a man in charge and now they have one—at least nominally.'

'More than nominally,' Ren corrected with a wry grin. 'Perhaps this means you've revised your opinion of me. Under *these* circumstances which have newly come to light, I'd think you would be glad to see me. Although yesterday, you led me to believe otherwise.' There was a teasing quality to his words, but the topic was serious: where did they stand with each other? And why?

Emma felt as if she were fighting a battle on two fronts. On one side, she had Gridley to contend with, an enemy she knew in full measure. On the other, there was Ren, a man who could be either enemy or friend. That decision was up to her.

She did need him. She needed him to stand between her and Gridley's proposals. She needed him to stand between her and the neighbours who felt a man, even a man who didn't know a thing about sugar cane, would be a better manager of the plantation than a woman who knew everything. He'd aptly summed up the battles that had consumed her since Merry had died.

She so desperately wanted to do this on her own, to show everyone who doubted that Sugarland could be run by woman, that a woman could do anything a man could do. Maybe then she could be left alone.

Emma clenched her fists covertly in her skirts, her nails digging into her palms, frustration mounting. She'd been managing decently until Ren Dryden had come along, now she had Gridley on her doorstep persistent as ever, obeah magic threatening her workforce and exploding chicken coops. How would she ever convince Ren she had it all under control when that control seemed bent on slipping away? The noose around her independence was tightening.

'The truth is, Emma, you need me.' He made the pronouncement sound like an invitation to sin, the way he'd made their discussion of cane crops on the bluff sound like foreplay. They were standing close, no longer side by side staring out over the dark lawns, but face-to-face, having turned during the course of the conversation. Ren's knuckles skimmed the curve of her jaw, his touch warm against her skin.

Emma felt the door frame hard at her back. He had her effectively trapped. There was no escaping his hot blue eyes or the thrum of her pulse as it raced in anticipation. 'What are you doing, Ren?' she murmured, although she knew very well. He'd been staking his claim all day in little ways, pushing all other claims out of the way by her own denial of them.

Ren's mouth bent to the column of her neck. 'I'm claiming my forfeit.'

Chapter Seven

'Give over, Emma.' His mouth was close to her ear, whispering his decadent suggestion, the feel of his body intoxicating as she arched into him, giving him full access to her neck, letting him trail kisses up its length to her earlobe. She let his teeth nip the tender flesh, his breath feathering against her ear. She couldn't give over any more without giving over entirely and that would be foolish. She knew what this was. The game of seduction he'd begun on the bluff was adding another delicious layer.

Tonight she seemed helpless to resist, even knowing better. Maybe that wasn't such a bad thing. Maybe it was best to get this first initial contact out of the way, remove all the anticipation and curiosity that often motivates first kisses. And perhaps she should play a little after all? She wouldn't know what Ren intended if she didn't let him advance. At least that's what she told herself as his mouth closed over hers, his tongue running over the seam of her lips. She gave him entrance, her own tongue eager to duel, eager to taste.

Surely, there could be no harm in letting her guard down just for a moment. She had been fighting for so long, been on constant alert to the hidden agendas of others. Ren was no threat to her forty-nine per cent, he already held the majority and she knew what he was playing for. His agenda was not nearly as secretive as those who'd come for the funeral. They'd come to assess the spoils, to assess how they could best use her for their own advancement. But Ren's agenda was clear even if she didn't agree with it.

Ren's hands were at her waist, strong and firm. It would be a very little thing indeed, only a matter of inches, to raise her hands to those broad shoulders. It didn't have to mean anything, just a few moments of freedom, a few moments for herself. That decided it.

Emma slid into his arms, revelling in the feel of his mouth, the caress of his tongue as it claimed hers with the confidence of an expert lover, a man sure of his reception, her mouth drinking him in as much as he drank her. He tasted faintly of dinner's wine, smelled of vanilla and clean, healthy male.

Her body moved against him of its own accord. This was a kiss that demanded full participation, not just mouths but bodies. She could feel the heat of him, the masculine strength of him where their bodies met, the power of his thighs where they pressed against her skirts, his body fulfilling the promises it had alluded to on the bluff. It was a potent signal that here was a man who understood pleasure was best when shared. Here was a man who would not seek pleasure only for himself. It was also a signal that this had gone too far. This was only to have been the experiment of a moment.

Emma broke the kiss with a little shake of her head. 'We have to stop.' Her voice sounded breathless to her own ears.

'Why?' Ren rested his forehead against hers, his eyes dark and dancing.

It was hard to think of a reason with him so close. 'We hardly know each other,' she said softly. Even that was a lie. She knew enough about him to know this was the road to no good.

'I think you underestimate how much kissing can tell you about a person, even strangers.' Ren gave her a wicked grin in the gathering darkness. He had one arm braced against the wall over her head, his body still indecently close to hers, giving her no quarter. 'For instance, you're an extraordinarily passionate woman. You do not kiss only with your mouth, but with your hips, your arms, with all you have.' His free hand had dropped to her waist, his thumb drawing lazy circles low on her hip, pressing firmly, erotically, through the fabric of her gown. 'You deserve a lover who is worthy of your passion.' His mouth was at her neck again, his implication blatant.

'You think you are that lover?' Emma fought to sound aloof when her body was surging with desire. Never had she'd been so overtly pursued and she found the honesty of that pursuit heady in the extreme. She was passionate, yes. An easy conquest? No.

'I could be, Emma. You've been alone too long.' His eyes lingered on her lips. 'I've issued a bold invitation, nothing more. The rest is up to you.' Then he was gone, levering his weight off the door frame and slipping out into the night, the Caribbean darkness swallowing him entirely the moment he stepped beyond the reach of the lamplight.

Emma stared after him, thoughts forming,

disintegrating and reforming in the wake of his departure. Gridley's aggressive visit today had reshaped her perception of what Ren could mean to her. Instead of seeing him as a second antagonist to fight, he could be an ally given the right incentive.

Ren could stand between her and Gridley by virtue of being the majority shareholder. And he would. He'd demonstrated as much already. But for how long? What if Ren decided to sell in the future, or what if Ren returned to London? How could she entice him to stay?

What a difference a day made. Initially, selling or leaving were things she'd favoured in order to maintain her independence. But she'd underestimated Gridley. If Gridley had told Ren he meant to push his suit, more trouble than she'd realised was brewing. Being married to Gridley not only put Sugarland under his control, but it put her under his control as well.

This was her greater fear. Having been under a man's control before, the experience did not recommend itself as worth repeating. Emma closed her eyes, pushing memories of Thompson Hunt and his cruelties to the back of her mind. Whatever Thompson Hunt had done, she had no doubts Arthur Gridley would be worse.

Thompson Hunt had been a selfish con artist with a malicious streak, nothing more. Arthur Gridley was a sadist and, in her opinion, a murderer. Those were two claims no one would believe if she made them as his wife, assuming she lived long enough to make them at all. She was certain their marriage would be a short one, just long enough for him to ensure Sugarland was his at last.

Emma opened her eyes and blew out a breath, refocusing her thoughts on the present. She needed Ren to stay, perhaps in a more permanent capacity than majority shareholder. How to ensure that, especially if he ever learned Sugarland wasn't as solvent as perhaps he'd been led to believe? Did she dare to risk with him what she would not risk with Gridley? Marriage was the most permanent bond she could think of.

But even then, marriage wouldn't prevent Ren from leaving her and sailing back to London, especially if it was an empty marriage done for convenience. It didn't have to be empty. If she could give him a passion to stay for, a warm bed he'd be reluctant to leave… He was a man unafraid of passion, of his own sexuality. Tonight had proven she could rouse those passions, ignite them. Her past proved sex could be a powerful weapon. It certainly had been when wielded against her. She would never stoop to Thompson Hunt's level, but she would fight with all she had.

Emma twisted a strand of hair that had come loose, an idea coming hard and fast. What had she thought earlier? *A woman could do anything a man could do...* Men seduced women out of inheritances all the time. Ren might even be trying to do that very thing. He had made it clear he couldn't be pushed away. Maybe he could be pulled in. Emma tapped a thoughtful finger against her chin. It would take time, she'd have to go slowly. Ren would never believe she'd done a complete about-turn so immediately. Nor would he trust a woman too loose with her favours. But it would be perfect. She'd use his own seduction of her as a smokescreen; while he was seducing her, she'd be seducing him. Into bed, and with luck, beyond.

'I believe he can be seduced to our side,' Arthur Gridley announced confidently to the men seated at the round table in his library: Miles Calvert, Elias Blakely, Hugh Devore and Amherst Cunningham. All Englishmen, all upstanding citizens of St Michael's parish, all of them bound together under the common standard of having suffered financial setbacks over the last five years and, most importantly, all of them having concluded that wresting Sugarland out of Emma Ward's control lay at the heart of any successful solution to their cash-flow problems. Outside of those commonalities, there were other private agendas that drew them together, politics making very strange bedfellows indeed, in some cases literally, and Gridley knew them all.

Cunningham nodded slowly, his dark eyebrows knitted together in thought. 'We'll have to act quickly before that hellcat gets her claws into him.'

'I am working on that,' Gridley said. 'Dryden and I had a long visit today.' He hoped a few salient seeds had taken root, particularly the one that warned Dryden off pursuing anything with Emma Ward. Emma was *his*. If anyone was going to wed her, or bed her, it was going to be him. He'd paid his dues. It had been unsettling to discover Dryden was a younger man. He'd been counting on someone older, less physically appealing.

'Does Dryden have money?' Miles Calvert asked. The light of the candles in the centre of the table cast his face in shadow, the whole of his expression inscrutable.

The darkness didn't bother Gridley. He knew without seeing Miles's nervous pale green eyes that Miles would be wondering if he could entice the newcomer to buy his moderate-sized plantation and add it to Sugarland's holdings. Miles had been privately contemplating a buyer so he could take the profits and return to England.

Fortunately, Miles had done that contemplating over absinthe in the evenings with him. So far, Gridley had dissuaded Miles from such a course of action in general. It hadn't been hard, there'd been no buyer until now. Miles was wondering if the arrival of Ren Dryden changed that. Gridley would have to make sure it didn't.

'I'm not sure,' Gridley answered truthfully. 'He dresses well and presents himself as an educated man. I would think he's not entirely without funds, but how much?' Gridley shrugged to indicate he thought it unlikely Dryden possessed enough to buy a plantation.

Hugh Devore broke in with a shake of his head, dismissing Calvert's financial concerns. He was a beefy, heavier-set man with greying hair and he spoke with a commanding voice. 'It's not money that matters, it's relationships. What I want to know is who Dryden's connections are. How well did he know Merrimore? We know he's a cousin, but were they close? Was Merrimore likely to have told him about us? If so, what might that have been? Are we friends or enemies?'

The last was said with the faintest hint of accusation. Gridley bristled at the implication that somehow he was to blame if they were exposed. 'I assured you months ago and I assure you now that the risks we so covertly refer to are secure. Merrimore suspected nothing, he told no one because in his mind there was nothing to tell.'

Hugh Devore was not satisfied. 'We took an *enormous* risk at your urging, Gridley, and we lost. You were wrong in your assumptions. Nothing turned out as you purported and now we have a cousin on the scene, one more person that stands between us and our goals.'

Elias Blakely nodded his head in concurrence. Amherst Cunningham said nothing, but looked distractedly at his hands. So that was how things stood these days. A little faction was growing within his group, Gridley noted. He would have to calm them with a reminder of what he held against them. He wasn't above a bit of blackmail to ensure compliance. But first, perhaps some soothing was in order.

'I don't recall seeing you in Merrimore's sick-room taking those risks,' he reminded Devore and Blakely. 'That was all me. In that respect, gentlemen, your hands are clean.' Never mind that they'd given permission for what he'd done in there. He'd remind them about that another time. Accomplices were just as guilty as those who executed the act.

Devore sat back in his chair, hands laced across a healthy show of stomach. 'Be that as it may, Emma Ward has refused you, making our risky efforts for naught. Sugarland, either through legal deed or marriage, is beyond our grasp at present.'

That statement had everyone's attention. The men at the table leaned forward in earnest. Six months ago when Merrimore's demise was imminent, they'd decided the best, least intrusive way to take Sugarland from Emma would be to marry into it. The most likely candidate had been himself. Devore and Cunningham were already married, Miles was a 'confirmed bachelor' and Elias Blakely wasn't much to look at and prone to ill health besides.

'I will renew my courtship now that she's had a chance to see what reality looks like,' Gridley replied. 'I will remind her of my promises to Merrimore and play to her sentimentality.'

'And Dryden?' Devore asked astutely. 'Does he have matrimony on his mind?'

'I'm not sure what Dryden has on his mind. I only spoke with him the once and he's only just arrived,' Gridley reminded the group with a note of censure. 'I'm not a mind reader, although at times many of you think I am. I think the best course forward is to hold a dinner party for him so each of you can take his measure. We can plan how to deal with him from there.'

Elias Blakely spoke for the first time. 'In the meanwhile, there must be something we can do to urge Emma Ward towards our conclusion. I don't need to tell anyone here that time is critical. We are poised at the beginning of the harvest. Once the harvest is in, decisions will be made about next year. All of us will be making those decisions, too, and money is tight. If we cannot secure Sugarland, some of us might make different decisions about the following year.' He swallowed and said quietly, 'Plantation prices are dropping. Some of us may decide to sell before prices drop further.'

Gridley fixed him with a hard stare. 'If anyone were to do that, it would ruin the cartel we've worked so hard to put together. All of us standing united can drive the prices of sugar back up. Then, we'll be in the money.'

'Only if Sugarland is with us,' Miles put in, his eye always on the bottom line. 'If Sugarland continues to stand alone, we'll never achieve the ability to control the prices.'

Gridley gave a tight smile. He was growing weary of the effort of dragging the group along behind him, but he needed them. It would pacify them if he resumed an active courtship of Emma, so he would do it. He would give her two weeks' respite from exploding chicken coops and obeah dolls before he launched his new campaign. His dinner party for Dryden would be the perfect venue for resuming his courtship.

Privately, he didn't think such measures would be enough. But there were other ways to urge Emma to the altar that had nothing to do with the delicacies of romance and everything to do with the hard choices a person makes to save the things they love.

Chapter Eight

Ren stood impatiently while Michael put the finishing touches to his cravat. Arthur Gridley's dinner party was tonight and Ren felt as if he were donning armour instead of evening dress.

The metaphor of battle was not amiss. The peaceful hiatus of the last two weeks while planters focused on their own crops had been a detente of sorts between Gridley and Sugarland. In the quiet of the interim, Ren had not forgotten Gridley and his self-serving intentions lurking just beyond the harvest. The dinner party marked the end of any reprieve. Gridley would be waiting to see how Ren would align himself—with the parish or with Emma.

'Be patient, Mr Ren. Mr Merrimore was a stickler for perfection and you should be, too.' Michael stepped back with the reminder that he was as capable as any London valet. 'I dressed Mr Merrimore for many of Sir Arthur's dinner parties. He liked to wear his stick pin just so. Perhaps I should adjust yours?'

Ren lifted his chin and tolerated the effort, a thought coming to him. 'Were Merrimore and Gridley good friends?' Who would know better than Merrimore's footman-cum-valet? Currently, he only had Gridley's word on the subject. Frankly, Gridley would be biased on that account.

Michael's brow knitted as he reset the stick pin. 'They were always friendly, but it wasn't until the last year that they were what you'd call close. Sir Arthur was here every day, playing backgammon or chess. When Mr Merrimore wasn't well enough to do that, Sir Arthur read to him. Sir Arthur would have me carry Mr Merrimore downstairs and they'd sit and read for hours. He was here when Mr Merrimore passed away and he was here every day after until Miss Emma couldn't stand it any more.' Michael stood back. 'That looks much better.'

Ren gathered up his watch and chain from the dresser. 'She kicked him out, did she?' He was starting to piece together where Emma's loathing for Gridley came from. He'd rather have had Emma tell him herself, but since she'd been reticent on the subject of Gridley except to say she would not consider his suit, Ren had to look elsewhere for information.

'She was grieving, Mr Ren, and Sir Arthur wanted decisions made. It was just too much for her,' Michael offered. 'They fought one day. We could hear them yelling at each other all the way down in the kitchen. We couldn't hear what they said exactly, just the rise and fall of voices. Then we heard something shatter. Later we found pieces of a vase when we were cleaning up. Miss Emma must have thrown it at him.'

Ren stifled a laugh. He could imagine Emma doing just that. She was a woman of passions and that included her temper. These weeks had seen progress on that front, too. The forfeit he'd claimed had accomplished its purpose. She was starting to reshape how she viewed him. That was exactly what he wanted. He wanted her to stop seeing him as an enemy and begin to see him as a man with potential, someone who could help Sugarland, help her if she'd let him. If that potential started with a kiss, so be it. If she would not welcome him as a business partner, perhaps she'd welcome him as a friend or something more. He'd left that invitation open.

She was an exciting woman, a woman aware of her own desires and she was not immune to him.

'Thank you, Michael. I can handle things from here.' Ren dismissed the eager footman-cum-valet with a smile and strict orders not to wait up. He could get himself to bed and he knew Michael would have an early day of it no matter when he got in. He'd learned that during the harvest everyone had early mornings. Regardless of one's usual status the rest of the year, everyone was in the fields these crucial weeks, including himself and Emma.

He'd been astonished by the amount of people needed to run the place. In part due to inherent labour shortage and in part due to the lingering effects of the obeah charm, Emma had ended up with only about two-thirds of the hands she needed. Everyone had been pulled to the fields. Jobs in other areas of the plantation went undone. The two of them had even joined in, stripping stalks of cane and tossing them on the wagons It was back-breaking work. His friends at home would have laughed to see him sweating in the fields.

Thankfully, Sugarland was nearly done, but other plantations might continue to harvest or even start their harvests at staggered intervals for the rest of the month depending on the readiness of their fields.

Ren stretched to relieve the soreness of his muscles, a testament to the long hours and hard work. He didn't mind. It felt good to be actively doing something on his family's behalf, to feel that he was making progress in achieving financial security for them. Soon the harvest would be in and there would be money to send home, a good chunk of it, too.

He was already imagining the relief on Sarah's face when the notice came, already hearing Annaliese's happy laughter as she danced through the hall dreaming of all the ribbons she could buy in the village. Sarah would buy those ribbons and licorice drops for Teddy but she would know what it really meant. They were saved. She could go back to London and carry on as if nothing had happened. She could have her pick of husbands and in a few years Annaliese could too.

This would be the first of many infusions. He would not be there to celebrate with them, of course. His efforts would be required here, but his absence was a small sacrifice for their security. He'd known quite well when he'd left England there would be no going back. Maybe for a short visit in a few years, but never to live. This new life would require all of him. And in truth, he didn't mind that either. London had paled for him long ago. If it hadn't been for his sense of duty, he might have left with Kitt. But he'd been the heir and Kitt a mere second son. Kitt's choices couldn't be his.

Ren took a final look in the mirror. The image made him smile. It had been five weeks since he'd left England and already he was changing. His hair was a little lighter—more the colour of paler winter wheat, less the colour of deep wild honey. His face was tan, his arms would be too beneath the sleeves of his shirt. Even his chest was tan after weeks of working shirtless in the equatorial sun. He doubted Arthur Gridley would sport such evidence of hard work tonight. Emma had said Gridley did not take an active hand in his harvest.

Satisfied with his appearance, Ren picked up his evening cape from the bed. It seemed silly to take the garment with the weather being warm, but Michael had assured him Sir Arthur's parties were formal affairs and one did not go to war without the proper weapons, after all.

Emma was waiting for him in the drawing room. She turned from the window and his

breath hitched. She was stunning, exotic. Gone
was any trace of the trouser-clad, boot-wearing
woman who'd sweated and laboured beside him,
although that woman had been appealing, too.
In her place was a lady London would find no
fault with.

Emma's dark hair was piled high on her head
and threaded with pearls. The *coiffure* was both
demure and seductive, showing off the elegant
length of her neck. At the base lay a thin gold
necklace, simple but expensive. No jewel could
have looked finer. The gold was the perfect foil
for the deep coral of her gown. In London, the
colour would have been scandalous, too bold
among the whites and pinks of debutantes, but
here among the lush colours of the island with
its rich green grasses and deep azure skies, the
vibrant red-orange seemed entirely appropriate.

It certainly suited her colouring: dark hair,
dark eyes and skin tinged a healthy shade of light
toast from days in the sun. It suited her figure,
too. The cut of the gown made the most of her
natural assets; a bare neckline exposed slender
shoulders, a tight bodice lifted her breasts high,
the fullness of her skirt fell sensuously over the
curve of her hips, accentuating the provocative
sway of her hips.

'I thought the man was supposed to wait for the woman.' She gave a throaty laugh and crossed the room, her eyes running over the length of him in silent approval.

Ren picked up her cloak from the chair and held it out for her, letting his hands skim bare skin as he settled it about her shoulders. 'I assure you, I'm worth waiting for.' He felt her telltale pulse leap beneath his fingers where they lingered.

'You're certainly the most arrogant man I've ever had to wait for.' She slanted him a coy look.

'I don't think you mind.' Ren smiled, enjoying the flirty sparring and gave her his arm. Perhaps tonight would be a chance to launch an offensive on this particular front. Goodness knew his body had been on edge since the night of their kiss, the proximity and long hours together since then working all sorts of magic in honing his physical desire to sharpness. Five weeks of enforced celibacy didn't help.

The carriage, an open-air landau, was already outside. He handed her in and took the rear-facing seat, determined to be the gentleman. Women responded to manners and, oh, how he wanted her to respond. *Give over, Emma*, he thought. *You know you want to, stop torturing us both.*

She wasn't the only one affected, not by a long shot. He was attracted to her, had been from the moment he'd stepped off the wagon and seen her standing on the porch. In all fairness, the kiss had not been all strategy. There was a certain thrill to seducing her, to feeling the infinitesimal tensing of her body as he'd come up behind her on the bluff, to seeing her pulse beat in anticipation at the base of her neck when he came near, to see those eyes darken in response to his innuendos.

The kiss had tested all sorts of waters and now he was waiting, rather impatiently, to see what she would do. The intervening weeks had been her test as well as his. He'd provoked her and, in turn, she was teasing him with a toss of her hair over breakfast, a lingering glance at dinner, flirtation and witty banter over backgammon, even a light brush of her fingers on his sleeve when she said goodnight.

All of which had conspired to leave him in a perpetual state of slow burn. He was starting to wonder who was playing whom. It was time, Ren decided, for her to take the invitation. Perhaps he could help that decision along tonight.

* * *

The drive to Gridley's took half an hour and Emma had filled it with talk about who he would meet. It was a briefing more than a conversation. Ren's head was swimming with names and details by the time the carriage pulled up to the impressive front of Gridley's neo-classical home with its pillars and fountain.

'The house makes quite a statement.' Ren helped Emma down from the carriage, letting his hand linger at her back in silent persuasion.

'It's a pretentious monstrosity if you ask me.' Emma shook out her skirts. 'No other great house on the island is built this way.'

Ren offered her his arm. 'Then that's probably why he did it.' He was starting to understand this neighbour a little better. Arthur Gridley was a man who coveted the best and the rarest of things. No wonder he had proposed to Emma. She was a rare beauty. Gridley would have coveted her even without the plantation.

The others were already assembled in the drawing room, drinks in hand. Gridley noticed their arrival immediately and strode forward. 'Everyone, our guest of honour is here!' The announcement was met with a small round of applause. Gridley shook his hand. 'It is good to see you, Dryden. You're looking well. Emma hasn't worked you to death yet.' He turned to Emma and bent over her hand, bestowing a kiss on her knuckles. Ren could feel Emma freeze beside him, unable to avoid the physical contact. 'You look lovely. I'm so glad you didn't wear black. Albert wouldn't have wanted you to mourn.'

'I'm very clear on what Merry wanted for me,' Emma answered sharply, pulling back her hand. 'Shall I introduce Mr Dryden around?' It was a ploy to escape Gridley.

'Let me do the work, Emma. You relax and enjoy yourself. The ladies will want a good coze with you. I know it's been ages since you've seen them.' He gave Ren a knowing, manly look. 'The ladies have little suitable company on the island, one of the drawbacks of living in the colonies.'

Gridley spirited him away to meet the gentlemen, leaving Emma to join the women gathered on one side of the drawing room. He met the neighbouring planters, shook their hands, listened to them discuss their harvests which were just getting under way while Sugarland's was nearly done. But Emma remained relegated to the other side of the room, a bright, brilliant burst of colour against muted blues and grays. It occurred to Ren that Gridley might be attempting to divide and conquer.

Dinner was much the same. Ren sat at Gridley's right hand with Gloria Devore on his other side, *her* hand resting occasionally on his thigh in blatant invitation. Alexandra Cunningham was across from him affecting the same sort of invitation with her eyes. Emma was at the other end of the table, holding court with Elias Blakely and Miles Calvert. By the time cheese and fruit were served, Ren did not doubt the meal, the whole event even, had been orchestrated and not solely for his benefit, but for Arthur Gridley's.

Gridley had trotted out the best china and crystal, he'd shouldered the expense of preparing excellent food and opening the finest imported wines in the hopes of getting something in return. *From him.* He was the guest of honour for a reason. Ren finished the last of the wine in his glass and shot a quick glance at Gridley. The man was watching Emma again. Ren had caught Gridley watching her all night. Perhaps he shouldn't be so egotistical and think it was only himself Gridley wanted something from. This was a display for Emma, too, a reminder of all he could provide for her, the lifestyle she'd have if she said yes.

Something possessive flared to life in Ren's core at the thought of Emma in Arthur's arms, of Emma kissing another the way she'd kissed him. Emma had made it clear she didn't want Arthur Gridley, but he still didn't know why.

Ren fingered the stem of his wine glass. Why *did* a woman turn down a man like Arthur Gridley? Gridley was wealthy, good-looking, well mannered, had a house that would impress a certain type of person, he even had a title. It wasn't one that could be inherited, but he'd demonstrated his upstanding citizenry by providing a valuable service to the Crown. What wouldn't appeal about that package? That it *didn't* appeal was far stranger than if she'd accepted his proposal, especially when it was made at what Ren considered a very opportune time.

Devore's wife rose from the table, her hand finally admitting defeat. 'Ladies, let us adjourn to the drawing room. Conversation at this end is quickly turning to dull business.' She flashed him a last look, invitation openly written in her hazel eyes as she led the ladies, Emma included, from the room. Gloria Devore was handsome, but Ren didn't make a habit of dallying with married women. Unlike Kitt, who actively sought a new woman every night, married or not, Ren preferred the mixture of adventure and stability that came with long-term mistresses. Kitt was easy and he was hard, damn hard these days when it came to Emma.

Chapter Nine

Ren's senses went on alert the moment the double doors were drawn behind them. Whatever purpose Gridley had in putting on this lavish dinner, it would be exposed shortly. It was just the men now and business would be discussed, talk would be freer.

Gridley began buttonholing the port around the table. There was general, unfocused conversation as everyone poured a glass. 'As you can see, Dryden, we are not without our comforts. We live well out here in the colonies.' Gridley raised his glass once everyone had served themselves. 'A toast, gentlemen, to our success, hard won as it is.'

Ren drank to the toast although he couldn't help but think Gridley's success was due to force more than the winning of anything, much less loyalty. The atmosphere at Gridley's was different from Sugarland. At Sugarland, the staff was much like a house staff in wealthy English homes. There was a sense of being in service, working for a wage, as opposed to being in slavery. Gridley might profess to follow the apprenticeship programme, but the climate of his home didn't suggest a sense of freedom or personal pride in one's work. It did, however, suggest a sense of fear driving the excellence that surrounded Gridley.

'I won't beat around the bush, Dryden. We want to discuss business with you.' Gridley put down his glass and refilled it. 'Sugar prices have fallen in the last few years. We are of a mind to form a sugar cartel in order to drive up the prices. We'd like you to join, to bring Sugarland in line with the other plantations in the parish.'

Ren sipped slowly, letting the rich port travel down his throat. So this was what Gridley wanted. What they all wanted. The others nodded their heads sagely. 'I will need to discuss that with Emma.'

Gridley gave a friendly laugh and leaned forward, his hand on Ren's arm in a gesture of familiarity. 'You control the majority of the estate. You don't need to ask Emma anything. Take charge, Dryden. Don't let her lead you around by the short hairs.' He winked and added conspiratorially, 'Although you wouldn't be the first man she had thinking with the wrong head, if you know what I mean.' There was general masculine laughter around the table.

Ren bristled at the remark. It was insulting on so many different levels he didn't know where to aim his anger: at slander against his masculinity and the idea that his head could be so easily turned or the crude reference to Emma. 'As the will stands, Emma and I are partners. The division of the estate is all but equal.' He made the protest even while his own sense of caution silently challenged him not to act rashly.

Was it slander or did Gridley speak the truth? Emma was no blushing virgin. He'd not thought it when he arrived and he certainly didn't think so now after the flirting and kissing that had passed between them. Emma definitely had a sense of her own feminine power. Did that mean she lacked virtue as Gridley suggested? Up until now, he hadn't realised how heavily he'd been relying on Merrimore's judgement to serve as Emma's character reference.

'But it's *not* equal when it comes right down to it. Don't you let her convince you otherwise.

Merrimore left *you* the majority for a reason,' Hugh Devore put in briskly. 'Emma's impulsive, she's emotional and we know she misses Merrimore. She's not equipped to make a good decision and we can't wait. We need the cartel in place before we sell this year's crop.'

Elias Blakely backed him up in softer tones. 'It's not as if we haven't waited. We've given her time. I think Merrimore would have joined us, but she's backed off. Sugarland is the largest producer in our parish. Without you, the cartel will have no teeth.'

Ren nodded noncommittally. The game wasn't a complicated one. They were trying the age-old back-door strategy. They couldn't get to Emma so they were trying to go through him. 'I will look into it.' He put enough steel into his voice to end the conversation.

Gridley understood the message and intervened before Devore could argue. 'Check the books at Sugarland if you haven't already, Dryden. You need the cartel as much as the cartel needs you.' He beamed at the group. 'Now that's settled, let's go join the ladies.'

Emma looked up with relief as the door between the drawing room and the dining room slid open. She wanted nothing more than for the evening to end. Being *inside* Arthur Gridley's home was nothing short of being in prison. There'd been a cold pit in her stomach all night, put there by the irrational fear she'd disappear inside these walls and never be seen again. It was what she feared if Gridley succeeded in marrying her.

Nothing all night had been able to distract her fear, not the fine food which she barely tasted, and certainly not conversation with the women. The women had bored her with their agenda of barely veiled concern over her being alone at Sugarland with a man. Emma had no doubt their husbands had put them up to it. They wanted her to move. Gloria Devore had offered her rooms with them. 'Let Mr Dryden run the plantation, you needn't be alone there any more,' she'd said with false sweetness. Emma had politely declined. Gloria probably would have preferred to offer those rooms to Ren based on the amount of time her hand had spent under the table tonight.

At least the men hadn't taken very long, only a half hour. She wondered if that was good or bad. Ren looked a little grimmer than he had at dinner. But whatever had happened had not got the best of him. With that grimness came an air of command. His presence dominated the room. She'd felt that presence before when they were alone. It was one thing to think he was powerful when there was no one to compare him to. It was another to think it when she saw him against the backdrop of the parish's leading men. He stood out even in the company of large men like Devore and supposedly attractive men like Arthur Gridley.

Ren's eye caught hers and the nerves in her stomach began to relax. She'd missed Ren tonight. After having had him to herself for dinners and days on end, she'd not had him at all this evening. He'd been whisked from her side the moment they'd walked in. She was sure it had not been accidental. She'd not realised how used to him she'd become. They'd worked together, they'd taken their evening meal together, they'd played backgammon games together before retiring. One might say they lived in each other's pockets.

And yet, she worried. What she would have given to hear what had been said behind those doors! How had Ren responded? She might know his backgammon strategy, but she had no idea how he'd answer the leading members of the plantocracy. Would he undo all of her hard work? Would he use his fifty-one per cent to force her into accepting decisions she would not have made? Would he have betrayed her? Men had betrayed her before. Would Ren prove to be the same?

Betrayal was a strong word with only a kiss between them, yet betrayal was the emotion she felt when she looked at him; this strong, masterful stranger who'd entered her life. Would he betray her? Ren was speaking with Gridley. She smiled at him, hoping to signal that he should join her but it was Gridley who approached the sofa where she sat.

'My dear Emma, come take a turn about the room with me. I don't think you've seen my new painting.' She couldn't refuse, nor could she ignore the warm glances the women cast her way as Gridley led her apart from the group. It was no secret everyone's lives would be easier if she accepted Gridley or if she disappeared, leaving them free to pursue their cartel at the expense of the backs they built their empire on.

The knot in her stomach returned. She felt vulnerable in his home with him, even surrounded by others. Who would come to her aid if Gridley decided to act less than gentlemanly? Would Ren? Had Ren decided over port that life would be smoother if her stubbornness was re-moved? Emma thought of the knife strapped to her thigh beneath her skirts and drew a deep breath. She would use it if she had to. She had no doubt she could plunge it into Gridley's black heart if the need arose.

'Is this the beginning of another courtship?' Emma asked sharply. 'If it is, you may also con-sider it the end. You already have my answer.' She pretended to study the painting.

Gridley stood close, too close. She fought the urge to move away, so unlike her response to Ren. 'You should re-examine your options, Emma. Look at all I have to offer you. My wealth is on display for you tonight. I can provide for you the way Merrimore wanted you to be cared for.' He lowered his voice. 'I am a patient man and I do not think you'd find my presence in your bed intolerable, my dear. I'm asking for so little in exchange for so much.'

Her temper began to override her fear. 'Do not play the lovesick suitor with me,' Emma an-swered in low, angry tones. 'How dare you stand there, acting as if nothing else were at stake but your heart when we both know it's Sugarland you want.'

Gridley gave a dry laugh. 'You underestimate

your charms, Emma. I assure you, I want you. I lie awake at night, dreaming of how it will be when you are mine.' He lowered his voice, his eyes glinting with evil desire. 'Shall I describe it for you?'

'No!' Emma almost shrieked. Only the steel grip she kept on her self-control prevented her from causing a scene. In her mind, she willed Ren to approach. Surely this didn't *look* like a normal conversation to anyone, further proof that no one in the room particularly cared how Gridley achieved his ends, only that he achieved them.

Emma opted to play her one ace in an attempt to regain some control. 'You are a slave-master and a murderer. If you continue to pursue this issue between us, I will be forced to go to the magistrate.' She sought to walk away, but Gridley held her arm tight, his grip a vice.

'Is that what you think you saw in Merrimore's bedchamber?' he hissed, his breath warm and sour on her face.

'You killed him.' Emma held her ground. Let him be scared. 'I saw you with the pillow.'

A leer spread across his lips. 'I saw something a little different. I saw *you* put the pillow over the old man's face.'

'Liar!' Emma all but spat in his face for the accusation.

'Who is to say who the liar is, Emma?' He shrugged. 'You say I killed Merrimore and I say you did. Who will the magistrate believe? A knight of the realm who has shown you every courtesy, including the protection of marriage, or you a woman who has a dubious past and who doesn't exactly reek of good judgement? I think we both know to what I refer. I would think this line of attack over more thoroughly if I were you.'

She tugged but he wouldn't let go of her arm. Instead he smiled as if the conversation were friendly. 'You haven't shown Dryden the accounts yet. How long do you think he'll stay after that or even want to consult your opinion? I imagine he'll lose interest unless you've offered him some other incentive?' The type of incentive he referred to was obvious. 'That's what you offered Thompson Hunt, wasn't it?'

'How dare you imply—'

'How dare *you*!' Gridley interrupted, his fingers digging painfully into her arm. She would have bruises. 'I am tired of hearing what I dare when it is *you* who insults me at every turn. You need me more than you think. Some day you will beg me on your knees for help.' He licked his lips, his eyes dropping to the low swell of her neckline. 'I will wait for that day. After all, I am a patient man with a vivid imagination.'

The fear her temper had held at bay clawed at her stomach. She'd seen Gridley angry before. There had been that one quarrel when she'd thrown the vase. But this anger was different. There was an unholy light in his eyes, a fierceness in his grip. He'd never laid hands on her like this. Gridley was a strong man, a tall man. In the past she'd always thought her word was enough to stop him. No meant no. Now, she wasn't sure.

What if Gridley decided not to wait for her capitulation? What if he could physically force her to his will? No one would stop him. Everyone supported Gridley's quest to see their lands united, to see *them* united. The others either didn't see the evil in Gridley or they didn't care. Who would stand up for her if Gridley came for her? She felt a presence behind her as if in answer to the question. Ren.

'I think Emma has recovered her balance sufficiently to stand on her own.' Her knees nearly buckled from relief. 'You did lose your balance, my dear, didn't you? Are you feeling faint? I can't think of any other reason for a gentleman to grip your arm so tightly.' The last was said strictly for Gridley's benefit, a threat neatly wrapped in polite enquiry.

'I'm fine now.' Emma edged closer to Ren and took his arm, her courage returning. 'The painting was most, ah, enlightening.'

Gridley looked from her to Ren, trying to gauge their level of involvement. She felt her pulse catch. She was playing a dangerous game, pitting them against one another. Ren would not appreciate being used. 'Just so, I think I'd like you to take me home,' she appealed to Ren, eager to be away from this nest of smiling vipers.

Ren saw to the carriage and they were off within ten minutes, their lanterns lighting the way in the darkness. She was grateful for his efficiency when it came to arrangements. She was a little less grateful when it came to conversations. The driveway was hardly behind them when Ren started the questions. 'What were you and Gridley discussing so intently?'

Emma shook her head. 'Nothing. He's jealous, that's all.' She fought the urge to spill everything to Ren, but that would give him power he might not deserve. *Not yet*, she cautioned herself. She had to be sure of him first. Not yet.

Ren's eyebrows arched in the shadows. 'Why would he be jealous?' There was a hint of teasing beneath the question, their conversation taking on a lighter, flirtier edge now that Gridley's house was behind them.

Emma smiled and moved to sit beside him. 'Because he thinks I prefer you to him.'

'And do you?'

Emma slid a hand up his thigh. 'Yes, as a matter of fact, I do.' This was a dangerous gambit too, but she had to be sure of Ren. There was so much at risk, she would do whatever it took to secure her future—which was a far better justification for her actions than simply admitting to herself that she wanted him, but far less true. She would have wanted him without the plantation between them. In the back of her mind, she knew she had planned to make her intentions known tonight regardless of the evening's outcome at Gridley's.

Ren's hand covered hers in caution. 'Emma, do you think this is a good idea?' Good idea or not, it didn't matter. It was the only idea she had, if sex would be something irrevocable to bind him to her. Besides, it seemed an natural evolution of their relationship at this point. Everything since their kiss had been leading to this.

He had started it with his wicked forfeit over backgammon, but by heaven, she would finish it. Her safety and Sugarland's security demanded it.

'It's the best idea I've had in a long time.' She leaned forward and kissed him hard on the mouth, as if everything depended on it, because it did.

Chapter Ten

This was a bad idea on multiple levels, starting with the most obvious: there'd been *a lot* of wine served at dinner. They'd both imbibed thoroughly. There were more complicated reasons, too, Ren knew: whether she admitted it or not, Emma's encounter with Gridley had left her feeling vulnerable, feeling in need of a hero. He was aware he'd been that hero for her in the drawing room, coming to her side when he'd noted the conversation had taken a less friendly turn. Perhaps the hand running up his thigh was being grateful for his assistance. Perhaps she felt she needed to offer recompense.

Mentally, Ren knew he should put a stop to that hand before it reached a more critical juncture. His mind didn't want 'grateful' sex, but his body didn't seem capable of making those distinctions. His body was responding to her with the wholehearted enthusiasm of a healthy man who'd been celibate for over a month.

Emma had managed to get a leg over his lap, straddling him, with her coral skirts riding high, her hand between them cupping the hardened ridge through his trousers, her mouth on his in a full-bodied kiss, her tongue in his mouth, his own tongue giving as good as it got. As much as his mind willed, his body would not be mounting any resistance to her intimate assault.

Emma ran a thumb over the outlined tip of him and he moaned. It had been so long since anything had felt this good, this physically inviting. His hands ran up her legs past the curve of her calves to her thighs and came to an abrupt halt as one hand made contact with a leather sheath. 'Good lord, Emma, what is this?'

'An old habit,' she murmured between kisses. Why did a woman take a concealed weapon to a dinner party? He should have pushed the issue right then, but his mind had finally registered the sensual reality of bare flesh. His hands had moved on, clenching around the soft swell of her buttocks, 'You minx!' Ren nipped at her bottom lip with his teeth. 'You've been naked beneath this dress all night.'

She gave a throaty laugh and squeezed him, her eyes dark with desire. 'I'm hungry for you, Ren Dryden. Are you hungry for me?'

'Oh, yes.' Ren groaned. She was bold, beautiful, sure of herself, all the things he liked in a woman. The nakedness beneath her skirts confirmed it. She'd planned to have him, a most titillating and flattering realisation. Confident lovers were hard to come by. Apparently so was privacy.

They both recognised they'd reached the limits of what could decently be accomplished. There was no question of taking this any further in the open-air carriage with the driver's back so near. Emma flashed him a frustrated glance. They had another mile to go before they were home.

Inspiration struck. There was one thing he could do. 'Can you be very quiet?' Ren whispered at her ear, his hand sliding again beneath the bunched fabric of her gown to the damp, hot core of her. Whatever reservations his mind had about taking her, there was no arguing she wanted this, wanted *him*. His fingers were wet with her honey as he found her secret place, the centre of her pleasure. He ran his thumb over the hidden little nub, watching her eyes widen, feeling her body shudder with delight.

She arched against his hand, her body instinctively wanting to be closer to the source of pleasure. He revelled in her response, intoxicated by the knowledge he could render this beautiful woman boneless. *She wanted him,* without any inkling of who he was, or what his title meant.

He stroked her again, and the tiniest of mewls escaped her lips. 'Shh,' Ren warned with a wicked grin. He silenced her with a kiss, long and deep, while he stroked, while he rubbed. It became an intense, intimate game to see who would break first. Emma writhed against him, the kisses coming hard and fierce as her climax neared.

'Do *not* scream,' Ren instructed hoarsely, feeling her body tighten. Her hands dug into his shoulders in an effort to keep her silence. She gave a gasp and Ren smothered it with a kiss as she collapsed against him, her relief palpable. Ren was almost jealous. She was momentarily sated while he was still very much aroused and painfully so, craving her touch, craving the release that would come. His mind urged his body patience. This was good, but there was better waiting. This was just the beginning.

They pulled into the drive, the carriage coming to a stop in front of the house. He helped Emma down, the sight of her, ravished and dishevelled, fuelling his desire to the brink of breaking. Her hair had come down in dark glorious waves, her lips were swollen from ardent kisses, marks of his possession, signs that she was his. And she burned for him still, her eyes hot with wanting as they mounted the front steps. The momentary release he'd given her now becoming only a prelude, a sample of something greater to come.

She might have sparked what had happened in the carriage, but Ren had become the master of it, driving her to the edge of pleasure and over it, but even that hadn't been enough for his wild Emma. She was burning, her body on fire for more, for him. Knowledge of it stoked his passion to the breaking point. He was a well-primed powder keg of male desire by the time they gained the hall. She tugged at the lapels of his evening coat, dragging him to her for a hard kiss. Any thought he'd entertained about making it upstairs to bed vanished in the wake of his wanting.

Ren answered her with a devouring kiss of his own, his mouth claiming primal possession. Her arms were about his neck. Her body pressed into his, her hips undulating in an unspoken request. 'Take me, Ren. Here.' Her voice was a feverish murmur against his mouth.

It was all the invitation he needed. Desire rode him hard. He bore her back to the wall, lifting, balancing, as her legs wrapped about him and her skirts fell back to reveal bare skin, the grip of her thighs urging him closer. He released the fall of his trousers and, by all that was holy, he couldn't recall wanting a woman with such uncontrolled abandon. He felt rough and wild as he thrust into her, not in the least a gentleman.

Her head went back, her neck arched, a feral cry escaping her. He was a king in that moment, watching her thrash in passion, knowing that the wildness was not his alone. He thrust again and again, pushing both of them to the completion that waited just beyond the wildness. He gave a last, rough thrust, his body pulsing into hers as she screamed his name one last time.

They could not stay here, locked in an intimate embrace in the hall. It was Ren's first thought once sanity returned, a thought mobilised by necessity. His muscles were starting to ache from the strain of balancing her against the wall.

'Emma love, let me help you upstairs.' He disengaged as gracefully as possible and gently lowered her until her feet touched the ground, but she was boneless in the aftermath of their exertions. While he might take manly pride in that accomplishment, it had its own consequences. She gave only the slightest of protests, his muscles giving rather more, when he swept her up in his arms and mounted the staircase.

By the time he'd tucked a sleeping Emma into bed still fully dressed and reached the *garçonnière*, Ren's brain had started to register the fullness of what he'd done, what they'd done. It was perhaps more sobering than any amount of coffee. From the wicked game they'd played in the carriage to the unrestrained lovemaking in the hall, the interlude had been savage and uncivilised in the extreme.

Ren supposed he could chalk it up as the natural repercussion of a healthy man and woman living and working in close proximity. There was bound to be curiosity. They certainly had been aware of each other from the start and heavy flirting had followed. Under those conditions, what happened tonight had been inevitable. But now that the curiosity was satisfied, what next? How did they go on from here?

Was this to be a one-night experiment or was it the beginning of an affair, or even the beginning of something more, a relationship? Ren undressed for bed, carefully laying aside his evening clothes for Michael to brush in the morning. He wished his thoughts could be set aside just as easily.

Had this evening been only about the physical? His thoughts might have strayed in such lusty directions, but in the end Emma had started it. *She'd* been the one to straddle him, to intimately cup him. One could not mistake an overture like that. Even exhausted as he was, his body roused to the memory. What had she been looking for? Satisfaction? Appeasement? A safe harbour?

She might have started it, but don't forget you finished it. You were the one to play a decadent game of 'don't scream'. You were the one to push her up against the wall, to thrust into her until she cried your name, his conscience scolded. It wasn't done. *Whatever tonight was, you enjoyed it far too much for it not to matter.* His pleasure was not inconsequential. Tonight had been as much about his pleasure as it had been hers. At the end, his own climax had ripped from him like a river breaking its banks and for a while it had obliterated everything in its path—common sense and reality.

The truth was, tonight had been a moment out of context. He knew deuce little about Emma Ward beyond the present. Ren lay down on his bed, his hands behind his head, his eyes fixed on the stuccoed ceiling. He knew of her only what their short time together had taught him. What he'd learned were attributes. She was strong, determined, independent. But attributes were not history. How did those traits translate into events? Had those traits worked for or against her? Sir Arthur Gridley suggested those characteristics led Emma to be impulsive, to make rash decisions in business and in sex. Gridley believed she needed to be protected against that rashness. Was Gridley to be believed?

Gridley would be livid if he knew what had transpired here tonight. Ren drew a deep breath and exhaled, making the argument with himself. He hadn't poached on another man's territory. Emma had made it plain she did not welcome Gridley's attentions, but Gridley wouldn't see it that way. Ren wondered if that had been some of Emma's impetus. Had she merely been caught up in the moment and looked for a quick way to strike out at Gridley?

He didn't relish thinking of himself as a pawn in her neighbourly war. Yet, that was the one thing he didn't doubt. Tonight, Emma had been frightened. The war between her and Gridley was real, suggesting the stakes for Emma were high. Ren had seen her fight fire and marshal her troops without hesitation. She was not a woman who scared easily.

That Gridley unnerved her spoke volumes, some of it rather difficult for his ego to contemplate. Had fear forced her into his arms tonight? The idea that her seduction had been planned was starting to pale from its original flattery. Had she been scared long before this and decided to seduce him as security?

'Oh, Merrimore, what have you sent me into?' Ren mused, feeling a bit guilty. No matter how pleasurable it had been, he'd acted rashly this evening. Would he have dared such a thing if Merrimore had been alive? What would Merrimore think if he knew Ren had tupped his ward in the hall, nonetheless? That was something Kitt Sherard would do. It wasn't that he wasn't an imaginative lover. He was. He just wasn't normally an exhibitionist, given to performance in potentially public places. Good heavens, what had he been thinking? Any late-night servant could have run across them.

But that was just it. He hadn't been thinking. Every ounce of his being had been focused on succouring his desire, sating his want. Tonight, the pursuit of pleasure had stripped him of all logical thought. He hadn't even possessed the decency to do it in a bed in a private room with the door shut. Not that those details made it better in the end. In the final analysis, he'd bedded—he did use that term loosely since there had been no real furniture involved—a woman he knew very little about and knew even less what he meant to do about it.

To make matters worse, Ren had to be honest. Despite the afterthoughts, he *would* do it again, even though it might be best if he didn't. If sex with Emma Ward was so consuming he forgot all decency, celibacy might be in his better interests. He had a plantation to learn to run. He had a family back home relying on this money-making venture. *He* was relying on this venture. If he wanted to escape the clutches of the York heiress, he had to think with his brain, not his—

A memory from earlier in the evening stirred; something Gridley had said. *Don't let her lead you around by the short hairs.* Initially, Ren had thought Gridley was merely referring to the division of the estate and the comment about who was really charge. Given Gridley's longer-standing relationship with Emma, Ren had to wonder if that was all he'd referred to.

An uncomfortable feeling began to take up residence in his gut. Gridley had implied Emma was not above using seduction and had done so on at least one occasion. He had to exercise caution. He knew logically the interlude was a mistake, yet he also recognised he'd willingly make that mistake again if the opportunity arose.

She started it. Another discomforting truth presented itself. Emma had planned this. She'd gone to dinner stark naked under her gown. It was fair to say there'd been some premeditation there. A woman didn't forgo undergarments on a random whim. Had she anticipated that when the act came it would be fast and furious, no time for undressing or for dealing with inconvenient underclothes? If she had, what did it mean?

The truth crashed about him in the darkness of his chambers. The longer he thought about it, the clearer it became. All roads led to the same conclusion. He, Ren Dryden, one of London's most sought-after lovers, had been seduced by a master.

Chapter Eleven

Emma gave a languorous stretch, letting the morning sun caress her body. She'd slept better last night than she had since Merry passed away. She felt rested, in both body and mind. It was the first morning she could recall where she hadn't awakened with her mind an immediate riot of lists full of things that had to be done. She gave another long stretch and stopped mid-action. Something didn't feel right. She felt confined as if she was wearing a tight garment instead of her loose nightgown.

That was funny; she couldn't remember putting her nightgown on last night. Emma ran hands down her body, her fingers halting when they met with satin instead of cotton. She looked down and confirmed her suspicions. She was still in her dress. Ren! The latter part of the evening came back to her in hot, vivid flashes; Ren's naughty game in the carriage, Ren taking her hard and swift up against the hall wall. All the pent-up passion that had lurked beneath the surface of their interactions since his arrival had been given its head last night to the delight of them both.

There was no ignoring that what had happened last night had been rough and spectacular. There was also no ignoring that she'd started it. She'd been the one who had slid her hand up his leg, who had boldly straddled his lap. But he'd not been resistant. He'd been more than ready for her when her hand had found him through his trousers.

Emma sighed and sat up, ringing for Hattie. She couldn't get out of the dress on her own. She'd have to tell Hattie something to explain it. She'd have to tell Ren something, too. She doubted she could let the interlude go unremarked. One didn't have sex against the wall with a guest living under one's roof and *not* address it.

Hattie came and exclaimed, as expected, over the crumpled gown. Emma murmured a vague excuse about being late and tired and not wanting to wake her. 'I just laid down for a moment...' Emma offered an apologetic smile 'the next thing I knew, it was morning.'

'Well, I can press most of the wrinkles out.' Hattie undid the fastenings in the back and helped her slide the gown off but the scowl of disapproval on her face suggested she suspected far more had happened.

Emma offered no further discussion of the evening. Her mind was already examining and discarding possible explanations she could give Ren for her behaviour as Hattie combed out her hair. She could blame it on Arthur Gridley. No, she would sound weak, desperate for a man to solve her problems. Ren would take that opening to further increase his involvement at the plantation.

She could blame it on the wine. That would sound irresponsible, but plausible. It would be better than blaming it on her curiosity, her physical attraction to him, or on the idea she'd been alone too long. All of which implied she wanted him to stay, even needed him in ways that superseded the practical tasks of running the estate. She had started this with the intent of using it to bind him to her, but she had to admit her plans were only a part of what had compelled her boldness last night. There'd been other, selfish, personal reasons, too. Those reasons also implied she might want to continue what they'd started in the hall.

A little shudder went through her at the thought: Another night with Ren? Is that what she'd wanted? He'd been a lover nonpareil, giving her exactly what she'd been after, a rough, impetuous joining, and doing it most thoroughly. She'd been completely lost. She might have started it, but he'd taken control almost immediately. Instead of satisfying her curiosity, the encounter had merely made her hungry for more. What would it be like to lie with him, skin to skin, to linger in the act of lovemaking instead of sharing a brief, heated encounter?

'Miss Emma, are you all right?' Hattie was staring at her in the mirror. Emma focused, embarrassed to see twin pockets of colour rising on her cheeks.

'I'm fine.' Emma stood up from her dressing table. 'I'm just hungry.'

Hattie nodded, giving her a considering look. 'There's breakfast downstairs. Mr Dryden already ate. He had a big appetite this morning, too.' Ah, she wouldn't have to face Ren right away.

'Where is he now?' Ren was up early for such a late night.

'He said he wanted to look through some of his cousin's personal belongings. Michael showed him where Mr Merrimore's room was.' Hattie paused. 'I hope that was all right?' Merry's chamber had been shut up since his death. At first, Emma hadn't been able to bring herself to enter the room. Later, she simply hadn't had time, at least that's what she told herself. Perhaps she still wasn't able to face it. It seemed she'd have to, though, if Ren was in there.

She smiled at Hattie to relieve the other woman's concern and maybe her own. She'd not planned on bearding that particular lion today. 'It's fine. I'll go see how Mr Dryden is doing.'

She had only the length of the hallway to decide how she wanted to handle facing Ren after last night. Did she want to excuse the encounter as a one-time slip of moral judgement or did she want to go ahead with her initial thought of seducing Ren as a means of binding her to him?

When she'd had that idea it had been before she actually knew what she was getting into— it had been before he'd carried her up the staircase and put her to bed, before he'd claimed her so thoroughly against that hall wall. She might have meant to seduce him last night, but in the end, it had been difficult to tell who was seducing whom. She needed to remember he had his own gambits in motion as well. If she continued on the path of seducing of him, she'd be allowing him to do the same with her.

Merry's door stood ajar, making no secret of the room being open and occupied. The coward in her had hoped Ren would have finished before she arrived. She pushed the door all the way open, drew a deep breath and stepped just inside. She could not will her feet to go further than the threshold.

The room was unchanged except for the basics. The big bed was made up. The bureau and the table tops were straightened, the medicines that had marked Merry's last months were gone, but his personal brushes and other sundry items still decorated the room. Sunlight streamed through the large window, toying with fluttering dust motes. If she threw open the wardrobe and bureau drawers she would find Merry's clothes pressed and ready. It was as if the room itself was waiting for Merry to walk through the door. But she knew better. This had not only been a place of death, it had been a place of murder.

She spotted Ren seated at Merry's small escritoire near the window, reading through a book. To reach him, she'd have to cross the room.

Emma opted to call out, 'Good morning, I hear you were up early.' She tried to sound cheery and nonchalant.

Ren looked up from his reading. Seeing her, his face broke into a smile, his dimple deepening. He didn't seem nervous at all. Perhaps he had more experience than she with morning-after encounters. And, of course, the room wouldn't mean the same to him.

Ren held up his reading material, a brown leather journal. Not a book, but a personal diary. 'I've been looking for answers and I think I may have found some.' Emma knew a different kind of anxiety. She'd never looked through Merry's personal journals, deeming it too great of a privacy violation when he was alive and not having the heart to do so when he was dead. Had he written about her in there? If so, what? She had her secrets and she preferred to keep them that way.

Emma forced a smile. 'What kind of answers? Perhaps you'd care to show me over breakfast. I'm starving.' She wasn't nearly as hungry as she had been earlier, the room had sucked most of her appetite out of her, but it was a clever ploy to get Ren out of the room and herself, too. Her breath was coming fast. She put a hand on the door frame to steady herself.

Ren rose from the desk, journal in hand, and moved towards her, concern etched on his face. 'Breakfast is a good idea. You look a bit peaked. Are you sure you're all right?'

He took her by the elbow and ushered her downstairs. In the breakfast room, he insisted she sit while he fixed her a plate.

'What would you like this morning? There's sausage, eggs, fresh toast.' He rattled off a list of offerings. Her stomach rumbled, her hunger returning.

'Sausage, please, and some eggs. Breakfast was always Merry's great weakness.' The good aromas of morning cooking were triumphing over the evil of Merry's bedroom. 'We serve many local dishes for dinner, as you've probably noticed, but Merry could never give up his English breakfast.'

She took the plate from Ren. 'Thank you.' It was filled perfectly if not excessively with a balance of the things she liked: eggs, two slices of toast, two sausages and a slice of melon on the side. She was impressed. This wasn't their first breakfast together. Apparently, he'd been paying attention.

Ren smiled at the mention of Merry and resumed his seat with a plate containing his second breakfast of the day. 'I'm sorry if I was out of line by going into my cousin's room. It clearly upset you and I must apologise.'

'No, you have every right,' Emma stammered. 'This is your home, too.' Although it was still hard to imagine it as such, it was a necessary part of her plan that he did see Sugarland that way. He'd be far less likely to want to leave a place he felt a connection with. She needed to foster that connection on any level she could. Emma summoned her courage. 'What were you looking for?'

'Cousin Merrimore's thoughts.' Ren paused to take a drink of coffee. 'It was suggested to me last night that my cousin would have supported the sugar cartel Gridley has in mind. But you don't. I am hard pressed to reconcile the idea that Merrimore would have sided with Gridley over you, but I have no real evidence for that.' He held up the journal. 'I was hoping this might provide some objective illumination.'

He studied her, his face sombre. 'It is difficult to be the newcomer. Everyone is eager to share their versions of the truth. In most cases, that truth is no more than a pretext. I have no context for assessing its value or validity except my own intuition.'

Emma swallowed, moved by his admission. He was vulnerable in that moment. He was letting her see how exposed he really was. She'd not thought of him that way. He'd been in command since the moment he'd arrived, never showing an ounce of self-doubt, never backing down from her or from Gridley, or hard work, never once showing weakness as he adjusted to a new life. As a result, it had been easy for her to overlook what he'd given up to come here: the family he must have left in England, his home, his friends, all of his comforts. She'd been so focused on herself, on what his arrival meant to her, she'd not thought about what it meant to him.

Careful, Emma, her conscience warned. *This might all be part of his game. If he shows you vulnerability, perhaps he hopes you will show him your vulnerable side, too.* She'd almost made it easy on him. Emma set aside her napkin. 'Did the journal provide you with any answers?' She kept her tone businesslike.

Ren gave a polite, tight smile, disappointed in her response. 'Yes. Cousin Merrimore makes it clear he had concerns over the cartel. He saw it as temporary success with no likely long-term viability.' Ren opened the journal to an early entry about a third of the way through the book and passed it to her. A footman came in to begin clearing away the sideboard.

'Is that as far as you read?' Emma scanned the date—February of last year.

'Yes.' Ren hesitated, his voice dropping in deference to the lingering servant. 'Is there more I should know?'

'I don't know what Merrimore wrote about,' Emma answered vaguely. She could guess though. 'I have never made a habit of reading someone else's private journal.'

Ren shook his head. 'That's not what I meant. What else do you know that I don't? What is really going on with Gridley?'

Emma shot Ren a warning glance. Her servants were loyal, but she didn't like them worrying over bits and pieces they might overhear. In the last year of his life, Merry had made it a practice to discuss business with her away from Sugarland. She supposed that ritual had rubbed off on her.

In a louder voice, she changed the conversational direction entirely. 'There's nothing like a good breakfast to set things right. Thank you for suggesting I eat something.' She gave Ren a broad smile.

He took his cue admirably. 'I must say that I agree. After Oxford, I did a grand tour through Europe. Nowhere else did breakfast rival the English version in my mind. Elsewhere it was a small meal: some bread, some cheese, maybe a piece of fruit.'

'You've travelled then?' He'd not mentioned it when they'd talked of her travels with her father.

'Just the usual venues.' Ren wiped his mouth with his napkin. 'Paris, Vienna, Rome, Greece, Ephesus.' Usual venues? Hardly. They sounded far more glamorous than the destinations her father had been posted to. Ren leaned across the table, a handsome smile on his face, a little spark leaping in his blue eyes. 'I've been a lot of places, but I've not seen much of the island since my arrival. Why don't we take the day and you can show me around? We'll pack a lunch and explore.'

The suggestion caught her off guard. Nothing this morning had happened the way she'd envisioned it. Her first thought had been to confront the issue of the prior evening, but they had yet to do that. They had instead addressed other concerning issues of business: the cartel and Gridley. It was just a matter of time before Ren asked her about the unpleasant conversation with Gridley last night. 'I don't know, there's work to be done—' Emma stalled.

'There's always work to be done,' Ren interrupted before she could begin to list all the things that needed doing. 'I've checked with Peter. There's nothing that can't wait, nor is there anything that needs your especial attention. Peter can handle it, it's his job after all.' Ren leaned back in his chair. 'When's the last time you had a day off?'

She hesitated too long and Ren laughed. 'That's what I thought. You can't remember. I'll give you twenty minutes to get ready and then I expect you in the front hall.'

Chapter Twelve

Expectations fulfilled. Precisely twenty-one minutes later they set out, a covered basket and towels in the small bed of the gig. Emma hadn't even considered protesting. Ren might ask politely, but she was certain he'd have come looking for her if she'd not shown up. In truth, she hadn't wanted to protest. After the surprises of the morning, she wanted to get out of the house, away from the dark memories.

'I want to see the island,' he'd said and he turned over their direction to her care. She decided their first destination would be the limestone caves between Sugarland and the beaches. Along the way, she pointed out the natural flora, saying things like, 'That tree with the pink flowers is frangipani. Those long red-orange leaves belong to the croton plant.' They passed a cluster of yellow-and-purple flowers. 'That's allamanda. It has no smell.' It was an easy conversation to make. There was no risk to it. Flowers were harmless and the small talk helped her relax.

'You're amazing. You know everything,' Ren complimented. He steered the gig beneath a tree and got down to picket the horse in the shade. 'I'm duly impressed with your botanical knowledge.' He bent down and plucked a flower from a nearby bush. 'Allamanda, right?'

'Yes, but be careful!' Emma jumped down from the gig. 'It's a milk flower. Its nectar can blister you if you're not cautious.' She grabbed the flower from him.

Ren laughed and held up his hands. 'I am at your mercy, my dear.' He glanced around, taking in the lush green surroundings. 'Where is this cave of yours?'

'We'll have to hike the rest of the way. It's not far.' She led the way, the path winding through tall grasses and over stones. The hike was only about a quarter of a mile. She found the entrance and stepped inside. The cave was cool and it was far larger than it appeared. Emma reached for the old lantern that was left on a hook near the entrance and struck a match, illuminating the area.

She moved to the side, wanting to catch a

glimpse of Ren's reaction. She had been here several times since coming to live on the island, but it never ceased to dazzle her.

'Oh my.' Ren's words came out in a gasp of delight. 'It's beautiful.' Long stalactites hung from the ceiling, stalagmites rose up from the ground in ponds of milky-turquoise water.

Emma led the way, holding the lantern out. 'There's more to see.' She led him past pools and along a trickling river, their voices echoing off the cavern walls. The underground river gathered and grew until they came to a ledge. 'Look down there.' The water cascaded in a fall, dropping into a pool twenty feet below.

Ren put his hand in the water. 'It's warm.' He sounded surprised. He looked at her and back at the water. 'Can we get down there?'

'I don't know,' Emma said honestly. 'I've never gone any further than this.' She'd always been with Merry or with her father. They'd always stopped here.

Ren took the lantern from her and swung its arc of light around. 'Look, over there. It's some sort of natural staircase.'

Crude but wide stone steps were cut into the wall. 'I've never noticed them.' Emma advanced towards them, eager to see them, but Ren put out an arm to stop her.

'Let me go first. Take my hand.' It was Ren who led them to the bottom of the stairs, her hand in his firm grip, warm and reassuring on the ancient steps whenever she stumbled. The trip down the stairs was worth it. The waterfall pool steamed in the lamplight, looking magical.

'It's like a fairy grove,' Emma exclaimed in quiet, awed tones.

'An underground hot spring.' Ren slanted her a naughty look. 'It would be a shame to have come this far and not try it out.' He was already tugging at his boots. 'Are you game, Emma? How about a swim?'

It was all the invitation Emma needed. She hadn't swum for some time. She'd used to love it. 'You'll have to help me with my dress.' She was envious of the speed which with Ren was able to undress. His shirt was gone, his boots off before he came to work the fastenings at the back of her gown. She shivered a little at the warmth of his hands, competent and sure as they worked the buttons. How many women had he undressed? His prowess last night suggested he was more than gifted at bed sport.

She shrugged out of her dress and set it aside

with her shoes. Ren stood at the water's edge, pushing down his trousers, revealing taut, muscled buttocks and long legs. It wasn't polite to stare, but she couldn't stop herself. There'd been nothing to see last night, only feel. She couldn't help but wonder what the source of all that pleasure looked like. She wished the lantern light was stronger. If he would just turn around... Darn it, Ren stepped into the water, not turning towards her until he was up to his waist in water.

'It's warm!' he called back to the shore. 'Let me swim out and see how deep it is.' In a few powerful strokes, he reached the waterfall and waved. The water reached mid-chest. 'I'm standing just fine. It's maybe five feet.'

But Emma hadn't waited. She'd stripped out of her chemise and undergarments and was feeling self-conscious standing on the shore naked, never mind the light didn't show much. It would be better to be naked in the water. She executed a shallow dive and swam out to him, revelling in the warm water. 'This is heaven. We have a giant bathtub all to ourselves.'

They swam, they raced, they dived beneath the surface. They floated lazily on their backs when they tired of their games. They were having fun, Emma realised. There was nothing in their way today: no politics, no Gridley, no plantation. She hadn't had this much fun with a man, *ever*. Men were creatures to be guarded against, to be used perhaps, but never enjoyed. One always had to be wary of the strings attached to any pleasure they offered. She'd learned that lesson first with Thompson Hunt and her dealings with Arthur Gridley had reinforced it. In the end, she didn't expect Ren Dryden to be any different, but for today he was. Today there was a truce.

Ren swam up under her and grabbed her leg. She let out a scream before she realised it wasn't a sea monster. He popped out of the water, hair streaming while he laughed. 'I got you!'

'You scared me!'

He hauled her to him, wrapping her in his arms. 'I didn't think anything scared the great Emma Ward.' He kissed her then, more slowly, more intently than last night or the night he'd claimed his forfeit. Oh, this, too, was a kind of heaven, to be held in his arms, to have her mouth ravished with his kisses, the water lapping against her body.

He lifted her in those arms and carried her to the shore, finding a soft, sandy patch. He laid her down, his hair dripping on her skin as he rose over her. 'They're like stalactites.' She laughed, reaching a hand up to squeeze the water out of the strands. His eyes burned into hers, hot coals of desire as skin met skin, wet and slick. Her tone turned husky. 'But I don't mind.'

Ren's mouth sealed itself over hers. He raised her arms above her head, shackling her wrists in one hand. Their bodies had no choice now but to meet and to meld. Her breasts thrust upwards against his chest, her legs parted to cradle him. He felt right, as if he belonged with her. Maybe it was the magic of the falls, the sense of being part of an ancient world here in the cave. She wanted, she *hungered*. Her body throbbed for him.

He was nuzzled against her entrance, but he wasn't done playing, wasn't done stoking her fires. His mouth sought her breast, his tongue working her rosy peak, sucking and tugging ever so lightly until her hips arched up into his in protest. *No more waiting, only claiming.* Her body was eager to see if the magic would happen again. She'd shattered for him not once, but twice last night. Would it always be like that?

Ren chuckled at her impatience, his lips pressing kisses to the column of her neck, but she sensed his own desire was pushing him. She spread her legs wider, an invitation he could not refuse. He slid into her and she sighed, luxuriating in the feel of him filling her, of her body shaping itself around him. She wrapped her legs around his waist, urging him, securing him. He thrust once, twice, and she picked up the rhythm, raising her hips to meet him, to join him. This— lying naked in a primeval cave, joined with a man in the oldest pleasure on earth—was decadence defined, sin at its very best.

Their rhythm increased, moving them towards the edge of ecstasy. She bucked hard beneath him, wanting her hands, wanting to bury her nails into his shoulders as an anchor against what was to come, something to hold on to while she broke. But he held her fast, forcing her to free-fall into the pleasure. And she did, one cogent thought in her mind—it was indeed possible.

Chapter Thirteen

Emerging into the sunlight and heat was akin to being born into another world and almost as difficult. Ren would like to have remained by the waterfall, savouring the magic of their cavern glade, but the horse would be getting restless and reality called. They kept silent as they climbed back into the gig and resumed their drive towards the beach.

Ren was reluctant to the break the spell, perhaps Emma was too. He cast a sideways glance at her profile beneath her straw hat, the slim nose, the sweep of her jaw, all conspiring to create the sharp beauty of her face. But there was tenseness, too. Whatever the reason for her silence, she was absorbed in her thoughts, breaking her contemplations only to gesture toward the cut-offs leading down to the water. He wondered if her thoughts followed the same pattern as his. Was she thinking about them, too? What did the events of the last two days mean to her? Or was she thinking of something else? She'd been frightened last night with Gridley and she'd been frightened again this morning, although a less perceptive man would not have noticed. Emma was a master at using boldness, her bravado, as her shield against that fear.

They rounded a final curve and the ocean opened up before them, sparkling in deep blues and greens beneath the sun, the sand nearly white.

Ren couldn't help but smile at the incredible view. 'I thought the cave was breathtaking, but this easily rivals it. The average person in England can't begin to imagine the beauty here, it's so vibrant. Even the colours are different. Our ocean is dark and cold, hardly inviting.'

He jumped down and unharnessed the horse. In this secluded cove, the horse couldn't go far. He went around to Emma's side and helped her down, his hands lingering at her waist, looking for some sign of what was going on behind her dark eyes. She was by far the loveliest, most mysterious woman he'd yet to meet, but that also made her the most complicated and the most intriguing. 'Will you walk with me, Emma?' Ren asked quietly.

They made short work of their shoes. Ren rolled up his trousers and Emma tied her skirt in a knot to keep it out of the waves. Everything *was* different, not just the colours of the ocean, Ren reflected as they made their way to the water, the sand warm between his toes. Emma was different, too. She'd not hesitated to take off her shoes, to knot up her skirt. No English girl would have dared such immodesty, certainly not the heiress in York. But modesty was often impractical here. He couldn't picture Emma *not* enjoying the beauty of the ocean for the sake of keeping her toes covered. Propriety was not worth the sacrifice.

'A penny for your thoughts...' Ren began as the waves gently lapped at their feet. The warmth of the water was a marvel to him. His brother Teddy would be in awe.

'A pound for yours. You smiled just now. What were you thinking?' Emma bent down and picked up a white shell.

'I was thinking of my brother and how much he would love this place. We'd never get him off the beach.'

Emma threw the shell out into the water. 'Do you miss them? Your family?'

Ren gave a short laugh. 'Not yet. I am sure I will, though. Back home, I saw them every day. It can be overwhelming to have a house full of females, especially when one is used to living alone.'

Emma knit her brow, not quite understanding. He elaborated. 'When my father was alive, I kept my own apartments in London. It was the right balance of distance for a young man. I like my family, but I like my freedom, too. A young man's pursuits aren't always appropriate when surrounded by nosy sisters. When my father passed away, I moved into the town house so I could take care of the family.'

When he'd become the earl, everything had changed right down to his way of life. 'Overnight I went from being a carefree buck to a man of responsibility.' Great responsibility. He not only had a family to look after, he had estates, investments, debts to manage, decisions to make, his sister Sarah to launch into Society. That had been four years ago, four years of trying to make ends meet and realising that traditional methods of aristocratic money management weren't going to work.

Emma looked up at him from beneath the brim of her hat, her eyes thoughtful and sincere. 'I'm sorry. You never mentioned your father had died. Were you close?'

'We were.' Ren couldn't help but smile. He could see his father in his mind, tall, striding about vigorously, laughing, wrestling with Teddy, teasing the girls, full of life. 'He loved us. None of us doubted it. My father saw that I was ready to take his place some day, that I was educated and prepared for life, socially, academically. He did the same for his daughters. But it was all so sudden.'

His voice dropped, the memory of those first moments flooding him. 'I'd met him for a drink at our club the previous afternoon. We'd talked about a horse he wanted to buy. I was supposed to meet him and my family at a ball that night, but he didn't feel well after dinner and went to lie down. The next morning he was gone.'

He felt Emma squeeze his hand, her words quiet. 'We're never prepared, sudden or not.' She looked away, her eyes going out over the ocean. 'It *is* beautiful here, but it's dangerous, too. Sometimes I'm not sure we were meant to be here. There are hurricanes, deadly insects, fevers and there's nothing to be done when they strike. We can't hold back the storms, we can't stop the fevers. We are so very vulnerable.

'My father was a strong man. He'd weathered the rigours of military life for years and yet the fever took him within a week. People told me I was lucky. We'd had a chance to say goodbye, he'd had a chance to make last plans. Merry sat with him, writing furiously when my father wasn't delirious and reassuring him when he was. But in the end, it didn't matter. I still missed him, still grieved. I suppose that gives us something in common.'

They moved a little further along the surf line, hands interlocked. He felt connected to Emma in those moments in a way that defied any other connection he'd felt. Perhaps it was the lingering intimacy of the caves that had provoked his disclosure. Perhaps it was something else. He only knew he'd not planned to tell her such a thing when they'd come down to the water. In truth, he'd meant to draw *her* out. He knew, too, that he'd never shared those feelings with another, *ever*. Kitt had left before his father died, and he'd not wanted to burden his sisters in their own grief with his.

They turned back towards the wagon and the picnic basket. His stomach was rumbling. Breakfast seemed ages ago, part of a different world. Ren spread the blanket and helped Emma set out the food. She wanted to hear more about England. 'I haven't been there since I was a little girl,' she confessed, biting into a cold ham sandwich. 'I don't remember much except that it was gloomy and it rained a lot.'

Ren laughed. 'Then you remember it pretty well. It hasn't changed. But summer in the English countryside is not to be missed.' He regaled her with stories of his family, their country home where they picked strawberries and rode horses and swam in the river.

His tales took them through the sandwiches, the mangoes and the sponge cake the cook had packed. Ren finished his cake and set aside his napkin. Emma had already stretched out on her side of the blanket, propped up on an elbow, her hair falling over one shoulder. She looked utterly provocative on that blanket. His body stirred with a thousand possibilities. Actually, he wasn't sure it had stopped stirring since the caves. Her every move, her every glance, touch, word seemed to keep him on the edge of arousal.

Ren stretched out beside her and she welcomed him with a smile. Ren fought the urge to give in to that welcome. What she wanted would have to wait. 'I think we have to talk before things go any further.'

She did not protest. Part of him had hoped she would. 'I thought we had been talking,' she said coyly, dropping her eyes to the blanket.

'We have, and it's been good. We haven't talked, not like that, since I arrived. Sometimes I'm struck about how little I know about you and you about me, considering how much time we spend together and our circumstances.'

Her eyes came back to his, her gaze direct. 'By circumstances you mean having made love?'

'Among other things.' Ren met her directness with a bluntness of his own. 'We have a plantation between us, we are partners whether we choose it or not...' he made a back-and-forth gesture with his hand between them, 'and now, we have *this*. It's profound and heady and I don't have a word for it, just "this" and "it". What are we doing, Emma?' He paused, watching her pleat the blanket between her thumb and forefinger. 'Is this an affair, something to entertain ourselves with? Is it guided by real feeling or is it part of some political agenda against Gridley? Maybe it's just a personal agenda. Which is it, Emma?'

'You think too much, Ren.' Emma gave a slow

smile to take the edge off her response and perhaps to distract. 'Can't it just be sex? Very, very good sex?'

'I wish it could be, but I don't believe it can be, not for a minute. There are too many strings pulling at us.'

Emma scooted closer to him, the heat of his body rising with her nearness. Her arm went about his neck. He could smell the scent of water and salt on her, the scents of the Caribbean in her hair. 'Were there strings pulling at us in the cave?' Her voice was husky as she dropped slow kisses along his jaw.

Ren swallowed hard. This conversation was going nowhere—well, not *nowhere*, it was going somewhere quite nicely, just not the place he'd hoped. He was starting to think resistance was pointless. 'Emma, you know what I mean.' It was a half-hearted attempt to call upon her own sense of reason.

She gave a throaty laugh against his neck, her hand reaching for him. 'I shattered for you twice last night, and you brought me to it again this morning. Is that something secret agendas can control?' Her words were an aphrodisiac as she thumbed him, the friction of cloth and her hand driving him to the edge of insanity. Her next words, whispered at his ear, sent him over that cliff. 'I've never experienced anything like it before. Does that mean nothing?'

She bit his earlobe with a gentle nip. 'Only you, Ren Dryden. I've shattered only for you. Forgive me if I don't want to look for reasons for it.' She worked the fall of his trousers. 'Let me return the favour. Shatter for me, Ren, no strings attached.'

It was the fantasy every man must dream about: a beautiful woman in a setting that rivalled Paradise, taking him in hand. Before now there'd only been moulding, cupping. There was no material between them this time, just her warm, firm hand on him, easing itself up and down his length. He would shatter for her. There was no doubt in his mind she would bring him to climax.

That didn't mean everything was settled between them. He should probably stop her; force her to keep the contract that nothing could happen until they'd decided what this was going to be between them. She thumbed the tender tip of him, spreading moisture over the head, a shudder of absolute delight taking him. He knew there was no chance of stopping her just as surely as he knew he would shatter under her touch. Their discussion had been postponed. Which was just as well. A moment later he was beyond any coherent thought, his hips bucking upwards against her hand, a groan ripping from his throat as she brought him to completion.

Emma's eyes were dark with excitement, a little smile hovering on her lips as she watched him. He was not the only one who had received pleasure from the act. The look she gave him was almost as moving as what had just occurred. It was an honest look, a look of having been swept up in the moment. In his experience, there was much about pleasure that could be contrived or feigned, but not *that*. It went a long way in alleviating his worries over there being a larger, more sinister agenda at work. After this, Ren didn't want there to be. He didn't want to face a reality where this pleasure had an ulterior purpose. He'd already faced one in the York heiress and found such a situation cold, lacking.

For once, he wanted something to be pure and unadulterated. He'd been pursued by women since he'd come into the title—not because they wanted him necessarily, but because they wanted what he represented. He, too, had been forced to pursue certain women because of what *they* represented as well—fortunes that could redeem the earldom.

Here, in the Caribbean, he could have the best of both worlds; he could escape that fate as Kitt had escaped it and he could save his family from social ostracism. But he wanted Emma to want him, no strings attached. He certainly wanted her. He'd have wanted her with or without the plantation. He wanted her still, even with Sugarland acting as a barrier between them. She was used to independently running the place, she did not easily welcome his interference and yet, wanting her overrode those concerns. He wanted to believe the passion they shared overrode those concerns for her, too, that passion could lay the groundwork for trust. But even if it did, he was right back to where he'd started. What did this mean for them? An affair, or something more?

In his world, a gentleman's world, 'something more' implied marriage without exception. A man didn't behave with a woman as he had with Emma without offering her the protection of marriage unless that woman was of a certain sort and class, a class Merrimore's ward didn't fall into by any means. Had Merrimore been expecting her to now fall under Ren's protection as his proxy? Or had Merrimore thought something more?

Emma moved into the crook of his arm, her head on his shoulder. 'You're thinking again, Ren.'

Ren kissed the top of her head, breathing in the light floral scent of her hair. 'Only about you, surely that's fair enough.'

She nestled closer, running a hand up inside his shirt. 'As long as the thoughts are good ones.'

It was on the tip of his tongue to ask why they wouldn't be, but his mind wasn't entirely finished with the previous ones. What if Cousin Merrimore had brought him here for more than just the plantation? What if Merrimore had brought him here for *her*?

Chapter Fourteen

The more Ren thought about it, the more the idea had merit. It was still on his mind as he paced in the drawing room, waiting to take Emma into their usual dinner for two. The question was— what shape did that inheritance take? Had Merrimore wanted him to be a proxy protector? If so, Ren had done a poor job of it. He'd been here a handful of weeks and he'd already bedded Merrimore's ward, hardly a sterling recommendation for a protector, which raised another question. Had Merrimore wanted him to be something more permanent? A husband, perhaps?

Ren wasn't sure how such a possibility sat with him. In part, he'd left England to avoid an arranged marriage. It seemed the height of irony to have come all this way only to have another arrangement waiting for him. It was a much prettier arrangement, a more passionate arrangement to be sure, but it was still an arrangement, *someone else's arrangement*, that would guide the rest of *his* life. Ren very selfishly wanted to make those sorts of arrangements on his own.

Had that been what Cousin Merrimore had wanted? Ren trailed his hand over the curves of a porcelain figure of a dog sitting on a small side table. He'd been so sure Merrimore had been looking for a plantation manager. Had Merrimore instead been looking for husband material for his rather wayward ward? It had not escaped Ren last night or this afternoon that he'd not been her first lover. She'd been sure of her skills and he'd thought from the first that such sensuality didn't come with virginity, but from confidence and experience. He had no complaints. Virgins had never held much charm for him, but society adored them. His cousin might have been anxious about Emma's future based on that social preference.

Ren did, however, chastise himself for not seeing the possibility sooner although he knew the reasons for it. He'd been self-absorbed in the adventure; overly focused on the plantation and what it could do for the salvation of his family in England, overly focused, too, on his own freedom, his narrow escape from the clutches of the York heiress. The busyness surrounding his arrival hadn't helped things. There'd been the exploding chicken coop, the burning fields, the neighbours to meet, new and unexpected circumstances to adjust to. He'd been swept up immediately into the daily processes of plantation life. There'd been no time, as one of his professors at Oxford was fond of saying, 'to see the forest through the trees'. The larger scope of why he'd been called here had escaped his notice, lost in the technicalities and events of the daily routine.

It was only now when things had slowed that he could see the patterns and the subtle intentions.

A swish of skirts alerted him to Emma's arrival. He looked up, a slow smile taking his face. She always managed to look stunning in gowns, or the breeches she wore about the estate. He couldn't imagine Emma *not* looking stunning. Tonight she'd done it in a gown of pale blue that turned her hair impossibly dark and her skin beautifully tanned. A single, slim strand of pearls rested at the base of her neck, calling attention to the fact that there was quite a lot of skin artfully revealed in the sleeveless vee cut of the bodice. There were no trimmings or flounces to disguise what was on display. As a result, the gown was far less girlish than the silly London confections designed to be demure.

Dinner was waiting for them. Tonight, it was a spicy rice dish liberally filled with shrimp, accompanied by fresh baked bread, fried okra, which had been new to Ren, and a light white wine.

Ren took a bite of the rice and shrimp, savouring it as if it were a great luxury. 'I think I like the food in Barbados, especially the seafood dishes.'

Emma laughed, her eyes twinkling as she leaned forward. 'You haven't tasted pudding and souse yet. Do you know what that is?'

Ren grinned and leaned back in his chair, waiting to be regaled. 'You know I couldn't possibly.'

'It's a special Barbadian dish made of pig parts for the pudding and pig's head with trotters boiled down for the souse.' Emma smiled and took another sip of wine, waiting for his reaction. He almost gave it. The dish sounded positively disgusting but that was what the little minx wanted. Ren fought the urge and opted to tease her a bit.

He merely fingered the stem of his glass and said, 'Ah, a Barbadian version of haggis, is it? Why do you suppose so many cultures seem bent on stuffing things into intestines?'

The comment caught her entirely off guard as he intended. She'd not anticipated a humorous response from him. If she had, she might not have taken that sip. Wine spewed out of her mouth, just missing her plate of rice and shrimp. She choked, gasping for breath, until Ren had to come to her side, patting her on the back as if she were a small child. 'I'm sorry. I should have timed my remark better.' Ren offered her his napkin, but he couldn't help laughing.

Emma was laughing, too, unable to stay angry. 'You timed it just when you wanted it. You knew what you were doing,' Emma scolded in friendly tones, wiping her eyes.

Ren took his seat. 'Well, maybe I did,' he confessed. 'Do you need a new plate? I could call Faulks.'

'No, I missed the plate.'

'This is one of the reasons I prefer eating this way, everything is on the table at once. Can you imagine resetting Gridley's table if you'd spat your wine out last night?' Ren shook his head in mock despair. 'One plate we could have managed, but all of his? And the glasses and the silverware?'

Emma laughed with him. 'I assure you I don't make a habit of spitting out my wine. But it's true, Gridley does prefer excess. He wants everyone to remember he is English and a knight of the realm.'

Ren laughed. 'So his house is too big, his art too ostentatious, his table too full.' Ren paused. 'He's jealous, you know. He wants everyone to remember he's equal to Sugarland. He told me during our afternoon visit that you had the best of everything. The best food, the best cook. No matter what he does, he still finds himself lacking when measured against you.' Ren gestured to the room about him. 'Sugarland is a stunning home. The dining room rivals anything one would find in London, as does the service.'

Emma smiled. 'Sugarland does sport the best dining room on the island. It was one of Merry's pride and joys. He had the Wedgwood specially commissioned and the crystal hand blown in Ireland.'

'My cousin had good taste or did he have you to thank for it?' Ren gave her a warm smile. He liked this easy conversation with her. They'd made progress today relaxing with one another.

'More like the merchants on Swan Street, but I certainly helped.'

They'd finished their meal and it was the perfect opening to move the conversation towards the questions in his mind. Ren rose and offered Emma his arm. They'd developed the habit of taking a walk about the lawns after dinner before settling into a game of chess or backgammon. Tonight, it seemed the perfect venue for a more intimate discussion. 'My cousin must have valued you a great deal. Tell me about Merry. I suspect you were closer to him those last years than anyone, even Gridley. I have difficulty understanding that friendship. It's rather odd to be friends with a man one is jealous of.'

It was still warm outside, but not uncomfortably so. The stars were starting to come out. It was somewhat of a magical novelty to Ren that darkness actually fell in a land so warm, but it did, a constant reminder of how close they were to the equator. There were no long or short days here, all the days were the same.

'Gridley always has a reason for his friendships,' Emma said, looking up into the night sky where the stars were beginning to come out. 'There's usually something he wants.' She was trying to sound blasé. Ren wasn't fooled.

The nonchalance was just another aspect of her brave facade.

'You?' Ren offered bluntly. 'His eyes made no secret of the fact last night. Even without his gaze following you around the room, he made that abundantly clear the afternoon we talked. In retrospect I see his confession more as a warning than anything else.'

Emma gave a nervous laugh. 'I thought we were talking about Merry.' He had her off-centre—interesting. What was he getting close to? He had meant to talk about Merry, but perhaps this was the opportunity to talk about Gridley the way he'd meant to earlier in the day.

'I think the two are inseparable,' Ren said, his voice low in the darkness. He wanted to build an aura of intimacy, wanted her to feel comfortable with a confession if there was one to make. 'What did Merry want for you? Did he want Gridley for you? Did he want you to go to London?' His mouth was next to her ear, his nostrils breathing in the clean scent of her. 'Did he want you to have me?' *I want to have you, to hell with what Merry thought or anyone else.* It was probably unfair to ask such a question standing here in the warm evening, their bodies close, primed with reminders of the day, but he asked anyway.

'I don't know what Merry intended. I was anticipating an older man.' She gave a short self-deprecating laugh. 'I wasn't sure if anyone would even come.'

'I'm sorry to disappoint you.' Ren chuckled.

She gave him a coy smile. 'You don't exactly disappoint, Ren Dryden. But if you're asking me what Merry intended for you or for me, or for us, I don't know.' Even in the darkness, intuition told him she was holding something back. She might not know in truth, but there were things she suspected. Ren tried to pry her thoughts loose with a little disclosure of his own.

'There were plenty of people who advised me not to come. My mother, my friends. Such a journey was too risky and unnecessary, they said. I should stay home and collect my portion of the profits and do nothing. But I sensed Cousin Merry hadn't willed me the interest in Sugarland for me to stay home. I don't know that to be the case factually speaking, but I *felt* it. It seemed to suggest itself based on circumstances.' He stopped, taking a moment to watch her profile. She was thinking, hard. 'Surely you must have some intuition about what Cousin Merrimore wanted for you? There must have been conversations in the past, even at the end that would at least suggest some answers?'

Ren was pushing hard tonight and it made her wary. He was using all the tools at his disposal: a day of exquisite sexual practice, the deepening intimacy of the night, the proximity of his body, the easy humour over dinner. It all combined to create a heightened sense of comfort between them. And it was working. She did feel comfortable with him despite what she knew he was doing. He'd seduced her and now he thought to use that intimacy to get his answers. Well, Thompson Hunt had already beaten him to that strategy and she would not be fooled twice.

She had her own strategies, too, for what their intimate encounters might be used for. Then there were her hopes that maybe here was a man who would be different from the rest. She'd never know unless she tested that hypothesis, too. Tonight, she'd risk a little more, perhaps risk a lot. She sensed the time for truth, at least about Gridley, had come. Emma drew a breath. 'Towards the end, Gridley was with him and the solicitor constantly. Those last days were fearful to me. I was afraid of Gridley's influence, afraid Gridley might convince Merry to do something foolish at the end.'

'Like what?'

'Something medieval like Merry compelling me to marry Gridley in order to keep the plantation or forcing me to join Sugarland to his. Gridley talked of it nonstop.' She said it casually, with a laugh to make it sound even more ludicrous. She might be ready for Ren to know what had transpired, but she wasn't ready for him to know how real that fear had been.

'Merry suspected Gridley had more than friendship on his mind, however. One day shortly before he died, we went up to the bluff and he told me about his concerns,' Emma added quietly. 'Whatever Merry wanted for me, it was not Gridley. I wonder, too, if Merry wrote those suspicions down in his journal along with his thoughts about the cartel.' Or if he'd had a chance. He'd seldom been alone. 'Every time the solicitor came, I worried. It sounds selfish, but I breathed easier once the will was read and nothing of the sort was mandated.'

'It's good to know that Merry knew,' Ren said after a while. 'I wouldn't have liked knowing that he died duped into a false friendship.'

Emma stopped walking and faced him. Ren meant the comment to be consoling, but it was far from that and she could not let it pass unaddressed. This was no ordinary land struggle or arranged marriage drama. It was time to disabuse Ren of any notion he harboured in that direction. It was time for the truth about Gridley. She took a deep breath, her grip on Ren's hand tightening. 'In the end, Merry knew Gridley's measure precisely. He lay there helpless, unable to do anything but watch while Gridley put a pillow over his face and snuffed out the last of his life.'

'Dear God!' Even in the dark, she could tell Ren was stunned. 'How do you know?'

'I saw the last of it. I saw him lift the pillow from Merry's face.' Her voice was starting to shake. Tears burned in her eyes. Even a few simple, unemotional words were too much for her. She could see it in her mind as if it had just happened.

There was a stone bench nearby and Ren led her there, forcing her to sit, his arm about her drawing her close for comfort and strength. 'You don't have to tell me,' he whispered into her hair.

'Yes, I do. You have to know what you're up against. Gridley is a monster.' She forced her thoughts into coherent sentences. 'The solicitor had come downstairs and stopped to talk with me. We spoke for maybe five minutes before he left. Then I went up to see Merry. It was time for his medicine,' she explained, although the detail didn't matter. 'I entered the room without knocking and that's when I saw him. It was plain what he'd done and Gridley made no attempt to excuse it.' Her voice caught and she swallowed hard. 'He looked at me and said, "The old man was bound to go tomorrow or the next anyway. It might as well be today." Then he winked at me and said, "This will be our little secret. We can't have anyone thinking you might have done this", as if he were taking the blame for me.'

She felt Ren's arm tighten about her in protection and anger. She'd been right to tell him. 'Oh, my dear girl, you must have been frightened beyond words. No wonder you were so pale in that room this morning.'

'I was too numb to be frightened,' Emma admitted. 'Gridley simply walked out of the room and went home as if nothing unusual had happened.'

She could feel Ren's breathing change as he began to think. She could almost predict his next question. 'Did you tell anyone?'

Emma shook her head against his shoulder. 'No. It's the one and only time I've ever done anything Gridley's asked. How could I have done otherwise? I was alone with no one to protect me and Gridley's threat had teeth. When I thought about it, who would believe me over Gridley? So I let it go.'

'And in doing so, you've given Gridley a tidy piece of blackmail to hang over your head,' Ren summed up. 'Why hasn't he used it to force your hand already? Marriage and Sugarland in exchange for not taking you to trial.'

'That's easy, Ren,' she murmured. 'Timing and you. He had to wait for the will to be read. He honestly thought it was going to be changed, that something had been agreed upon that last day. He was eager to see Merry removed before Merry could change it again. But he'd guessed wrong. The solicitor and Merry had outwitted him at the last.

'Then there were his promises to Merry. He'd been very public about having been charged with "watching over" me. There had to be an interval of decency. I think there's some fear for him, too, in making his claim public. I'd at least smear his reputation by telling everyone the murderer was him. I'd be the one who loses in court. I would hang, but he'd be ruined in other ways.

'Then just when that was ending, you showed

up to complicate things further. Blackmailing me into compliance isn't enough any more. You have the other fifty-one per cent.'

Emma felt Ren's hand still where it had been running up and down her arm in a comforting motion. His body stiffened. His voice was terse when he spoke. 'Is that why you slept with me?'

A blow to the stomach could not have been more effective. This was the pivotal moment, the moment where she could lose him. She could not lose him now! Not now when she'd invested so much in the hope Ren embodied for her future and when she'd invested so much of herself not just physically, but emotionally. She'd trusted him tonight. Emma disengaged herself and rose, combining truth and lie into the only answer she could defend. 'I slept with you because I wanted to.' The terse set of Ren's jaw started to relax. She played her ace. Regardless of his misgivings, Ren could not resist her. Emma held out a hand, putting his acceptance of her answer to the immediate test. 'And I would like to do it again, only tonight I might suggest something different.'

Ren stood, his eyes hot with rising desire. The crisis was past. A rill of elation surged through her at the little victory as he took her hand. 'What would that be, Emma?'

She smiled coyly and tugged him towards the house. 'A bed.'

Chapter Fifteen

Bed changed everything. Ren's blood ran hot with the thrill of deliberately taking a woman to bed, of watching her undress and undressing for her in turn. The mere prospect honed a man's arousal to a sharp edge of anticipation. There was a titillating intimacy to the formal art of sex in a bedroom that was absent from hotter, more spontaneous encounters—the sort of which had populated their couplings to date.

He liked those encounters as well. They didn't require thinking, only doing, only living in the moment of passion. One could be swept away, let oneself go and then use that very sponta-neity as a carefully constructed excuse later to explain 'the mistake'. One did not have such leniency in the bedroom where it was all clearly premeditated. One had to be honest with one-self afterwards.

A single lamp illuminated Emma's bedchamber, casting a rosy-gold light on the walls. Like the other walls in the house, they were white stucco. Wallpaper didn't last in the humidity. But the other items in the room leant the chamber its colour. A braided rug in oranges, pinks and reds lay on the polished hardwood planking of the floor. A quilt of matching colours lay folded at the foot of the bed.

Ah, the bed! It was a four-postered wonder done in teak, covered in an immaculate white quilt turned back to expose the thick mattress and tight fitted sheets. Pillows were plumped sumptuously against the headboard. But what stood out most to Ren was how high it was set up from the ground in what he was coming to know as the Caribbean style. His own bed in the *garçonnière* was set unusually high, too. Michael had explained it was for protection against anything that crawled or slithered: scorpions, snakes, stinging beetles. Necessity it might be, but it also precluded any romantic gesture of carrying one's lover to bed since getting into bed required a mounting block. A laugh escaped him at the humour.

'What's so funny?' Emma had sobered, too—perhaps she'd also realised what a bedding in the bedroom entailed.

Ren nodded towards the steps set beside the bed. 'I was just thinking how appropriate it was to need a mounting block for mounting of another sort.'

She tossed him a hot look. 'You have a wicked mind, Ren Dryden.'

'It makes me more interesting.' Ren tugged at the end of his cravat, pulling it loose and letting the yards of cloth slide around his neck, giving Emma ample warning of what was coming next. He tossed the strip of cloth on to the end of the bed. One never knew when a cravat could be put to other uses.

Emma took her cue and sat down in an upholstered lady's chair by the window. She spread her skirts about her, managing to look both demure and worldly as she prepared to watch him disrobe.

Ren started with his waistcoat, making her wait as he took off his watch chain and cufflinks, setting them in a trifle dish on the table next to the bed. He undid the buttons of his paisley waistcoat and started on the studs of his shirt, pulling his tails out of the waistband of his trousers as he went. His shirt came off. He heard Emma's breath catch at the sight of him.

He was magnificent! Emma's hands fisted in the folds of her skirts, her breath catching at the sight of him. There was something poignantly erotic about seeing a lover revealed for the first time, a gorgeous package being unwrapped just for her. Ren Dryden in clothes was a sight to behold. Ren Dryden without them was beyond words.

The dark shadows of the cave had not done him justice, nor had their lusty half-clothed couplings. Here was a man who knew how to take care of himself. His chest was a sculpted atlas of muscles, his shoulders blatantly displaying their breadth. *This* was what she'd lain her head against at the beach, *these* were the arms that had held her against the wall and carried her up the stairs to bed.

Ren's hands went to the waistband of his trousers, his eyes on her making it known that part of this seduction was this decadent voyeurism—him studying her studying him. A slow smile crept across his face. 'Watch me, Em.'

As if she could do otherwise. Her throat was dry with anticipation, her eyes riveted on his hands, taking in every minute motion of those long fingers as he undid the fall of his trousers and pushed them down past narrow hips, muscled thighs and well-shaped calves. She couldn't recall when his boots had come off, but they must have at some point. It was hardly important when there was so much more to look at, to wonder over. Her eye was drawn to the manly core of him, to that nest of dark hair and what was jutting up sharply from it. She needn't be shy, he meant for her to look, to drink her fill. A trill of feminine possessiveness took her. *Her* lover was extraordinary.

Ren climbed the steps to the bed and stretched out, posing on his side and letting the lamplight fall over the length of his body; every plane, every angle, every muscle of him on display as he propped himself up on an elbow, resting his head on his hand, one leg bent. There wasn't an ounce of modesty to him. He was all brazen male. He gave her a nearly imperceptible nod. Now it was her turn.

Emma rose from her chair, thankful she'd inadvertently chosen a dress she could get off by herself. She'd not planned this when she'd dressed for dinner. The idea of taking Ren to bed had been spontaneous, a product of the warm night and their quiet disclosures and, to be honest, a product of distraction. His questions were getting too close to disturbing subjects she'd rather not discuss until she must. Already, she'd told him so much. And yet, a secret or two remained.

Emma reached behind her, freeing the three hooks that fastened the gown. She let the dress slide over her body and down, leaving her in the soft, thin cotton of her undergarments. 'Move into the light,' Ren instructed in low, hoarse tones from the bed. 'I want it to play behind you, my very own erotic chiaroscuro.'

'Ah, an artist's distribution of light and shadow.' Emma replied, complying. She knew full well what the light would do, what it would expose: the deep rosy brown of her nipples pressing against the thin linen of her chemise, showcasing the dark juncture between her legs.

Emma lifted a leg to the middle step of the mounting block and began to peel off her stocking. She felt Ren's eyes following the roll of silk down past her knee, down slim calves. She did the second one, hearing the sheets rustle as Ren shifted his weight. She was careful not to look at him, inviting him to participate in a different sort of voyeurism than the kind he'd invoked.

She undressed as if she was alone in her room, unaware of a man watching her private ablutions.

Emma raised the chemise over her head, letting the lamplight catch her breasts in profile. She discarded the undergarment and cupped her breasts, lifting them, palming them as if studying their suitability, something she'd done a hundred times in front of a mirror, testing her own attractiveness. But in front of a man, the act took on something bolder, wilder.

'Goodness, Emma. You'd drive a saint to sin,' Ren growled appreciatively from the bed, lust lacing his words. She pretended not to hear, her hands moving to the delicate string of her pantalettes. She turned her back to him and moved her hips, drawing the loosened pantalettes downward over the slim curve of her buttocks until they pooled in a white puddle at her feet.

'Come to bed, Minx.'

'Not yet,' Emma said softly, knowing he was enjoying the view from behind as much as he'd enjoyed the other views she'd presented. She reached up to her hair and pulled out the pins, letting the heavy tresses fall down her back, a dark curtain. She heard Ren moan. After a moment more, she turned to face him for the first time, fully naked, enjoying the desire that flared in his eyes, knowing she'd been the one to put it there. 'I shall take pity on my poor subject and grant him a boon. What do you want? Name anything.'

'I want to be your steed, my lady. Will you ride me?'

Emma climbed the steps to the bed and straddled him, her knees sinking into the soft mattress. 'Gladly. I will ride you and more,' she promised. His hands were warm where they framed her hips. She lifted herself over him, rising over his rigid shaft and lowered, slowly slipping on to him, letting herself savour the slide of him as she took him inside. Oh, this was exquisite! This was power! One look at Ren's face and she knew he shared the sensation, too. There was awe and amazement written there, as if nothing had ever felt this good, this right.

Emma began to ride, up and down the length of him, his hands holding her hips so she didn't stray too far. She clenched about him, delighting in the gasp of surprise that claimed him. Ren had not anticipated such a show of feminine strength. She did it again and felt him respond inside her. His grip tightened on her hips and she gave a little scream as he rolled her beneath him, a swift move that kept them joined.

'I thought you wanted *me* to ride you. You lied!' Emma protested, looking up into his blue eyes.

'I didn't lie. I changed my mind,' Ren clarified with a wolfish grin.

She adjusted her legs about him, shifting ever so slightly to accommodate this new position. 'You're a most demanding subject.'

Ren bit at her neck. 'You're a most tempting queen who needs to be taught a lesson about provoking said subject.'

Emma raised her hands above her head in surrender, her voice a husky whisper. 'Then teach me.'

Ren didn't have to be asked twice. He stretched out his arms, reaching up to capture her wrists in his grip. Using her body as leverage, he began the rhythm she craved; thrust and withdraw, each cycle building the delicious tension. She felt herself die a little each time he pulled back and live again when he surged into her, her body flowing about him until the tension he'd wrought was unbearable, pushing her to the breaking point. Ren's voice was harsh at her ear, a victim of his own efforts. 'Let go, Em.'

That was when she broke, taking him with her over pleasure's cliff. A strangled cry escaped her. She was falling, falling with only Ren to hold on to, her anchor in the free fall into pleasure's oblivion. Her one cogent thought, brief and fleeting: how was it that a game of seduction, a game she'd designed to counteract his own efforts to render her vulnerable, a game designed to *protect* her, had failed her completely, leaving her exposed to the very things she sought to avoid?

How, in heaven's name, had this happened? But she knew the answer in part already. This was what happened when one dared to use sex as a weapon, forgetting that quite often weapons are turned on those who wield them.

'How the hell has this happened?' Arthur Gridley brought the palm of his hand down hard on the polished mahogany surface of his desk. The inkstand jumped, the heavy paperweight gave a shudder.

The man standing before him played with the brim of his straw hat, too nervous to meet his gaze, as well he might be. The man had nothing good to report. Ren Dryden had turned out to have a voracious sexual appetite if the man's information was to be believed. But then, Dryden couldn't take all the credit. Arthur imagined Emma Ward could bring out the best in any man's more intimate appetites.

'They went out into the gardens and when they came back in, they went upstairs.'

'Which room?' Arthur interrupted.

'Second room on the right in the front.'

'Her room.' Arthur nodded his confirmation, his groin tightening at the image of Emma taking a man into her private chambers.

The man coughed discreetly. 'There was a lamp, sir, there were shadows visible from the front lawn. There's no doubt what they got up to.'

'And what was that?' Arthur Gridley pressed. He was making his messenger uncomfortable, but he wanted the details, wanted to know exactly what Emma and Dryden had been doing. He listened intently, his mind providing the erotic images of Emma undressing against the light, her hair coming down, her hands on her breasts, teasing Dryden in ways she ought to be teasing *him* instead; Dryden stripping out of his trousers, his naked, muscled body covering Emma. Dryden was a well-made man. Arthur was flexible enough to appreciate Dryden's physical features, although he'd appreciate them more if they weren't being used to seduce Emma out from under him.

In fact, once his lurid fascination was appeased, there was only anger left; anger at

Emma, who had betrayed him by throwing herself after an Englishman she barely knew, yet again; anger at Ren Dryden who fashioned himself a gentleman and ought to have known better than to accept the offer. Arthur pulled a quill from the inkstand, playing with it. A gentleman didn't take advantage of a woman on her own, especially when the gentleman in question had been told she was taken. The quill in his hand snapped. Well, the gloves were off now. If Ren Dryden didn't feel the need to act like gentleman, neither did he.

It was difficult to strike against Emma as he would like. To destroy her cane crop, for instance, would bring her to her knees financially and quite possibly in other ways. She'd be begging him to help her through the season. But the move seemed illogical. To hurt Sugarland would be to strike against himself. He would ultimately pay for any destruction he did to the plantation and that defeated his purposes. He wanted Emma Ward in his bed, but he wanted Sugarland in his bank account. He would have to pull the financial rug out from under her in other ways.

He doubted Ren Dryden would be as eager to take her to bed if she wasn't a plantation heiress. The reported activities of the last two days suggested Dryden had not yet taken his advice and looked at the books. Arthur tapped the broken end of the quill against the desk. It was time to make sure Dryden did. A glimpse of financial reality might also encourage Dryden to join the cartel regardless of the pleasures Emma provided in bed. When money talked, men usually listened. He would be there first thing in the morning to make sure Dryden didn't prove to be the exception.

Arthur undid his trousers and put a hand on himself. He leaned back in his chair, eyes closed, his mind conjuring up a vision of Emma on her knees before him, her hair unpinned, begging him, pleading with him. His hand slipped up and down as a dialogue formed in his head. She was sorry she'd given herself to the wrong man. He'd been right; Dryden had only wanted her for her money. Dryden had made a whore of her with his demands. She'd forgotten how powerful Arthur was, how she should have come to him from the start, how he'd always been there for her. If he would only forgive her, she would spend her life showing her gratitude.

Arthur began to jerk in his excitement. In his

fantasy, he saw himself place a priestlike hand on her head, offering absolution. 'Take me in your mouth, Emma, and all will be forgiven.'

Chapter Sixteen

Ren could almost forgive the sun for rising when he recalled the night that had preceded it. Shortly before dawn, he'd found enough willpower to drag himself to his rooms in order to maintain a facade of decency and to rest. What he couldn't forgive was being awakened by Michael after what had seemed like only a few minutes of deep sleep.

'Sir Arthur Gridley is here.' The rush of Michael's words mirrored his actions. Michael was hurrying through the room, laying out clothes. 'He wants to see you.'

Ren pushed himself up, his eyes squinting against the bright light from the opened blinds. 'If he wants to see me, he can wait,' he said, sounding grouchy.

'But it's Sir Arthur.' Michael's comment vacillated between a protest and a warning. Apparently, Sir Arthur sat at the top of island society.

'And he's waking *me* up. Maybe he should think about that before he comes calling.' Ren stretched, starting to feel more awake as Emma's revelations flooded to the fore of his mind. That murdering bastard was not going to jangle the keys to *this* kingdom any longer. 'I'll see Arthur Gridley when I'm ready to see him and not a moment sooner.' Protectiveness of his realm and his woman surged and he dressed quickly. Gridley didn't call the tune at Sugarland, but neither did Ren want that snake wandering the halls unaccompanied.

Something was afoot. Even in his groggy state, he knew that much. What he knew about Gridley's personal habits did not recommend the man as a morning person. If Gridley was here so early, it meant something. Ren swung his feet out of bed. 'Did Gridley say what he wanted? There hasn't been an emergency, has there?' He would feel terrible if there was truly a crisis and he'd decided to play a little game of social one-upmanship just to prove a point.

Michael shook his head. 'He didn't say. Faulks told him to help himself to breakfast and you'd be there presently.'

'And Miss Ward? Did Gridley ask to see her, too?' Ren held out his arms and let Michael help him into a shirt.

'It was only you he asked for.'

If he hadn't asked for Emma to join them, he'd likely come for his answer about the cartel. 'We'll let him wait, but not for too long.' Ren sniffed at the air. 'Is that coffee you brought? I think I'll have a cup.' He wanted to meet Gridley with his mind fully functioning. After Emma's disclosures about Gridley, Ren was starting to feel as if he were caught in the middle of something that ran deep and sinister. The depths to which Gridley had sunk suggested he was desperate for Ren to choose a side. Gridley could not make his next move until Ren did.

Ren sat down, waiting for his customary shave. He closed his eyes as Michael bathed his face in warm water, the ritual giving his thoughts a chance to regroup. Gridley wasn't the only desperate party. Emma was desperate, too—desperate for protection against Gridley, desperate to save her home. She was certainly the more innocent party here. She hadn't committed murder or forced another into a completely untenable position, but what *had* she been willing to do in her desperation? When he'd asked her point blank in the garden last night, she hadn't really answered.

After a night of unbound lovemaking, thoughts of having been used or having been manipulated through that lovemaking were unsavoury ones to wake up with. Yet, Ren could not dismiss the potential. Emma had motive. *But she'd wanted you*, his male ego was quick to argue. *That sort of response could not be feigned over and over again, not once, not twice, but multiple times.*

But why? He hoped he didn't know the answer. He didn't want Emma in his bed because she was desperate. That brought him up short. He paused in the hall, reluctantly contemplating his train of thought. He wanted her in his bed because it meant something to him to have her there and he wanted it to mean something to her, too. As Ren approached the breakfast room he couldn't help but feel that something was not all it seemed and that he and Emma were poised on the edge of something that transcended the problem of Gridley and his sugar cartel.

'Ah, Dryden, there you are. I'm green with envy. Your cook has the English breakfast down to perfection.' Sir Arthur's booming tones met him as he entered the room. Usually, Ren had taken Gridley's easy bonhomie at face value. Today, with his new knowledge, Ren fought the urge to plant the man a facer and throw him out of the house. He'd not counted on such a visceral response.

'I am glad you have availed yourself of the hospitality.' Ren schooled his features, deciding to play the gracious host. How had Emma managed to tolerate the man for so long? No wonder she carried a knife beneath her skirts. If he'd had a knife on him, it would now be embedded in Gridley's black heart. Being in the same room with his cousin's murderer curdled his stomach.

The fist at his side clenched and unclenched at the sight of Gridley tucking into his food. But Ren couldn't give in to those baser emotions. He couldn't give any hint Emma had shared that information. Intuitively, he felt to do so would place Emma in grave danger. He fixed himself a plate since it would appear odd not to and sat at the table, even though sitting down with his cousin's murderer caused the bile to rise in his throat. Ren hoped he could give a decent facsimile of eating.

'What brings you over so early in the day?' It couldn't hurt to point out the hour, a subtle reminder that Gridley had called without an appointment.

'Early?' Gridley's sandy eyebrows went up. 'Eleven is hardly early.' He leaned forward with a chuckle. 'But maybe your nights are more exciting than the rest of ours. Is that it, eh?'

Ren met the implication with a stiff reply. 'I sense there is an inappropriate innuendo underlying your comment. If so, I take offence at it.' Not only did Gridley make a habit of arriving without invitation, he also seemed to be in the practice of slandering Emma in her own home. All minor sins, of course, compared to the one that lurked beneath the surface of those questionable behaviours.

The other man was not put off. He waved his hand in one of his dismissive gestures. 'Come now, Dryden, we are both men and we can be honest with each other. Emma Ward is past the first blush of innocence and a beauty besides. You wouldn't be a full-blooded male if you didn't notice the way she walks through a room, the sway of her hips, those lips, those eyes. You don't need to pretend with me.' He nodded at Ren's plate. 'Are you finished? If breakfast doesn't appeal, perhaps we might adjourn to the library?

I have some things to discuss with you that require more privacy than a dining room affords.'

The movement offered a chance to drop Gridley's latest slur of Emma's character. Ren was beginning to think he'd have to call the man out. Such comments would not have gone unchallenged in London, to say nothing of murder. As hot as his blood was running right now, a duel was starting to look like quite the appealing option.

'Ahhhh,' Gridley exhaled as they stepped inside the library with its smells of leather and books. 'Albert and I spent hours in this room. His collection is excellent. He took a regular shipment of books that came every three months.' He smiled fondly at Ren. 'But these aren't the books I came to discuss. I came to discuss the accounts. Have you looked at them?' He ran a hand over the spines in a casual gesture. But Ren had Gridley's measure. Everything about the man was a facade designed to conceal the evil within.

'No, not yet. I imagine Emma and I will sit down and do a thorough rendering of them once the harvest is settled,' Ren said honestly. 'I don't have reason to think I'll find anything amiss, however.'

'I think that depends on your definition of "amiss", old chap.' Gridley faced him, his eyes friendly, tinged with the slightest hint of pity. Really, the man was a master at dissembling. 'We've all been losing money, the whole plantocracy. The hurricane four years ago was a costly disaster, which we might have survived if the Crown hadn't gone and abolished slavery and instituted this mixed-up apprentice system which is bleeding us dry with wages. All of it taken together has created something of an economic depression for us. Sugarland is no exception no matter what Emma tells you.'

Gridley was eyeing him, watching for a reaction. He was expecting shock, outrage. Ren was careful to show him neither, although inside he was starting to reel. Phrases like 'losing money' 'bleeding us dry' and 'economic depression' were digging a pit in his stomach. There was no need to panic yet, he told himself. 'It can't be that bad. You seem prosperous enough.' Ren smiled affably. 'I've seen the boots you wear, the opulence of your fine home. Those are not the signs of a man suffering hardship.'

Gridley met his smile with a patient one of his own. 'I suppose the quarterly cheque sent to your bank account didn't look desperate either.'

Ren tensed. He'd only received one quarterly cheque, the one issued after Cousin Merrimore's passing. It had looked fairly healthy. It had arrived after news of the will reached him. That cheque had been the deciding factor in his decision to come, to use the plantation as the bulwark that would stabilise his family's failing finances. He did *not* want to be told the cheque was a fraud.

He wasn't concerned about the money. It had been real enough when he'd spent it. However, Ren feared what that cheque represented wasn't. He'd been lured here under false pretences of prosperity. The feeling he'd experienced upon arrival of having been Trojan Horsed, resurfaced. His sisters, Teddy, his mother, were all counting on him, on this.

Consider the source. What does Gridley gain if you panic? The realisation carried a calming quality with it. Anything out of Gridley's mouth was highly suspect.

'Albert wouldn't tell you, although I insisted he should,' Gridley went on. 'Albert wanted to make sure you received the full share. I told him it would give you the wrong impression.'

Ren found Gridley's knowledge of his cousin's finances almost as disturbing as the news.

'I appreciate the insight.' Ren studied a shelf of books, gathering his thoughts.

'Of course, the cartel is an opportunity to turn things around,' Gridley offered in consoling tones. 'We're all in the depression together, we all might as well be in the success, too. This time next year, things could change if we all come together. It's true plantation prices are plummeting. There was a fellow in another parish who sold last year, a mere pittance really. It doesn't help that we're not the only ones growing cane any more. Now the Americans have crops and the other islands in the West Indies have turned to cane. But a cartel that can corner the market and control the supply can balance those scales.'

Ren nodded absently. In theory, Gridley spoke the truth. The venture was economically sound. It was the ethics of it that bothered him. He'd be throwing his lot in with people who treated their workers like slaves, people who for all intents and purposes, behaved as if slavery had not been abolished. There would be blood on any of the money he made through them. Yet, if he didn't take this opportunity, who would save his family? Who would help his sisters make matches worthy of them? Who would give his mother the comfort of her own home in her widowhood, or send Teddy to school? 'As I said, I haven't looked over the books.'

Gridley had taken up residence in a chair. 'I'm not sure at this point that looking over the books even matters. You need the money and even if you didn't, the rest of us do. Joining the cartel is the neighbourly thing to do. It would be selfish to hold the rest of us back.' Ren heard the threat. If he wasn't *for* them, he was *against* them.

Gridley studied his nails in another pose of feigned casualness. 'Miles is thinking of selling as it is. I'd hate to lose him. We've all been through a lot together, we're like family out here.'

A weird sort of family full of covetousness and lust, Ren thought. Family didn't make comments about one another that bordered on lecherous. He and Gridley must disagree about what family denoted.

'I know Emma doesn't want any part of it and I know that's why *you're* hesitating.' Gridley adopted a tone somewhere between a well-meaning older brother and a wise uncle. Ren thought it sounded condescending. 'She's got her delicious claws into you, there's no shame in admitting it. You're not the first man who has succumbed to her charms. You should ask her about Thompson Hunt some time.' Ren didn't want to hear about Thompson Hunt. Gridley's words were uncomfortably close to his own ruminations this morning.

'Don't play the offended gentleman with me, Dryden. Your defence of her honour does you credit, but she gave away her virtue long before you. She knows how to bring a man around to her point of view.' He held up a hand to stall Ren's burgeoning protest. 'You seem like an ambitious, smart man, Dryden. Think about it. Seeing the books would naturally be one of the first things a man like yourself would do in a venture like this. Don't make any more excuses. Yes, there was harvesting, but now it's over. She knows it's just a matter of time before you ask to see the accounts unless she can distract you, make you forget.'

Gridley paused. 'Face the truth, Dryden, regardless of what she's indicated, she doesn't want you here. Why would she? You threaten her autonomy. Where else on this earth can she be the mistress of her destiny, own property, have a man's life? She has two choices. She can send you packing or she can find some way to emasculate you and render your fifty-one per cent impotent.' Ren wondered if Gridley's crass references were deliberately sexual. The man seemed to have a one-track mind where sex and Emma were intertwined.

Gridley looked at him thoughtfully. 'Is she that good? Is she worth social castration? Because I assure you, that is exactly what will happen if you throw your lot in with her.'

'And yet you seem quite eager to marry her,' Ren ground out, fighting the urge to plant Gridley a facer for the umpteenth time that morning. If he'd had his way, Gridley's face would be black and blue and his mouth short a few teeth.

'I'd marry her to tame her, to control her,' Gridley answered. 'She's impulsive, wild and she will ruin the district if she's not brought to heel.' Something hot and lurid leapt in his eyes.

'I think you should leave.' Ren stood up.

Gridley rose and held out his hands, palms up. 'Remember, Dryden, I'm merely the messenger. Sex is her weapon. *You* look at the books, *you* talk to Emma. When you've seen the facts, you will come to the right decision.' He tapped his skull with his forefinger. 'Just make sure you're thinking with the right head when you do.'

Gridley was as audacious as they came. He probably should have taken a swing at the bastard anyway for marching in here, thinking he could dictate terms, thinking he could insult Emma, thinking he could insult Ren's own masculinity. There were so many reasons. But hitting Gridley for any of them accomplished nothing. The niggling worry that had taken up residence in his brain had become full bloom. *What if Gridley was right?*

One did not hit a man because he was right. An opinion wasn't necessarily wrong just because he didn't like the man who held it. Ren's mind reeled with *what if*s. What if Emma had been using the attraction between them for her benefit? It wasn't as if he hadn't wondered that himself. What if she was miraculously able to fake such pleasure time and again? What if she was distracting him from seeing the truth of the accounts? What if Sugarland was indeed foundering in economic seas as Gridley suggested? He would be betrayed on all fronts. The few bites of breakfast sat like a rock in his stomach.

Ren drew a deep breath. He'd never know if he sat in the library sulking. He needed to see those books. Ren made his way to the office, half expecting to see Emma materialise on the stairs, but there was no sign of her. He was glad she had not been present for the interview with Gridley. The beginnings of a self-satisfied smile played on his lips. She was sleeping late because of him, because he'd kept her up half the night and then some; further proof that she felt *something* for him at least, further proof that Gridley wasn't entirely correct about the nature of their relationship.

In the office, Ren found the books behind a glass cabinet, each one neatly labelled by year. There was something reassuring, solid, about seeing decades of ledgers. Ren ran his hand over the spines. A place that lasted this long, that had passed from owner to owner through centuries even, couldn't be in dire straits. He found the ledgers from 1831 to present and pulled them out, deciding he would test Gridley's supposition that things had started to fail after the hurricane.

Ren seated himself behind the desk, opened the first ledger and began to read. He recognised his mistake right away. He needed to go back a few more years and see what the norm was before the hurricane. He went to the cabinet and pulled out the three years preceding 1831.

Those were good years. There was hope in the stories told by the columns and balances. But there was another story, too. The plantation did not diversify. It relied almost exclusively on cane for its export profits.

Ren sat back in his chair, absently rubbing at his temples. He'd file that bit of information away for another time. When it came to business, putting all of one's eggs in a single basket was not solid practice. It worried him that Sugarland had done so, especially if Gridley was right. It worried him, too, that the cartel was seeking to do the same thing. A monopoly might provide short-term financial solutions, but it wouldn't solve long-term problems. There would be other hurricanes, there would be other places establishing their own sugar-cane trade.

Ren reluctantly reached for the post-1831 ledgers. He suspected he'd read the good news. Now it was time for the bad, if Gridley was to be believed. He opened the first book.

An hour later he pushed the ledgers aside, fighting panic along with the facts. The money he'd thought Sugarland had was a myth. What would happen to his family now? Sarah and Annalise, Teddy and his mother, were all counting on him, on something that had never been.

The great adventure had failed before it had really begun. The ledgers told the whole story. By 1834, the downward pattern was clear. Gridley had been right. The pit in Ren's stomach clenched in sickening realisation. Ren reached for the bell pull. He had to confront Emma. If Gridley was right about the economics, what else was he right about?

A footman came right away. 'Tell Miss Ward I'd like to speak with her in the office immediately.' His voice sounded hollow even to himself. He'd been Trojan Horsed after all. The next question was how deep did the deception go? Had everything been a lie?

Chapter Seventeen

Emma answered the summons with no small amount of trepidation. She wanted to be angry. She wanted to rail: how dare he act with such presumption! How dare he think a night in her bed meant she was at his beck and call. It would be easier to be angry over the summons, but it would also be a lie.

She wasn't angry, she was nervous. What did Ren want? Hattie had told her Gridley had been here early. She'd opted for the coward's way out and let Ren handle him. Had Ren called for her as a result of Gridley's visit? What kind of vile rumour had Gridley let loose this time? Or had Ren called her for another reason? The thought of that reason set butterflies fluttering in her stomach in girlish anticipation. Perhaps that reason had to do with last night? The night had been erotic and beautiful and, heaven help her, it had meant something to her despite her vow to the contrary. Had it meant something to him, too?

Emma pressed a hand to her stomach, trying to still her nerves as she made her way down the hall toward the office. It wasn't supposed to be this way. She wasn't supposed to have fallen for her own ploy. She was to have been neutral and calculating, treating the sexual attraction between her and Ren with cool detachment. He was supposed to have been the one who was seduced.

Emma pushed open the office door and all thoughts of seduction fled at the sight of the ledgers spread open before him. This was not about Gridley or last night, but something else altogether.

Ren looked up at her entrance, his jaw tight, his skin ashen beneath his tan. 'Sugarland is losing money.' It was part accusation, part questioning disbelief.

He knew! Her stomach tightened. Yet another of her secrets was up. Would he blame her for it? Would he opt to use this as proof of her inability to run the place? Or use it as proof to force her into the cartel? Emma fought the urge to give any outward show of dismay.

'Sugar prices have dropped.' Emma decided to play it coolly. She would let him come to her with whatever had provoked this sudden desire to look in the books. She took a seat in a chair and arranged her skirts. *Show no fear!* It was the number-one rule of engagement with any man looking to get the upper hand.

'I can see that. Based on these numbers Gridley's cartel seems a good idea.' Ren's tone was cool as well, his blue eyes shrewd as they studied her, his demeanour distant. It was hard to believe this was the same man who'd been so passionately alive in her bed last night, who'd cried her name at climax, who had teased her so sinfully with his body.

The man behind the desk was detached and businesslike as he went on. 'But, of course, there are ethical, personal reasons why we can no longer pursue a cartel arrangement with Gridley no matter how much profit it offers. We will not do business with a murderer.'

Emma met his gaze calmly. Inside, she was a roiling mess of emotions. She hadn't lost him yet. He was still saying 'we', and he was aligning himself with her on the position of Gridley. Whatever Gridley had come to say, it had not swayed Ren into betraying her. She held Ren's gaze and went on the offensive.

'What prompted this sudden look at the accounts? I have to say it isn't the usual response after a night of rabid lovemaking.' She let her eyes flirt a bit, her gaze lingering on his mouth. Perhaps it wouldn't hurt to mix a little business with pleasure and strengthen the lure that currently bound him to her.

'Arthur Gridley paid me a call this morning before I was even out of bed.' Gridley had put Ren up to this? It was the worst prompt Emma could think of. She'd far rather have had the peek into the accounts prompted by his own curiosity. If Gridley had made the suggestion, it no doubt came with a personal commentary as well. She could imagine how Gridley would have shaped his case. But Gridley's arguments were for naught. Ren had already indicated as much, which meant Gridley hadn't provoked the ashen pallor beneath his tan.

'You should have sent for me. I would have met with him as well. If we are to be partners, we need to show a united front. Clearly, Gridley called for *you*, thinking we are not united.' Blame and misdirection were usually standard tools for launching an offensive. But Ren was quick to respond, not in the least stymied by her shift.

'Partners?' The anger rose in Ren's carefully controlled voice. 'You hid this from me. You led me to believe Sugarland was doing well.' He made a sweeping gesture towards the open ledgers in front of him. Emma's heart sank. This was about money. Well, now at least she knew.

'Omissions seem to be a habit for you. These ledgers are not all you haven't mentioned. You didn't tell me about the cartel and your efforts to resist it. I had to learn that from Gridley. You didn't tell me there isn't really a choice when it comes to that cartel. Despite our ethical reservations about doing business with a murderer, lack of participation in the cartel will make life unbearable for us, if not downright dangerous.'

Ren had risen, ticking off on his long fingers the list of her omissions.

'You're upset...' Emma began, hoping to placate him. His face was positively thunderous and she was reminded of the power of his presence. Ren's hand slammed the page of an open ledger in a forceful movement. She jumped, startled by the sound.

'Damn right I'm upset. I've travelled halfway around the world to discover I've not inherited a plantation, I've inherited a viper's nest!' He moved around the desk, halting in front of her, his height accentuated from where she sat, forcing her to look up. 'Everywhere I look, you're at the heart of it, Emma—you and Arthur Gridley with your schemes and secret histories.'

Oh, no, she was losing him. He might as well have stabbed her with a knife if he was going to compare her to the likes of Gridley. Emma felt herself pale with real, desperate fear.

He narrowed his eyes, twin cobalt flames burning into her. 'Tell me, did you seduce me? I asked you last night, but you didn't give me a straight answer. Is this the reason why? Did you hope once I had a taste of your charms I'd not care what I found in the ledgers or anywhere else?'

'That is the outside of enough!' Emma rose swiftly, her hand making hard contact against his cheek with a resounding slap. 'I will *not* allow you to stand in this room and call me a whore when you know what I've been through, what I've had to fight. A woman has far fewer weapons at her disposal than a man.'

They were standing toe to toe, chests heaving with emotion. She could see a tic jump in his cheek. He was keeping himself barely leashed, the imprint of her palm red on his cheek.

'Answer the question, Emma,' Ren growled. 'Did you seduce me?'

Oh, mercy. She had hurt him, and in doing so she hurt herself, too, something she hadn't thought possible when he'd arrived. He'd been an object then, a stranger. The realisation that he had become more made her uncomfortable. She was a good person, she wasn't in the habit of scheming, of perpetrating evil, that was Gridley's market. Even more than that, she didn't want to hurt Ren, not even to protect Sugarland.

'It wasn't like that, not last night…' Emma began, resuming her seat. The heat of the fight had left her. How to do this? Did she dare the truth? It would expose her entirely in ways that left her vulnerable. She drew a breath to steady her voice, her decision made. She would risk the truth if it meant keeping Ren. 'All right, maybe in the beginning I thought I might be able to use our attraction to my advantage.'

'Aha!' Ren accused.

'Let me explain,' Emma protested the interruption. 'If you want answers, you can't twist the facts.'

Ren nodded, backing off, giving her space

while he opted to pace by the window and listen. 'That night when you claimed your forfeit, you wanted me, it was there in your eyes. I thought I could do it, I thought I could use that desire to keep control of Sugarland. But when it came right down to it, I couldn't.'

'And yet, we've had quite the last three days.' Ren's tone was cynical. 'I'm having trouble believing you had difficulty doing it. You seemed to be "doing it" quite well.'

Emma crossed the room, coming up behind him, her hands on his arms, her lips pressed to his back. 'Then believe this. I couldn't do it for the reasons I'd set out to do. I'd meant to use you, to bind you to me. But when the moment came, I only went forward because I wanted you for myself too much. I couldn't be neutral, detached. Everything that has happened, happened because I wanted it, not because it furthered some hidden agenda.'

He had to believe her! She'd given him the truth—what more was there to give him? If he refused to accept it, something valuable would be lost, broken beyond repair even if Sugarland was saved.

He turned, his body as stiff as his tone as he

disengaged her hands and stepped away from her. 'All right. I will take that into consideration.'

It wasn't what she was hoping for. Desperation galvanised her. 'Ren, this is Gridley's divisiveness at work, I feel it.'

Ren merely nodded. 'I will take that into consideration, too. If you will excuse me, I have to go into Bridgetown.'

'Why?' Panic gripped her. He couldn't leave, not now when everything was a mess. She hated feeling this way. She was not one given to panic. It was testament to how deeply he'd affected her, how quickly his opinion had come to matter.

He fixed her with a steely stare. 'The way I see things, there're two problems at work. We have a plantation and a burgeoning relationship, both in jeopardy. I think I can save the former. I'm not sure about the latter. The plantation is worth my effort, I don't know if the relationship is.'

His words made her feel small and petty. She'd misplayed her hand with him from the start and now she had to pay. 'I'll come with you. We can talk over your ideas for the plantation on the way. I can help.' Emma stood up and smoothed her skirts, eager to mend fences, eager to earn back his trust and respect, assuming she'd had it in the first place.

Ren shook his head. 'No. I want to go alone. I think you've helped enough.'

Emma stood in silent shock, watching Ren walk away. It was the most complete dismissal she'd ever received. Goodness, it hurt. Never mind that she might have deserved it. In all fairness, he *had* walked into a viper's pit. There was much she had deliberately held back and even when the revelations had come out one by one, he'd borne each one reasonably. Except today. The money had bothered him greatly, the proverbial straw that had broken the camel's back. Why had the money mattered so much? At the moment, it seemed to matter more than her, more than her soul-exposing disclosure.

To her credit, she had meant what she'd said today. She had not given herself to him in the hopes of playing his desire against him. She welcomed his passion, welcomed the fire he raised in her. She'd taken him to her bed because she'd wanted him, because her body cried out for him. He made her feel alive, free.

A tear slipped down her cheek. Now he was gone. What had she done? 'Is that why you did it, Merry? Is that why you wanted him to come? To protect me?' she said aloud to the empty room. From the start, she'd seen Ren Dryden as a nuisance while Merry had seen him as something more. Not just for Sugarland, but for her, too. Emma had the sinking sensation that in her desire to protect the plantation, to protect herself, she'd inadvertently chased away the one man who could save them both.

Chapter Eighteen

'I need a secondary export to save Sugarland,' Ren said over ale in one of Bridgetown's less glamorous public houses where he'd found Kitt Sherard. When he'd left the plantation he'd known only that he needed to talk, needed to be listened to and needed to listen in return. In short, he needed a friend and Kitt was it. He'd hoped the entire five miles into town that Kitt would be in port.

'Is it as bad as all that?' Kitt eyed him over the foaming tankard.

'It will be. Sugar prices have continued to drop, the cost of labour will rise. The books are already showing the effects.' Ren pushed a hand through his hair. 'I think diversifying is an obvious answer. A second export would give us something substantial to fall back on in hard times.'

'May I suggest rum?' Kitt offered. 'Sugarland has its own still, if I recall.' He leaned forward and lowered his voice. 'Around here, most planters produce rum for themselves and for local businesses. But I'm talking about mass-producing the rum. Sugarland is large enough to have the molasses to do it. A lot of places don't have the resources to go big.'

'Where do I sell all this rum? It wouldn't be enough to just sell it here on the island.'

Kitt laughed and dropped his voice to a whisper. 'To the British navy, you numbskull. They're the world's largest consumer of rum. I also think you work on a special line. Sell the regular stuff to the navy. Their rum doesn't have to be fancy. Then start to make another rum designed for a finer palate, something that might appeal to all your snob friends back home. Run up the price on that. Snobs like to pay for their pleasures.'

Ren nodded slowly, processing the idea. They could start right away. With the harvest finished and the cane just now going to the mill, there would be fresh sugar-cane juice, a fresh supply of molasses. 'I don't suppose you could arrange for me to meet with the naval quartermaster?'

Ren asked drily. He didn't think for a moment Kitt had offered this out of sheer humanitarianism.

Kitt's grin widened. 'Stay over in town with me tonight and you can see him tomorrow. I have an appointment to discuss other business with him.'

Ren leaned back against the wall, studying his friend. 'Is this what you've been doing for five years, Kitt? Running rum?'

Kitt nodded, unashamed. 'Pretty much. It's not illegal any more. But everyone in the islands needs it, wants it. Not everyone can produce it. The best rum in the islands comes out of Barbados. What I've discovered in these parts is that transportation is the key. It takes time to get from one point to another. The first thing I did when I arrived was buy myself a boat. I just started hauling whatever people needed delivered to wherever it needed to go.'

Ren didn't want to ask what some of that might have been. Kitt's code of ethics was a little different from his. But at least Kitt had one. Ren was starting to think that was a rare commodity on the island. He reached across the table and gripped Kitt's forearm. 'Thank you for this, my friend. I won't forget it.' One problem was potentially resolved if he could deliver the rum.

'What else is on your mind?' Kitt asked quietly. 'Is there more to this than finding a secondary source of income?'

Ren stared into his emptying tankard. Why not tell Kitt everything? It was surprisingly hard to talk about this latest intimacy, even with Kitt. They'd shared talk about women before plenty of times back in London, but those had been casual liaisons, society games. He and Emma were...different. What they had shared was sacred somehow, more personal, something he had just begun to realise before the doubts had set in.

Ren braved the disclosure with a carefully couched sentence. 'Things with Emma Ward have become complicated.' An understatement if ever there was one.

Kitt gave an embarrassingly loud hoot of laughter that drew stares towards their table. 'You bedded her! After all your protests about how you didn't think you had time for a woman.' He winked at Ren. 'There's always time for a woman when she's the right woman, isn't there? Emma's as pretty as they come and as prickly, too.'

Ren rubbed the back of his neck. 'I think she

seduced me to minimise my power. I think she
hoped if I bedded her, I wouldn't contest her authority.' He didn't want that to be true. Hearing
the words out loud made them sound so cold,
the complete antithesis to what he and Emma
had shared.

'That you'd be too caught up in her charms?'
Kitt nodded knowingly. 'That's no good, my
friend.' He thought for a moment before leaning
back in, his voice thankfully lower again. 'Why
do you think that? Did you come up with that
idea on your own or did someone suggest it?'

'In part, both. You know me, I'm an analyst.
I'm always thinking of things from different
angles. She wasn't pleased to see me the day I
showed up and then a couple weeks later we're
in bed. One might say that's quite an about-turn.'
Only he hadn't seen it that way. He had been
caught up in her flirtation and he'd been so sure
of himself he hadn't thought to question things.

Kitt shrugged. 'You know how to turn a lady's
head, Ren. I've seen you do it countless times in
a ballroom. Even the stiffest old matron melts for
you. I wouldn't underestimate your charm. Perhaps she saw your, ah, "potential" and changed
her mind. But you said in part. What else influ-

enced your conclusion? It wouldn't be Arthur Gridley, would it?'

'I had a rather unpleasant interview with him this morning,' Ren said. 'The subject came up, not for the first time.'

'Gridley's hot for her, has been for ages. He won't like her choosing you over him. I wouldn't let his opinion colour mine too much since he's got an agenda.' Kitt had made his point. 'As for me, I don't think it seems like something Emma Ward would do. If anyone in these parts has a social conscience, it's her. She supports an honest application of the apprenticeship programme, she pays a fair wage. She doesn't use people, but Arthur Gridley does.'

Ren thought about the day the chicken coop burnt down, how Emma had understood the request for time off and a chance to practice local customs. He thought, too, about his earlier argument with himself. She could not have feigned such passion.

He thought, too, about what she'd told him regarding Gridley. She didn't merely loathe the man, she feared him. She stood to lose more than a home if Gridley succeeded. She stood to lose her freedom, maybe even her life. Under those circumstances, even if she had used him, he could hardly blame her. In her situation, he might have done the same, although she'd suggested this morning that she'd not gone through with it for those reasons.

He might have lied to Kitt when he'd told him Emma had thought to prevent his usurping of her authority. He saw now that she hadn't set out to emasculate him, far from it. She wanted him to be her buffer. She didn't want him to run, she wanted him to stay. And he'd done just the opposite. He'd left her to fend for herself against Gridley. But perhaps he could remedy that situation ,too.

'Kitt, what do you know about Arthur Gridley…?' he began hesitantly—he'd already asked Kitt for so much.

Kitt shook his head. 'Nothing good. His background is a little murky, but that's true for a lot of folks out here looking for new beginnings. Beyond the obvious, why do you ask?'

'I have reason to believe he killed my cousin. I'd like to investigate, but…' Ren let the implication hang in the air.

Kitt nodded knowingly. 'I'll look into it and see if Gridley has the magistrate or the police force in his pocket.' Before they could bring charges, they had to determine if it would be safe to do so. If the officials were bribed, it would be dangerous and futile.

He'd done what he could for now to help Emma, a mere peace offering after their quarrel. Guilt swamped Ren. He'd been too hard on her. He'd been in financial shock, upset over the reality of Sugarland because it wasn't what he needed and he'd channelled some of that disappointment in her direction. He groaned when he thought of the hot words they'd spoken, the things he'd accused her of. They were not things a gentleman accused a lady of *ever.* 'I may have some apologising to do,' Ren murmured into the last of his ale.

'I know someone else who might have some to do, too…' Kitt began slowly. 'I know you have lady problems of your own. I hate to add one more, but there's something you need to see. Just don't kill the messenger.' Kitt slid an opened letter across the table. 'This came in my post. I happened to intercept the mail packet a little sooner than the rest of you.'

The letter was from London. Ren swallowed, his heart starting to race. There would only be a few reasons why Kitt would show him a personal letter. 'It's from Benedict,' Kitt supplied as Ren scanned the contents. Ren felt his nerves ease. Benedict DeBreed was wild, always up to something crazy.

'What has Ben got himself into this time?' Ren gave a chuckle.

'Matrimony.' Kitt answered. 'To your sister. It's all in there. He even included the announcement from *The Times.*'

Ren looked at the newspaper clipping in disbelief.

Mr Benedict DeBreed announces his engagement to Lady Sarah Dryden, sister to the Earl of Dartmoor.

'Apparently, Benedict has come into some money, a tin mine or something.' Kitt said tentatively.

Sarah was going to marry one of London's most notorious bounders? How had this happened? But Ren knew. Rumour of their finances must have got out. 'I asked Benedict to watch over the family, not to marry into it,' Ren muttered. Benedict was a good friend, a loyal one, but that didn't mean he wanted a rake marrying his sister. Sarah must have felt forced to it, must have felt there was no other choice. Ren looked at the postmark. They might be married already if Benedict had proposed in haste. Even so, there was nothing he could do at a distance.

'This is my fault.' Ren groaned. He should have been there. He was feeling selfish. He'd come for a lot of reasons, but especially to escape his own matrimonial entanglement. Now, his sister had gone and done the unthinkable. 'I should have come up with a better solution.'

'Short of marrying that horse-faced heiress out of York, I don't know what that solution would have been.' Kitt reminded him.

'Perhaps I should have. Then Sarah wouldn't have had to marry DeBreed.'

'Maybe she wanted to. DeBreed's handsome, now he's rich. He's a legend in bed.' Kitt shrugged, not taking the issue with half as much seriousness. Then again, Kitt didn't have sisters.

'Shut up, Kitt,' Ren growled.

'What? You don't want your sister to enjoy marriage?' Kitt was brimming with laughter. 'If I had a sister, I'd want her to enjoy certain aspects of marriage.'

'Well, you don't, so you hardly know what you're talking about.' Ren tried to keep a straight face. The conversation was so ridiculous it was hard to scold Kitt for his crassness. Ren lost the battle, his face breaking into a grin. 'I had forgotten just how pathetic you are, Kitt. Thanks for reminding me.'

Kitt reached over and clapped him on the shoulder. 'Don't worry. DeBreed might be wild, but deep down inside, and when I say deep, I mean pretty deep, it is DeBreed we're talking about after all, he's a decent fellow. Besides, Sarah's a big girl. She can take care of herself and you have your new rum enterprise. I think you're missing the silver lining here. Sarah's married money and you're making money. The great Dartmoor line will be in the black in no time at all.' Kitt raised his hand and called for another round. 'Tonight, *you* should be celebrating.' He grinned. 'And I'll help.'

It didn't help matters that Ren hadn't come home the previous night from Bridgetown. How could she apologise? How could she win him back if he wasn't here? Emma looked out the front-room window for the millionth time since the sun had started to sink. There was no sign of life in the long drive. To hell with peeking out the windows. She was going to sit on the porch and stare down the road until he showed up. And she did, until it was too dark to see. So much for that idea.

The sun was completely gone and even with the assistance of a lantern, there was only so much visibility. That was when she decided it: she would wait for him in his bed. That way, even if she fell asleep, she wouldn't miss his return and he wouldn't be able to overlook her. For the first time since his arrival, she was regretting putting him in the *garçonnière*. It would be far more convenient to have him in one of the bedchambers in the main house near her.

Emma smiled when she entered his rooms. At least this would be private. Privacy would be welcomed if everything went well. She changed into her nightgown, a filmy white confection of lace and chiffon. She took down her hair and brushed it out. Then she settled into his bed to wait, knowing full well it would be hard for him to resist. She'd seen herself in the long mirror in the corner, her hair loose, her gown doing little to conceal her feminine assets.

She breathed in the scent of the linens. They smelled like him, all vanilla and sandalwood. She looked around the room, noting the little changes he'd made with the furniture, seeing the personal effects he'd set out. It was tempting to get out of bed and look at those items up close. Emma talked herself out of it. If she was going to earn back his trust, the last thing she needed to be caught doing was going through his belongings.

Waiting was boring. Snooping was starting to look more appealing. She had to do *something*. Emma opted for the book on his bedside table. She hoped for poetry, or a novel. What she got was an agricultural treatise on the Caribbean, interesting as far as research went. In other circumstances she might have enjoyed it. But in terms of keeping a girl awake, Emma had her doubts about its effectiveness. She made it through two pages before she began to yawn…

The sound of booted feet woke her with a jolt. She experienced a moment of panic, a sense of being invaded before she realised where she was and who was coming through the door. Ren! He was home. A surge of elation replaced the panic. She rose up on her elbows. 'Hello, stranger,' she said in her best sultry tones.

Ren grinned. 'You make coming home worthwhile. I could get used to a sight like that. I was starting to think I'd never make it back.' He came over to the bed and sat down. He did look exhausted. She couldn't recall ever having seen him look so entirely unkempt even after a day of riding the estate. His clothes were wrinkled, his shirt cuffs looked dingy where they peeped out from his jacket sleeve.

He leaned forward to pull his boots off. 'Those were the longest five miles ever. I misjudged how much time I'd need and I left it too late to get home before the sun set. I misjudged the darkness, too, that's pitch black out there. No lamplights, no nothing.'

Emma smiled and scooted over to him. 'I'm just glad you're home. You are right, though, the darkness can be dangerous. People get lost, wander into the interior, stumble on to a snake, and it's too late by the time we find them.' She meant to put her arms about his neck, to hold him close, let him feel the press of her breasts and remind him of what they could share but she recoiled at the last moment. 'Eww, you stink! Ren Dryden, you're drunk!'

Not even on the good stuff either. His clothes reeked of cheap ale and brandy—well, maybe the brandy was higher quality, it was hard to tell. No wonder he'd misjudged the time, no wonder he looked so dishevelled. Emma threw back the covers and slid out of bed. 'I'm disgusted with you! You left here and went straight to Bridgetown for a drinking binge without even telling me how long you would be gone. I've been here, worrying while you've been out doing who knows what with who knows whom.'

But she did know with whom—with the disreputable Kitt Sherard. And she probably did know what, too. Had he really left her bed and found another so quickly? Her heart sank, her visions of a happy reunion fading. Could she blame him? He'd left Sugarland believing she'd used him, believing there was nothing between them that required any loyalty.

She started towards the door, only to feel Ren's hand close over her arm. For a drunk man, he moved fast and in a straight line. 'Em, wait. It's not like that. Yes, I've been with Kitt. He spilled an ale, it got all over me, and, yes, things got a little wild, but I wasn't on a binge. I was at a meeting Kitt set up.' He forced her to turn and look at him and those beautiful blue eyes, which were clear. It would be easier to stay angry if he had been drunk.

'Em, listen to me. I found a way to increase our revenue. I have a contract with the British Navy to sell them rum, casks and casks of it.'

She stared, her brow knitting as she tried to process what he had said. Then the implications hit her and she felt her mouth drop. 'We won't have to rely solely on sugar any more. Ren, do you know what this means?' She hardly noticed his smelly clothes as her mind raced with the possibilities. 'We could branch out, make a special label for a finer-quality rum.'

Ren laughed. 'You might not like Sherard, but you sound an awful lot like him. That was his suggestion, too.'

There was hope after all. She wasn't fighting a losing battle. Ren had come back and he'd brought an answer with him. She threw her arms about his neck and kissed him full on the mouth. But Ren did not respond. Instead, he put his hands on her hips and set her away from him.

'Emma, this is an answer to *one* of our problems, not all of our problems. Even if we're successful with the rum, the cartel will not be happy. Gridley has suggested quite openly they will retaliate if we don't comply.'

Emma shook her head. 'Tonight I don't care. Tonight I'm just glad you're home. Ren, I'm so sorry.' She reached for him again and again he sidestepped her advances.

Ren looked at her, his eyes serious. 'Are you? Are you excited about the rum, or about me? I need you to be sure. No man wants to be appreciated solely for his fifty-one per cent.'

Emma answered his stare with an even gaze of her own. 'I came to this room to wait for *you*. You know it's true because I had no knowledge of your deal with Kitt, or if you would be back tonight. I don't know what we can be to each other, or even what we want to be to each other. You're right. That remains to be sorted out. But I do know what I want from you has nothing to do with your fifty-one per cent and a hundred per cent to do with the man.' Emma took his hand. 'I want you naked in bed, Ren Dryden. But before your ego gets too inflated, it's because you'd stink up the sheets otherwise.'

Ren swept her a bow. 'Your wish is granted. Naked I will be. It's no trouble since I sleep naked anyway.' He winked.

'Yes,' Emma said drily, climbing up on the bed to watch. 'I seem to recall it was one of the first things I learned about you. You were so eager to impart that piece of information at the time.'

Ren pulled off his coat and tossed it to a corner. 'I will bathe if you want me to,' he offered, his fingers working the buttons of his shirt.

Emma shook her head. 'Here's a little something you should know about me. I'm impatient and I've waited too long for you already.' To prove it, she pulled her nightgown up over her head and tossed it into the corner with his coat.

Chapter Nineteen

Dryden was back. Gridley's little spy had reported first thing in the morning. He wasn't surprised, but he'd hoped to get a lucky break. The mail packet was due in soon and it would be perfect timing for Dryden to make his exit.

Gridley drummed his fingers on his desktop. The fact that Dryden had returned worried him. It meant there'd been a reason to come back even after the nudge he'd given the man. What more could he do to convince Dryden? He'd shown Emma to be a woman of loose morals, a manipulator of men. He'd all but opened the books and put them under Dryden's nose to round out the impression Emma had deluded him. All the things Dryden had come to believe in had been exposed and found wanting. Yet he'd come back. Did it mean he was going to join the cartel? Or did it mean he'd found a way to revive Sugarland's flagging profits outside of the cartel? Or worse, there was always an outside chance Dryden had come back for Emma. If he had, it was only a matter of time before Dryden knew Gridley's dirty little secret. He couldn't rely on Emma keeping that quiet forever.

He looked up as a servant announced the arrival of Hugh Devore. Normally, Arthur liked to plan alone and announce his intentions after the fact. Today, he'd felt the need for reinforcements.

'Dryden has certainly thrown a wrench in our plans.' Devore settled into a chair and crossed a leg over one knee, cutting straight to the heart of the matter. 'It was one thing when we thought he'd be gone, or that we could rely on Emma helping us along with her own desire to be rid of him. But it seems that has changed. He means to stay and Emma has figured out he can be an ally.'

'Exactly,' Arthur agreed with Devore's assessment. 'The problem is what to do next? Anything we do, short of ignoring Sugarland's choices, will commit us irrevocably to a path of division. It will openly be us against them.' He preferred more covert tactics that relied on assumed friendships, the building of trust and then the ultimate betrayal with him riding to the rescue, no one the wiser as to his part in bringing the crisis about in the first place.

Devore thought for a moment. 'We need to re-shape the way we've looked at our options. We have always built our assumptions around the premise that Sugarland had to be factored into our plans. We've tried to buy it, tried to marry into it, tried to partner with it. None of those options have worked. What if it was just gone, no longer a variable to contend with?'

Interesting and risky. Arthur leaned forward. 'How would we do it? Eliminate the players or the thing we're playing for?' He was a little nervous, too. He'd always engineered the plots, making sure he was in a position to use Sugarland as leverage to force Emma. 'With Sugarland gone, I would lose a powerful piece of persuasion.'

'Would you?' Devore queried. 'She'd be completely exposed without the plantation, her source of income gone, her source of stability gone. She'd be homeless, nothing more than a rabbit flushed from the brush running without cover. Perhaps she'd see what you have to offer differently. Right now, a home doesn't mean much to her because she has one. Neither does an income, or a lover,' Devore said pointedly.

'We could have done without the last,' Arthur growled. It galled him to know Dryden had superseded him in all ways.

Devore steepled his hands over his stomach. 'It's a simple case of supply and demand. Everything is in the end.'

Arthur gave Devore's advice a considering nod. 'We get rid of Dryden, we burn Sugarland. But Emma remains unharmed. I must have that last condition. I promised Albert Merrimore…'

Devore gave a harsh laugh. 'Right before you put a pillow over the old man's face. Don't get sanctimonious on me, Arthur. You'd make promises to the devil if it advanced your cause. Not that I have a problem with that. I understand you and you understand me. We're businessmen, cut from the same cloth. We're both ruthless when it comes to something we want. Still, I want the cartel, you want the girl. I think that can be arranged.'

'When do we do it?' Arthur was warming to the idea now that he could see the benefits. Really, the plan was almost too good to be true. They would get their cartel, sugar prices would go up, Dryden would conveniently go away,

Emma would be his either by coercion or by persuasion.

'I think soon. Crop Over happens at the end of the week. All the workers will head to Bridgetown for the celebrations.'

'It should be a fire,' Gridley said. He didn't want Devore calling all the shots, it would give the man an exalted sense of his own power and make him forgetful of who led their exclusive coterie. 'They've already had one fire with that chicken coop. There's precedence.'

'Precedence for arson.' Devore gave an evil grin. 'I don't believe for a moment that coop burned on its own.'

Gridley returned the grin. 'It had help.' Never mind that the ploy hadn't worked as effectively as he'd hoped. The plan had been to have a minor catastrophe that would scare off enough of Emma's work force to subvert her ability to harvest. But Dryden had chosen that day to show up unannounced. Dryden had taken charge. There'd been little Arthur could do to work up panic among the workers by the time he'd arrived, short of making sure everyone saw the obeah doll he'd planted among the ashes. It had cost Emma a half day's labour, but nothing more. Until now. That fire was going to be useful after all.

'How do we take care of Dryden?' Devore enquired.

Burn him along with the house, lose him in the interior, set him aboard a ship sailing for parts unknown. Arthur could devise any number of unfortunate accidents. This would be one area, however, where he wouldn't mind Devore taking the lead. He'd handled Merrimore, clearing the way to leaving Emma open to the next layer of their attempts. Now it was someone else's turn. Devore could handle Dryden. Then, if it became convenient to expose Devore to Emma in the future to win her affections, he'd be able to turn on Devore. Ah, yes, things were starting to come together nicely.

The morning was starting well: Emma tucked against him, his body replete with sexual satisfaction. Two out of three wasn't bad. Any gambling man would take those odds. Unfortunately, Ren wasn't so much a gambler as he was a perfectionist. He'd prefer three out of three, but he couldn't get his mind to conform, to accept the here and now without looking forward to the future. How would the here and now affect the later? He was an analyst, too, along with being a perfectionist and both of those qualities were wreaking havoc with his mind at the moment.

Emma stirred against his shoulder, her dark hair grazing his chest. Ren looked down at his sleeping beauty. What was he going to do with her? She'd stirred his passions from the moment he'd laid eyes on her. But it had all happened so fast. In many ways she was a stranger still. Every revelation proved it. The very idea that Gridley's insinuations had the power to at least sow doubt reinforced that proof as did her own reticence to be forthcoming with him. And yet, he was drawn to her. He didn't want to let her go, but to what end?

His options were few. There was only one choice really. If he meant to keep her, to make her his, he should marry her. If he didn't marry her, he'd have to walk away. The island wasn't big enough for both of them. Walking away would mean returning to England. It was the more logical choice. He could open up an office in England to oversee the rum imports. He could build the business from that end and still be able to run the earldom as he should instead of at a distance through solicitors. He could be on hand to take care of his family, to make sure there were no more disasters, like Sarah marrying Benedict.

Perhaps he'd always known it would come to this. He'd wanted to believe coming here would be a new start, a new life for him. But deep down, perhaps he'd known it couldn't be permanent. He was the earl, he had responsibilities. If it came to choosing between Emma and his family, there wasn't really a choice. There couldn't be.

No matter that he honestly liked it here. Kitt was right, one got used to the heat. He loved the beaches, the ocean, the lush colours of sky and grass, the informality of life, the ability to work for that life. Did staying here preclude going home ever? That was the one issue he'd refused to address when he'd left home—would he ever return? It wasn't that he minded *not* seeing England again, but he did very much mind the idea that he would never see his family again, that his only contact with them would be through letters. He should have been there to negotiate Sarah's marriage settlement. He should have been there to head DeBreed off in the first place.

You could take Emma with you, came the niggling thought. *Why not become an absentee landlord like so many in the other parishes? Peter is a trustworthy overseer. With him in charge, you could keep an eye on the business from England.* Emma could be his countess in the truest sense. If he married her, she'd be a countess wherever they were, but in London it would count. London would require a certain lifestyle. He tried to imagine Emma there, navigating a ball, turning away the envious gentlemen that would flock to her side. He tried to imagine what his family would make of her. And he failed. Not because it was impossible to see her succeed, but because he couldn't see her being happy.

Gone would be the Emma who strode about the plantation in breeches. What would she wake up and do each day? He couldn't see her happily assimilating into a lady's routine of shopping, teas and charity work. The Emma he knew would be bored within a month. He knew in his gut, London would be nothing more than a cage for her.

In the light of morning, his choices seemed crystal clear. Keeping Emma meant staying here, making Sugarland his home and protecting Emma from Gridley. Marriage would be the best protection Ren could provide her. It would put her beyond Gridley's reach. Ren could see himself happily piecing together that life. Although there were trade-offs. Certainly, he might return to England occasionally as Merrimore had done, but he'd become an absentee earl in truth. It was possible to pull it off. He had good solicitors, a regular mail service and DeBreed would be there now with some legal power as a brother-in-law to oversee things until Teddy was old enough.

If he *didn't* marry Emma, it meant leaving and soon. It wasn't fair to her or to him to carry on this affair indefinitely if nothing was to come of it. He selected a deadline in his mind. The end of August. There would be time to deal with Gridley. He couldn't begin to think of leaving Emma alone with Gridley on the loose. Their rum business would be up and running by then, too; everything under control to a point where Emma could manage it and he would be waiting on the other side to receive the shipments. He might even make it home in time for Sarah's wedding if he wrote and told them to wait, that he was coming.

Emma lifted her head, her hair was tousled, her voice sleepy. 'You're awake. You should have woken me. We could have got our day started.'

'There's no hurry.' The logic of his earlier analysis started to slip. What man left *this* behind? What sort of man gave up a woman like Emma? He could almost hear Kitt laughing in his head—*only a fool, Ren.* 'Where did you want to start your day?'

She laughed, a low throaty sound, as she swung a leg over his hip. 'In bed, the same place I finished it. Then, we should ride out and see the still.'

It occurred to Ren as she straddled him that Emma was a woman who knew what she wanted and he hadn't worked that into the equation of his thoughts. He'd been concerned about what he wanted. Did *she* want to marry him? Maybe she'd be happy enough to see him leave in August? This wasn't going to be a decision he could make on his own. He would have to discuss it with her and her answers would affect the outcome. But in order to discuss it, he would have to tell her who he was in his other life and why he was really here. Rather belatedly, he realised the shoe was on the other foot now—his foot—and it pinched. Once she knew, she would be justified in pinning on him the same secrecy he'd accused her of.

His thoughts had come full circle. No matter how much he thought about it, they were still just two strangers in bed together and it was as much his fault as hers. Fortunately, Emma reached between his legs and stroked him into readiness, saving him from having to think too much with his brain. He was much preferring a different kind of logic at the moment.

Emma was almost giddy with excitement at the still. The prospect of starting up a new business was a heady one. She might have been entirely given to giddiness if she hadn't sensed Ren's distraction so strongly. He'd been distracted during lovemaking. She'd climaxed without him, their morning coupling lacking the intense connection that had marked their other joinings.

He was distracted now, too, although he was making a valiant effort to hide it. They'd talked about rum on the ride out to the distillery. He told her the details about his meeting with the quartermaster, how he'd already placed an order with a cooper in town for the casks they'd need. But his mind was only partly on the conversation. She wondered what else he might have done or discovered in town to bring on such distraction or if the distraction stemmed from something internal, perhaps remnants of their quarrel. She wasn't naive enough to think those more in-

terpersonal issues had been fixed just because
business had been resolved.

'There won't be an immediate profit, but you
should see one by next year,' Ren was saying as
they stepped outside the distillery and into the
sunlight.

Ah, that was it. Emma halted, her heart sinking. She caught the discrepancy right away.
'Don't you mean "we"? *We* will see the profit?'

'Of course, I meant "we".' Ren smiled and
tried for some humour. 'We'll be bound together
forever through this place. You'll never really
get rid of me.'

She knew instantly where this was leading.
The man who'd declared he was here to stay had
decided he was leaving. Maybe he wasn't leaving
tomorrow or on the next packet, but he was moving in that direction. How much time did they
have? Two months? Three? Everything had suddenly become short-term. 'You've decided the
Caribbean doesn't agree with you,' Emma said
matter-of-factly. Maybe it was the Caribbean that
didn't agree or maybe it was her. Perhaps he'd
decided they didn't suit. 'When did this happen?'

They stopped under the shade of a tall palm.
Ren took off his straw hat and ran a hand through
his hair. 'I didn't say anything about leaving.'

'Do not play semantic games with me,' Emma cautioned sharply. 'Something has happened. Is it Gridley again with his fallacious claims?'

Ren put his hat back on and shook his head. 'It's personal and it's more complicated than that. Emma, I can't stay and continue to compromise you. Already Gridley is spreading talk. I don't think I can just be your business partner. I can't be here and simply stop the affair. I want you too badly. It would be torture to live under that roof, to see you, to work with you every day and not have you. The sacrifice wouldn't be enough anyway. Even if I were to play the monk, no one would believe it.'

Emma turned away from him, her emotions stirring to the surface. Part of her was flattered. No man had ever shown her such a fine consideration. Part of her knew it was too fine. 'Your concern for my reputation is quite chivalrous, not that I have much of a reputation left to protect. But I'm not foolish enough to believe that is enough to send you back to England. There's more.'

She heard his hesitation in the silence that followed. 'My sister is getting married. Kitt had a letter arrive with the news while I was in Bridgetown.' He paused, perhaps realising as she did how incomplete that explanation was. People could travel. Weddings were not occasions that required him to stay in England permanently. A wedding did not explain his earlier chivalry. He started again slowly. 'Did Cousin Merrimore tell you anything about me? About my family?'

'No.' What she did know about Merry's family was very general. They were thousands of miles away and he had no immediate family. Knowing cousins and relatives Merry hardly knew himself hadn't seemed a priority. They'd had each other and that had been family enough. Until now. 'I think he said once that he was a relative of your mother.'

'He was a cousin of my mother's father,' Ren supplied. 'My mother's family is landed gentry out of the south-east of England, Sussex area. They're comfortable landowners with a nice income for their station. But my mother wasn't satisfied with that lifestyle. She went to London for a Season and aimed a little higher. She came home betrothed to the heir to the Earl of Dartmoor, one of the finest catches of that Season.'

Pieces slid together in a terrifying puzzle in her mind. Ren's father was an earl. Emma recalled bits of other conversations. His father was deceased; Ren had told her as much that day on the beach. His brother, the one called Teddy, was younger than Ren. She felt the truth overwhelm her. She'd always known he was a gentleman, it had been there in his clothes, his bearing, his manners, the way he'd taken charge the day of the fire. That wasn't surprising. She'd known Merry was from a comfortably situated family. It had stood to reason his distant cousin would share some of that comfortable life, but she'd not dreamed of the extent. Emma braced an arm against the palm-tree trunk, oblivious to the prickly bark cutting into her hand as she tried to take it all in. 'You're the earl!'

She felt him move towards her. 'I'm still Ren Dryden, I'm still just a man. This doesn't change anything.'

Emma whirled on him, not sure what emotion to feel first: anger, betrayal, hypocrisy. He'd been so worried about what she'd held back, so upset about the viper's pit she'd led him into and the whole time he'd withheld the truth of himself. 'Yes, it does. You've already admitted it. You wouldn't be leaving otherwise. *This* changes everything.'

Chapter Twenty

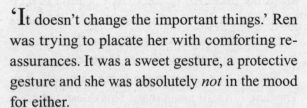

'It doesn't change the important things.' Ren was trying to placate her with comforting reassurances. It was a sweet gesture, a protective gesture and she was absolutely *not* in the mood for either.

'Stop right there. Do not give me platitudes about how it doesn't change your feelings for me. You have no idea what those feelings are.' Those feelings hardly mattered now. She should have refused the temptation of taking those feelings out and looking too closely at them before reality struck. Earls didn't marry daughters of colonels. They didn't marry women who hadn't set foot inside English society since they were eight and earls certainly didn't wed women who carried scandal for a calling card. If she showed up in England with Ren, there would be curiosity and curiosity would lead to enquiries. Eventually, her sordid past would come out. Earls needed pure innocent girls to be their countesses. Nothing could come of Ren's feelings even if they ran deep. It was best if he realised that before he decided chivalry could take forms other than leaving. Who was she fooling? It would be best for her, too.

'Perhaps we should talk about this back at the house,' Ren suggested. 'I've picked a poor place for this discussion.'

'No, we'll talk about it now.' Emma drew a deep breath to steady her mind. 'There's too great of an opportunity for interruption. We'll have privacy here.' Her thoughts were starting to move past the initial shock. 'What else don't I know, Ren? What are you really doing here?' Not for the first time, she wondered why he'd bothered to come at all, especially now when it was clear he had demanding responsibilities in England. Adventurers and businessmen could move around. But Ren was neither. Earls did not have the luxury of that freedom.

By silent, mutual consent, they started to walk. Ren was reluctant to talk. His words came haltingly. 'I'm here because the earldom is nearly broke and Cousin Merrimore's inheritance looked like manna from heaven at the time, a chance to restore our fortunes. I had to come and see if that was true.'

Guilt consumed her. She could have stopped that journey if she'd written, if she'd done more than wait around to see if he'd come or not. She could have written about the truth of that last payment to his account, that it reflected an illusion. She'd gone without her usual allowance to make that payment. He would have known from the start there was no real money. That would have changed everything.

Perhaps not for the best for her at least. What if he'd sold his share? What if he hadn't come? She would have had to face Gridley alone and possibly a second villain in the form of the new owner. She never would have stumbled on the rum contract. How long would she have lasted without Ren? She felt less guilty now, but a lot more selfish.

'I could have managed the inheritance from England, but I wanted to come. I was selfish.'

The words so closely mirrored her sentiments, Emma thought for a moment she'd spoken out loud. 'I beg your pardon?'

'I was selfish,' Ren repeated. 'This was an escape from an arranged but unwanted marriage.'

There was another woman! Her head swam. She'd desperately wanted to believe Ren was different from the men she'd known. She'd been terribly wrong. Did all men have women stashed in every corner of their lives? This was shaping up to be a rather unpleasant morning all around. 'How do you mean unwanted? Unwanted as in you didn't want to go through with it, or unwanted as in you *did* go through with it under duress?' She stopped walking and fixed him with a stare. 'I will not be a party to adultery or bigamy or anything of the sort.' The thought of encountering such circumstances a second time after Thompson Hunt made her stomach churn. She was supposed to have been smarter now.

Ren shook his head. 'I'm not married. I couldn't go through with it. There was an heiress in York who was willing to trade her fortune for my title, but we did not suit.'

Emma breathed easier. Not quite Thompson Hunt, then. She was still free to believe Ren was different; upstanding and noble. 'It's not selfish to avoid unhappiness.' She knew a thing or two about that.

Ren gave her a sharp look. 'It is when your sister sacrifices herself on the matrimonial altar in your place.'

'*She* married the York heiress?' Emma wasn't following the twist and turns of the story.

'No, she's marrying, or has already married, a man for his wealth in order to save the family from scandal. She did what I should have done.'

His remorse was palpable and it moved her. Above all, Ren Dryden was a responsible man. If the weeks of knowing him had shown her anything of the man it was that. 'Is the money that important?' She felt impotent. She would give him the world if it was hers to offer. But she didn't have the kind of money he was looking for. No wonder the ledgers had upset him. He'd come looking for the pot of gold.

'The money is everything, or was.' Ren paused. 'I suppose everything has worked out for now.'

But not the way he'd planned. Clearly, these new developments pained him. He'd been the one who had thought to provide for the family and given time, he would be, if he could just see that. Meanwhile, she hurt for him. When had she started to care so much about this man? It had been easier to fathom him when he was nothing more than an adventurer looking for fast money. She might be wary of such men, but at least she understood them. The islands were full of such men, every last one of them looking for an opportunity to make riches, men like Kitt Sherard. Ren Dryden was entirely out of her league. She didn't know what to do with a man of principle. Her experience there was admittedly limited.

'Is he a good man?' Emma could think of nothing else to say that would assuage Ren's guilt or feelings of failure.

Ren nodded. 'He's a good friend of mine.'

'Then he's a good man. I can't imagine you having bad friends.'

'What about Kitt Sherard? We went to school together.' Ren stopped himself from saying any more. Kitt had his secrets.

'You're trying to pick a fight now and we're not discussing Kitt Sherard. We're discussing you,' she gently reminded him. If they wanted to quarrel there was plenty of more immediate material to fight over than Sherard. 'Do you really see leaving as your only choice?' She brought the focus of the conversation into sharp relief with her words.

Ren faced her, his face serious, his eyes sombre. 'If I stayed, we'd be talking about marriage. We cannot live under the same roof without its protection. I could not do that to you.'

'That's definitely not the most romantic of

proposals.' Duty and obligation were written all over his suggestion and not an ounce of feeling, or love. However, she'd reached for the fairy tale once before and found it to be just that. Fairy tales weren't real. Neither were Prince Charmings. The fairy tale had been overrated. 'It would be no different from what you left England to escape, a marriage of convenience,' Emma posited.

Ren shrugged. 'Perhaps we can't really run from our fates.'

Emma shook her head and stepped away. If he touched her, she would lose control and she did not want to cry. It would be too easy to fall in love with him. She suspected she was already a good portion of the way there. To completely fall and to know he only saw her as an expeditious arrangement that suited him in bed and out would break what was left of her heart. 'I'm sorry, Ren. I couldn't do that to me. I am selfish, too. I need to be more than a man's convenience. In truth, I couldn't do it to you either.'

'I haven't even asked.' Ren tried to smile, but she could see that her outright refusal had surprised him. She realised he'd already tried the idea on in his mind and found the offer probable. He thought he could be comfortable with it. She ought to be flattered. An earl didn't come asking for her hand every day. But he was only asking because he didn't know better.

He studied her for a moment. 'I understand your reticence. I can only tell you I don't think it would be like that.'

They started walking again as if they could put distance between themselves and the awkward subject if they moved the space that had witnessed it. 'Have you ever thought Cousin Merrimore wanted us to marry?' Ren said after a while. 'Maybe that was why he divided the estate as he did?'

'No. It's a fairy tale of a thought, Ren, the perfect happy-ever-after is an impossibility under the best of circumstances. Merrimore knew better.' She paused, holding on to the last of her damning secrets for a moment. 'He watched my first marriage fall apart.'

It was her turn to stun him and that did it. If anything could trump the disclosure that Sugarland's majority shareholder was an earl in his other life, this was it. But all Ren said was, 'Perhaps you should tell me about it.'

She was glad they were walking. Talking was easier when the rest of her body had something to do. She didn't have to look at Ren and watch his reaction to just how ruined she was. What had happened had happened almost nine years ago and she'd thought she'd put her past behind her. More importantly, she'd thought she'd come to terms with it. Ren's arrival had shown her she had not. He tempted her to make the same mistakes again. More than that, he'd shown her what an imperfect shambles her life was without even meaning to do it. She was a treasure trove of scandal.

'I married at eighteen, perhaps too young, although lots of girls marry before they're twenty. I was dazzled by him and I rushed in. In retrospect, I think it was because I was lonely after my father's death. I had no family, no sense of place, except for what Merry had given me. But I was acutely aware of how temporary that might be. I wanted something solid of my own. I wanted to build a family that was mine, something to replace all that I'd missed in my nomadic childhood.'

The parallels to what was happening right now were overwhelming in their symmetry; the death of a close protector spurring her to subconsciously cast about for a replacement. Her father's death had encouraged her towards an early marriage, and now Merry's death was encouraging her towards Ren. She'd always thought of herself as strong and independent, but this pattern indicated otherwise.

She slipped a sideways glance at Ren. He nodded, focused on the outer story itself. 'You felt this man could give you those things?' He was taking it all in with a great deal of calm, she thought. But he didn't see the parallels yet. He didn't understand this story was a form of rejection, full of reasons why she couldn't marry him if for no other reason than to prove to herself she'd learned something from her past and would not repeat those errors.

'All that and more,' she admitted honestly. 'He was comfortably situated. He was older, in his late thirties. He'd been married before. He seemed to know everything about the world. He could make me laugh, he showered me with little gifts. He always had a little treat in his pocket, a ribbon or a bonbon. I worshipped him. He was Prince Charming, so handsome and gallant. Merry encouraged me to wait, to give it more time, but I didn't want to. I was afraid he'd leave and never come back. After two months of courtship, I married him. Merry gave us a lovely wedding in the gardens. Then it all fell apart.'

Very slowly, to be sure. Her new husband had been too smart to show his hand right away.

He'd helped Merry with the plantation, gradually usurping the role she'd held. He'd befriended Sir Arthur Gridley and the other planters in an attempt to be seen as the new face of Sugarland. After all, even nine years ago, Merry had been old. Then he'd tried to formalise that arrangement, pressuring her to get Merry to acknowledge him in the will.

'When that failed, the laughter stopped, the gifts stopped. He became an entirely different creature from the man I thought I knew,' Emma confessed. 'It was clear he'd married me to get to the plantation. It was a far easier route to land-ownership than starting up one of his own.'

'There'd likely been nothing to start from,' Ren put in. 'Gridley once mentioned there's no land for sale on the island.'

Emma nodded. 'It's true. The only way to acquire a plantation of any size is to buy it from someone else. But my husband wasn't interested in buying, only in taking. He thought he could woo Sugarland out of me. Fortunately, Merry was onto him. Unfortunately, too. Once he realised Merry wouldn't acknowledge him, he took his frustrations out on me.'

Those had been dark days. She'd tried to hide the bruises from Merry, but her husband had not been careful, or perhaps he had. He'd wanted his mark to be visible, wanted Merry to be coerced into reconsideration. She could feel Ren bristle beside her, his chivalry on full display. Ren's gentleman's code would not tolerate such treatment. 'Tell me how this story ends, Emma.' His voice was tight.

'Merry ordered him from the house at gunpoint one day. He was a coward at heart. He left. Shortly afterwards, we learned he'd gone to Jamaica and was living openly with a wealthy widow. Some even said he'd married her, but we have no real proof. I didn't care at the time. I was glad he was gone. Forever only lasted three years, and happy-ever-after lasted even less than that.'

'Where is he now?'

'Mouldering in a grave, shot dead by a jealous husband. It seemed the wealthy Jamaican widow wasn't enough for him. He had quite an enterprising career here in the Caribbean.' This was the more embarrassing part to admit. 'It's likely he was married to someone else while he was married to me. I can add bigamy to my list of accomplishments. Not everyone can claim they were a bigamist at eighteen or a widow by twenty-four.'

'You were an unknowing participant. It's hardly your fault—' Ren began.

She cut him off. 'Are you trying to absolve me or yourself? I don't need absolution, Ren. I made a mistake and married a bad man against the advice of those who cared for me. I can't pretend it didn't happen or excuse it. Society certainly won't. They feast on it.'

'He's lucky he's dead,' Ren said. 'If he wasn't, I'd have to shoot him myself. Even though he was gone, he kept you trapped in that marriage for two years after he left.'

'In name only was far better than having him here. But now you see the whole of me. You understand now why it's best I remain alone. I'm ruined and I'll never be anything but trouble to any man.'

Ren ignored the dismissal. 'What was the bastard's name?'

'Thompson Hunt.'

Chapter Twenty-One

He'd known the name before she spoke it. Gridley's last cryptic comment had been solved. Their walk led them in a loop back home. Ren felt as if their talk had led them in a circle, too. He knew so much more, but none of it brought him closer to resolution. He was still back where he started in all senses of the concept.

Emma gave a rueful laugh. 'You're a contrary creature, Ren Dryden. This morning you were talking of leaving, now you're talking of staying and marriage.' Her eyes were sad as she reached up to push an errant strand of hair back behind his ear. 'You only want me because you can't have me.' It was a comfortable, intimate gesture that fired his blood as surely as any erotic touch and it spoke volumes of what this relationship had become, something far more than bed sport, something he did not want to let go of, something he was willing to fight for.

In that singular moment, in that gesture, was the clarity he sought. She wanted him, she wanted what he offered, but she couldn't risk it, not just for herself and the fear of making the same mistake twice, but for him, too. She wouldn't allow him to be dragged down by her past. What woman turned down a countess's coronet? What woman gave up her own happiness in order to protect a man? That was when he knew. She was pushing him away because she loved him.

Emma loved him! Ren captured her hand where it lay against his ear, bringing it to his lips and pressing a kiss against her palm. Elation poured through him. She loved *him*, not his title, just Ren Dryden the man. His decision was made—go or stay, he wasn't letting her get away. When a man had a woman like Emma Ward, he had something worth fighting for.

The hall was unnaturally quiet. There was no one around, no maids polishing the bannister, no one moving in and out of rooms cleaning. 'Where is everyone?'

'They have the day off. It's Crop Over. Everyone has gone into Bridgetown for the celebration.'

A thought struck him. 'Did you want to go? I didn't mean to ruin any plans.' He'd been so excited about the rum still he hadn't stopped to think. 'We could get rooms at the hotel, you could shop.' Bridgetown was only five miles away, but life out here was so entirely consuming it might as well be fifty. If he could get her away, where it was just the two of them without constant reminders of the past, maybe he had a chance. Now that he'd made his mind up, he wanted that chance more than he wanted anything else except Emma herself.

He took her hands and danced her around the hall. 'What do you say?' He gave her a boyish grin. 'You deserve some fun, Emma and maybe we can think of something to celebrate.'

She was laughing, a sign she was starting to crack as he swung her about in a fast country-dance step. 'All right!' she conceded with a breathless gasp. 'I can be ready in half an hour.'

Bridgetown was a city besieged by revels and the atmosphere was contagious. Emma hugged Ren's arm spontaneously as he carefully navigated the gig to the livery off the crowded main street. 'I haven't been to the festival in years!' She twisted around on the seat, trying to take it all in at once. Street vendors filled every available space, calling out their wares, delicious smells peppered the air, there were handmade toys to buy, and street entertainers on stilts dressed in bright colours.

Ren laughed. 'You're going to fall off the seat if you aren't careful! There's plenty of time to see everything.'

They parked the gig and the horse at the livery and went to the hotel to claim rooms for the evening. Most people would be staying with friends or sleeping out in the open. There were plenty of rooms available and Ren insisted on getting two for propriety's sake, but they both knew one bed would be cold. No matter how things ended, Emma wanted whatever she could have. Oh, she knew what Ren *thought* he wanted and she knew what she had to do to protect him from his own chivalry. She hoped she had the courage to do it when the time came. Until then, however, there was no room for sad thoughts. Bridgetown at Crop Over was to be enjoyed, it was a time to be carefree.

Out in the streets, music was everywhere, on every corner; guitars and shak-shaks played as they wandered the bright market. They stopped to buy fishcakes wrapped in plantain leaves and fried dumplings, washing them down with tumblers of falernum. 'These are delicious.' Emma peered into her leaf wrapper, disappointed. 'I've eaten them all.'

'You've devoured them!' Ren laughed and bought her some more. 'This is quite the festival. Have you folks been doing it long?' His hand was at her back, ushering her towards a slightly less populated portion of the market.

'It's Crop Over, or Harvest Home, and we've been doing it since the sixteen hundreds,' Emma explained between bites of fishcakes. 'It's the celebration of the sugar-cane crop being in.'

'I love it, it makes our English fairs looked positively staid.' Ren took the last dumpling out of its wrapper and popped it in her mouth with a smile. 'I saved it for you since you like them so much.'

He spoiled her the rest of the day, dancing with her in the streets, buying her an endless supply of sweets, winning her a pretty green hair ribbon at a knife-tossing game and stealing a kiss when he did, much to the cheers of the crowd gathered around them. By the time they headed back to the hotel several hours later, her stomach was bursting from the food, her feet had started to hurt from all the dancing. She was tired and she was happy.

Best of all, they hadn't run into any of her neighbours. There hadn't been a sign of Devore, or Gridley, or any of the others. Ren was having fun, too, she realised. These efforts were not designed to entertain only her. *This was what it must feel like to be courted*, she thought. *What it must be like to be honestly in love with someone.* Did she dare trust that feeling? Did she dare reach for the happiness Ren offered? She believed she'd felt this way for Thompson Hunt once, too. But that had been blind infatuation. She hadn't known him, hadn't spent time with him the way she had with Ren.

They stepped into the hotel with its wide lobby and made their way up the curve of the staircase, both of them too tired for any more adventures in the streets. The hotel was full of whites, planters who'd come to town for the celebration. But still there was no sign of her neighbours. 'Does Gridley come to town for this?' Ren read her mind as he fitted the key into the door.

'Sometimes. He feels it's a bit beneath him.'

Emma slipped through the door in front of him. Ren followed her in and shut the door behind them, shutting out the noise of the hotel. It was just the two of them. The room was cool and dark, quietly intimate after the exuberance of the streets.

'Ren, this has been the most amazing day...' Emma began, unsure of what she meant to share. The silence was unnerving after a day of noise and sound.

'An amazing day, with an amazing woman.' Ren moved towards her, a finger on her lips. 'Shh, Emma. Just enjoy. We could have many more days like this. Did you think about that today? What it could be like next year with our rum venture underway and no worries? I did, I thought of nothing else.' He kissed her neck and she shivered. His touch could undo her in short order.

'Ren...' She wanted to protest, but could find no arguments. Of course she'd thought about it. It had been there in the back of her mind. This man could be hers if she would give up the fight. That fight had started out as a struggle to resist him, but it had since become a battle to protect him from her, from the scandal she'd bring and the danger. 'It's not a good idea.'

He had her in his arms now, peeling away her clothes with his hands, his mouth at her neck, at her ear, his voice thick with persuasion. 'I'm not him, Emma. I am not Thompson Hunt or Arthur Gridley or any other man who has wronged you. I promise. I will cherish you forever, starting tonight if you'll give me a chance.'

He pushed her dress from her shoulders, stripped away her chemise and undergarments until she stood naked before him, his gaze hot on her, devouring. He'd seen her naked before and in better light than this. But this time was different, this time *he'd* done the undressing. She felt claimed, the act marking her as his. Would he look at her the same way once the scandal started? If only she could be his without destroying him.

Ren's voice was hoarse when he spoke. 'Get on the bed, Emma.'

There was a hint of wickedness to his suggestion and a tremor of anticipation took her as she complied. Ren tugged at her legs, drawing her forward until her legs dangled over the bed, her *derrière* resting on the edge. He knelt between her legs, his hands resting on her thighs. 'When one finds something worth cherishing, one wants to start right away.'

He caught her eye, his intentions becoming clear. Oh, mercy, he meant to…Emma's mouth went dry. Never had she been approached so intimately, cherished so erotically. His breath was warm against her damp curls. Her head fell back on the bed, her legs utterly open to him. There was no point in resisting. She wanted this, wanted him. Neither of which were new revelations, but the intensity of them was.

His tongue flicked over her secret nub and she cried out, again and again as he repeated the delicious caress, each cry louder than the one before as pleasure rose, hope rising with it. Ren would stay for her—was she brave enough to let him? Could she believe in the fairy tale one more time? Her last cries were sobs, her control wouldn't last much longer. Then Ren was whispering to her, calling to her from somewhere within her pleasure, 'Emma, let go.'

She did. It didn't occur until later that if she let go, she might fall forever.

The morning came too soon, although it was more like late morning before Emma managed to rouse. She might have slept longer if her body hadn't subconsciously registered the absence of Ren's beside her. How quickly she'd become used to him, to his presence. She raised up on an elbow and searched the room, finding him by the open doors of the chamber that looked out into a quiet courtyard.

He seemed lost in thought as he gazed into the yard. From below, the sounds of a fountain burbled up. The quiet, the pose of her man, elbows resting on the railing of the small balcony, struck her as a moment out of time, a piece of serenity in this little paradise of theirs. Emma held still, closing her eyes tight to capture the image in her mind. No matter what happened, she'd always see him like this.

'Good morning,' she called from the bed. 'What has you up and about?'

He turned from the railing, a sheet of paper in his hand. 'I went out to get breakfast. There's coffee and rolls.' He gestured to the little table where he'd laid everything out. 'I brought the post, too. The mail packet came in yesterday in time for the celebration.'

'A letter from home?' Emma asked, trying to sound casual.

'From my sister. She wrote to tell me about Benedict DeBreed and their hasty engagement.' A little smile played at the corners of his mouth. 'It seems all's well that ends well. You and Sherard were right.' He folded the letter into squares and tucked it into his pocket. 'She has found happiness in a most unlooked-for place and with an unlooked-for person. I would not have imagined her with Benedict. It appears I was wrong.'

'I'm sure that doesn't happen often,' Emma teased, relieved there wasn't bad news, nothing to take Ren away from her before decisions were made. She wanted those decisions to be made between them and not because external circumstances dictated them. There'd been too much of that already.

'Of course not.' Ren smiled, picking up on her joke. 'After we eat, there's one place I want to stop before we head home.'

That place turned out to be St. Michael's Cathedral with its tall bell tower. If it wasn't the most perfect cathedral, it was understandable. 'It's survived quite a bit.' Emma stepped ahead of Ren into the dim interior. 'There was the hurricane of 1780. It took nine years to rebuild and then there was the hurricane of—'

'1831,' Ren finished for her. 'I wasn't even here for it and I feel like I know that storm personally.'

'It's how we define time in these parts,' Emma

said seriously. 'If I understand my history correctly, London marks time around the Great Fire,
is that not true?'

'Touché.' Ren laughed, putting a hand to his
heart. 'Your arrow has hit its target, my dear.'

'Why did you want to come here? I'm guessing it wasn't to assess the storm damage.' Emma
led him over to a stand of candles. Only a few
were lit. The church was quiet the day after the
festival.

'I don't want to go back.'

The words seared her. She'd not been expecting that. He was leaving now. Of course, the mail
packet was in port. It was just so much sooner
than she'd thought. It wasn't going to be her decision after all, even after everything he'd said.

'Not go back to Sugarland?' she stuttered
through the words, stepping away. What had she
misunderstood about yesterday, about last night?
Just yesterday, he'd been talking about forever
and she'd been the one hoping she'd have the
courage to let him go, but it seemed that courage wouldn't be required. He'd seen reason. He
understood her limitations whatever his fanta-
sies dictated to the contrary. It shouldn't be a
surprise. Earls didn't marry possible bigamists.

Ren gripped her hands, pulling her back towards him. 'I don't want to return to Sugarland and go back to how things were between us before we left. I want to go forward. I want to return knowing how things stand between us.'

In the candlelight, she could see for the first time the signs of strain on his face, how much this was costing him to ask. He wasn't sure of her, of how'd she answer. He might be the bravest man in the world, taking such a risk, sailing his soul into unknown waters. His next words confirmed it. 'I would like to go back to Sugarland knowing that you will be my wife and that we'll build a life together here in Barbados.'

She stared at him, stunned. He wasn't leaving. He was staying *for* her, *with* her, because of her. 'Why?' She barely breathed the word, her eyes never leaving his face.

'Because I love you and I want to stand up with you in this church, in front of God and everyone, and say, "You are my choice. This life is my choice." Will you marry me, Emma? Not because it's good for Sugarland, not because it will subdue Gridley's advances, not because I have money, because I don't, not right now at least. And not because I'm an earl, but because *you* want to, because you love me and I love you and that means something.'

It was to be her decision after all. Her knees threatened to give out. Could she throw caution to the wind? Could she grab a bit of happiness for herself with this man? He'd been brave moments ago, asking for what he wanted, knowing that his future hinged on her answer. He would go or stay on her choice. Now it was her turn to be brave in a far different way than the one she'd imagined yesterday. It required one sort of bravery to send him a way. It would require an entirely different type to let him stay, to let herself be happy. Emma seized her future with two hands and one simple word. 'Yes.'

Ren kissed her then, softly, reverently, on her hands, on her lips. 'You will always be safe with me, I promise.'

Chapter Twenty-Two

The day was promising to be one for the memory books, one of the best of his life. Ren was certain he'd look back in his old age and this day would be among the days that shone. He'd come to Barbados looking for a new life, a fresh start, and he'd found it. It wasn't the way he'd imagined it. His imaginings hadn't predicted a beautiful, headstrong woman waiting for him. Nor had his imaginings figured in the financial and social trials he'd faced. But he had triumphed. The woman dozing against his shoulder was proof enough, prize enough.

Ren mentally ticked off the blessings of the morning. His sister was happy, his friendships with Kitt and Benedict had proven true. His family was safe, although not through the means he'd expected. He was going to marry, not for convenience, but for love and for passion and for partnership, things he'd not thought to have or find when he left England. He was a satisfied man and the day was good indeed.

Two miles from home, Ren saw it; a grey funnel of smoke spiralling up into the sky, odd but not alarming. There were any number of reasons there'd be smoke this time of year. Someone could be burning leftover cane debris or clearing a field for a new crop. At this distance, it wasn't entirely clear the smoke even came from Sugarland, which of course it wouldn't. There was no one there. Workers would be trickling in later today, home from their holiday in Bridgetown. There'd be no real work until tomorrow, no real reason to wake Emma, who dozed against his shoulder.

One mile from home, the grey funnel became blacker, more intense, its location closer to Sugarland, although it was hard to tell with the twists and turns in the road exactly where the smoke was located. But Ren's anxiety grew. He was running out of counter-explanations. The plume was bigger, darker than it had been earlier. He thought he could even see the orange prongs of flames at the base of the funnel.

Beside him, Emma stirred, lifting her head and crinkling her nose. 'What is that smell? It smells like...smoke!' She caught sight the black cloud.

'Something's on fire. It's hard to tell where it's coming from.' Ren hedged, not wanting to panic her without cause.

Emma had no such reservations. She scanned the horizon and her judgement was instant. 'It's *Sugarland*. The estate is on fire! Ren, hurry!'

Ren whipped the horse up to top speed with the gig. He turned into the long drive, urging the sturdy chestnut to greater speeds. Beside him, Emma looked desperately for the source of the fire. 'It's out in the fields somewhere, I can't tell where.' Her voice edged with desperation. 'Gracious, Ren, how did this happen?'

The house came into view, untouched, but smoke was thick in the air, a precursor to impending disaster. Ren slowed the horse and they jumped down, racing through the house to the back veranda where any relief Ren felt at seeing the house safe evaporated into fear. Fire crossed the fields, racing towards them, eating up everything in its path. The flames ran horizontal, stretching the width of the fields, a great orange wall of fire.

Ren's mind was a whirlwind of thought. There was still time, but to do what? They couldn't fight the centre of the fire, just the two of them. If the fire kept on, it would reach the house, it would surround them given time. But perhaps they could flank it from a different location? He did not think they could save the home farm, it would be in the thick of the conflagration. But maybe they could save the still?

'We'll lose everything,' Emma breathed, her face white with panic as her mind registered the consequences of such a fire.

'Not everything.' Ren cast his gaze eastward. What to save? Should they try for the house, which seemed a futile battle, or the still, their source of income? The flames eastward seemed weakest. They could make a stand there, salvage something. There was no time to second-guess his instant analysis. He was running, already on his way to the office, calling instructions over his shoulder, 'Emma, you have two minutes, grab anything from the house you value: blankets, clothes, medicine. Meet me at the gig. We'll make our fight at the still.'

In the office, Ren grabbed a throw from a chair and spread it open on the floor. He opened the glass-fronted cabinet holding the ledgers and important papers and tossed items on to the throw. He flung open desk drawers, grabbing anything that looked official. He heard Emma's feet pounding down the stairs, her voice calling his name. Ren gathered the ends of the throw up into a makeshift pack and hefted his bundle onto his shoulder. He cast one more look around the room. Had he got everything? There was no more time.

Emma was outside, tossing her bundle into the shallow bed of the gig. She scrambled up and he leapt up beside her. They were off, paralleling the line of flames as they raced for the east edge of the property.

His gamble was well founded. The flames weren't as strong, weren't as greedy at this end, the smoke not as thick. The still was thick-walled. It would prove to be flame resistant to some degree, providing safety for them as well if they needed it. There were tools there, too: shovels and buckets, a rainwater barrel and the water for running the mill wheel.

'Do we have a chance?' Emma shielded her yes with a hand, watching the smoke.

'More than a chance. We can do this,' Ren said confidently, hoping to reassure her. It seemed a horrible irony that just two hours ago he'd promised her he'd keep her safe and now there were no guarantees he could keep even a portion of that promise. The best day had become a nightmare.

'We need help. The fire is too big,' Emma argued, but she took a shovel and started helping him dig an impromptu firebreak.

'We can fight for a while on our own and help will come. The workers will see the smoke plume and race to our side.' He hoped. She'd been a fair employer, they would come to her aid. He was counting on it. A ruined Sugarland meant no jobs for them. They had nothing to gain by not helping.

'They're five miles away,' Emma countered, flinging dirt into a pile. They'd passed people on the road, making the slow walk back to their jobs, no one in a hurry to see the holiday end.

'The neighbours are home,' Ren offered, remembering that Gridley and Devore and the others had not gone into town. 'They'll see the smoke.'

'And rejoice,' Emma said sharply, grunting between shovelfuls as a ditch started to take shape five hundred yards in front of the still. 'This is exactly the kind of catastrophe they've been waiting for. Without us to independently sell our sugar outside of their cartel, the cartel can control prices.

Ren leaned on his shovel, her words driving home with sickening reality. 'You think they set the fire? They would go that far?'

Emma met his eyes. 'Gridley would do it. He warned you, warned *us*, didn't he? And this is nothing compared to murder.'

Ren put his back into the shovelling. Emma was right. Aid was unlikely. They were on their own. This firebreak would be all that stood between the still and utter defeat. If the fire jumped the ditch... He didn't want to think about it. He would not fail Emma. But his mind hadn't given up trying to fathom the motives for such destruction. If Gridley had laid the fire, his decision was hard to grasp. It was drastic and counter-intuitive.

'Why would Gridley destroy something he covets?'

'To bring me to my knees,' Emma said simply, but Ren heard the unspoken logic. There was something, *someone*, Gridley coveted more than the estate: Emma. Without income, without an estate, the two things Merry had left to protect her, Emma was exposed. Ren could see Gridley's perverted reasoning. Emma would need him, be reliant on him for everything. But Gridley had forgotten one variable and that was Ren himself. *He* would stand between Emma and Gridley when the estate and the crops failed. He and the rum. He would fight for her just as he was fighting for her right now.

'He would go to such lengths, but I can't believe the others would allow it.' The depravity of the neighbourhood was hard to grasp. It bordered on madness.

'The Caribbean doesn't draw the finest of men. These are self-fashioned gentlemen who checked their morals at the dock and have given themselves airs.' Emma panted her words between shovelfuls.

He'd very much like Emma to be wrong. Ren stepped back from their digging and surveyed the work. It might be enough. 'Clear away any vegetation on our side. We don't want the fire to have anything to cling to if it crosses the ditch. Fires need fuel. If it's starved, it can't burn.'

Ren strode toward the gig and reached under the seat. He drew out the travelling pistol and tossed it to Emma. 'Here, take this. I hope you won't need it. I'll be back.'

'Where are you going? You're leaving me?' Emma cried in angry disbelief.

'I'm going to go scout the fire. I want to see how close it is and what else can be done.' The wind was picking up and it would either help them or hurt them. He hoped for the former, hoped the wind would blow the fire away from the still. If so, they might be able to leave it and make a second stand somewhere else, a chance to save one more thing.

Emma's hand was on his arm. 'I don't like it. Ren, fire is dangerous, wind is dangerous, it can change everything in an instant. Please, don't go. You could be surrounded and there'd be nothing you could do.'

He kissed her then, long and sweet. There was nothing else he could say or do. He couldn't make her any more promises. 'I won't be long. Don't worry, your defences will hold. You'll be safe here.'

'It's not me I'm worried about, you silly man.' She gave him a wry smile and released him. 'Go, then, but hurry and don't be a hero. Sticks and stones aren't worth it.'

The fire was magnificent, a work of art, Arthur Gridley thought as he and Hugh Devore sat on their horses watching Albert Merrimore's estate burn, the fields and the home farm, consumed in flame. From their vantage point, they could see the fire marching towards the main house. It would be a shame to lose that building, but if it stood Emma would never relent. The house couldn't generate income, but Emma was a sentimental fool. She wouldn't see the house as useless, she'd see it as a remainder of her inheritance. 'Dryden's gone for the still,' he told Devore. 'The gig headed in that direction.'

'Inspired, that. Dryden's a smart man. Too bad he didn't side with us,' Devore said, fingering the club he carried at his side. 'It will cost him.'

Gridley had to give Dryden credit there. The man had astutely decided to go for the still instead of the house. Gridley hadn't counted on that. He'd thought Emma would sway him to save the house. That was insightful. Perhaps Dryden carried more influence with her than Gridley had factored. Good to know. Ultimately, that would only help his cause. This was all going very well.

He and Devore had their men lay the charges under the cover of night. That hadn't been the risk. There'd been no one around to see. Everyone had been gone to town. It had been igniting them, the timing, that had contained the risk. That had to be done in the light of day. He wanted Dryden and Emma to see it, to know he'd made good on his warnings. He wanted them to rush towards it. The fire would play to their emotions. Both Dryden and Emma would try to fight it. Everything was going according to plan. They were down there even now, making a stand.

A breeze kicked up, drawing their eyes skyward. Clouds were moving in from the ocean, grey ones, heavy with rain. Well, let the weather come if it must. 'It's time.' He nodded to Devore.

Devore gave a devilish grin. 'I'll track down Dryden, you get the girl.' They kicked their horses into motion. Rain or not, the damage had already been done. Rain couldn't save much of Sugarland, and it wouldn't save Ren Dryden. It was time for phase two.

Emma checked the rain barrel and watched the sky, watched it darken with rain clouds. There was hope in those clouds. But the fire crept closer and the minutes dragged by. Where was Ren? Would he bring good news? Was the fire dying out? Was the house safe? If the house was safe, they might salvage something yet. How had this happened? But she knew how.

She had done this. In her arrogance and in her selfishness, she'd brought down the wrath of Arthur Gridley. She'd not been careful. He'd come for Sugarland and it was only a matter of time before he came for her, his prize. She would have nothing left to resist him with, nothing left to fight with, all her barriers stripped away. Except Ren.

Would he be enough? Would she *allow* him to be enough? There would be yet more danger for him, danger he didn't deserve. He'd come here looking to be a businessman, looking to save his beloved family, and he'd found peril after peril in knowing her. Her brashness this morning seemed ill founded based on the ruin around her. She should set Ren free, send him back to England where he'd be safe whether he willed it or not, whether her heart willed it or not.

Emma turned at the sound of noise behind her, the sound of someone coming. Ren! Her heart leapt even as her hand closed reflexively around the butt of the pistol and the first raindrops fell, flat and wet on her face.

'Emma, come away, this is foolishness! You can't save it.' It wasn't Ren, but Gridley who crashed into the courtyard of the still on his horse, concern pasted on his face. He slid off his horse, one hand on the reins, the other stretched out for her.

Another woman, a frightened woman, would have been fooled. Not Emma. He was here for her as she'd known he would be one way or another, one time or another. The last thing she wanted was to give up her ground and go anywhere with him. She knew in her heart this was to be the final battle. Better to face him on Sugarland ground even if it was burning. She raised her pistol, levelling at his chest. 'Drop the facade, Gridley, I am going nowhere with you.'

'You're not thinking clearly.' Gridley persisted in playing her friend, a role he'd played for months even when they both knew better. He dropped the reins of his horse and stepped forward. 'Put the gun down. Where's Dryden? We need to find him and get all of ourselves to safety. The fire will be here any minute. For the love of Albert Merrimore, come away with me. He would not want you to risk yourself needlessly.'

'You were never his friend! You murdered him in his bed.' Would she have to fire? Would Gridley call her bluff? The rain was coming down harder now, making it difficult to see, to hold the gun steady with slippery fingers. She would have to make her choice soon or it would be too late. Emma gathered her courage.

'I am done with you, Arthur Gridley. No one would think twice finding your body amid the ashes. I will make it clear to everyone you risked yourself to come to our aid. You will be a hero.'

Gridley laughed coldly. 'You won't shoot me. It's not in you, Emma. But gracious, the defiance! You *are* glorious. I've never wanted you as much as I do now with those dark eyes of yours staring at me from behind the barrel of a pistol.'

'I don't think she'll shoot, Gridley,' Hugh Devore called out, edging his horse around the corner, drawing both their attention. 'Not when she sees what I've got.' He shook his head in mock regret, revealing the body slung across the horse's hindquarters. 'Poor Dryden never saw it coming.'

Chapter Twenty-Three

'Ren!' Emma's scream tore the air. She dropped the gun and ran to him, hauling his limp form off the back of the horse with both hands. The weight of him nearly staggered her once she had him down. She got her hands under his arm pits and dragged him away from Devore and Gridley, panting from her efforts. 'What have you done?' The fire, the rain, the mounting wind, all of it ceased to matter. Only Ren mattered.

'What have *we* done? I think that's easy enough to see. We've disarmed you, for starters.' Gridley smiled evilly, stooping down to pick up her discarded pistol. He tossed it to Devore. 'Looks like we've also exposed her weakness, Hugh. Appears she has a *tendre* for our Englishman, after all.' He smirked. 'We did wonder, my dear, if it was just a romp in the sheets or something more. Apparently, it's something more.'

She barely registered the crass commentary. Emma ran her fingers through Ren's thick hair, searching for evidence of Devore's club. She found a bump on the side of his head. Ren groaned as she touched it. Sound was good, it meant he was alive, but in pain. Those bastards! Her anger surged. How dared they hurt him like this? But she knew how they dared and why. *All* of her defences were gone.

Gridley was stalking her like a big cat. He circled her, all pretence of niceness gone. There was nothing to stand between her and Gridley now. There was only her to stand between Gridley and Ren. Devore stood to the side under the eaves out of the rain, an interested spectator. How did she take on both of them? If it had just been Gridley, maybe she would have thought of something. She'd been managing Gridley for years.

The rain was coming down hard now. The fear of the fire reaching them receded, replaced by worry over taking a chill. Ren was soaked. She shivered, cold. She needed to act fast. 'What do you want, Gridley? Name your price.' She might as well cut straight to it. She had to get Ren to a warm bed.

'You know what I want. I want you.' His eyes glinted dangerously as he circled.

'What do I get in return?' Emma held his gaze, matching her footwork to his so that she began to circle with him, both of them moving around Ren's still form.

Gridley cast a disparaging glance at Ren. 'You can have Dryden's life. See him nursed back to health and put him on a boat. That's what you want, isn't it? What else is there to bargain for?'

'There's Sugarland.' Emma dared to push her luck. 'You've destroyed it. You should rebuild it for me.'

'As a wedding gift.' Gridley gave her a mocking bow. 'The place will be ours, after all.'

'It will be Dryden's,' Emma corrected. 'He owns fifty-one per cent and you've already promised me his life.'

'You ask for too much, Emma.' Gridley reached out a boot and kicked Ren in the stomach, laughing when Ren groaned. 'I have let you bargain for your lover. I didn't need to allow that. I could simply have taken you. You can't stop me.' As if to prove it, he lunged for her across their circle.

His sudden movement took her by surprise. She was no match for the weight of him in motion. Emma went down, crying out as Gridley landed on top of her. She struggled, kicking with her feet, jabbing with her knees, her hands. But Gridley was stronger. He got her hands, imprisoning them in his grip. 'Come hold her, Devore.'

'Not man enough for me?' She spat at Gridley, earning her cheek the back of his hand.

'Hellcat!' Gridley's eyes were dark with lust and anger as he straddled her in the mud.

Devore was there, laughing as he took her hands and stretched them over her head. 'You've got a live one, Arthur. Are you sure this is the one you want?'

She kicked out against at Gridley, not giving him a chance to answer. 'What do you get out of this, Devore?'

'I've already got it. Sugar prices will go high and that's all I wanted.'

She'd liked to have spat on him, too. But he was above her head, out of range. 'You disgust me. What sort of man thinks sugar prices are worth watching a woman being raped, a home burned, a man nearly killed?'

'It's hardly rape. He's going to marry you. Consider this your engagement. Besides,' he chuckled malevolently, 'you promised him. I think it's time you started holding up your end of the agreement.'

Gridley reared back, his hand working the

flap of his trousers. 'You did promise, my dear. I've let the Englishman live, but perhaps I should reconsider. A shot to the knee would hurt and it might convince you to keep your word. Do you have her, Hugh?' He rose up slightly, reaching around for his pistol. 'I don't think Dryden will thank you much for a permanent limp.'

'No!' Emma screamed. Gridley was absolutely over the edge of sanity. A leg wound could finish Ren. 'Don't do it, don't.' She sobbed.

Gridley laid the gun down, his attention back on her. 'Don't what, my dear?'

'Don't, *please.*' Emma gritted her teeth. She hated to beg, hated to be helpless. But only helplessness would save Ren.

'And?' Gridley ran a finger down her jaw. Her skin crawled.

'I'll be good,' she said meekly.

'That's more like it, isn't it, Hugh? Now where were we? Ah, yes, I was just about to share intimacies with you and you were going to let me and Devore was going to be my best man and watch.'

Ren pushed up to his hands and knees, his vision a blur, his head pounding. But he could hear perfectly well, enough to know Emma was in danger, that Gridley had her, that she'd bargained herself down to the rudest denominator to save him.

Mud squished between his hands as he inched forward. They were paying no attention to him. Devore and Gridley were far too intent on degrading Emma. He just needed a few more feet and enough strength to launch himself at Gridley. What happened after that hardly mattered as long as he pulled Gridley off her in time.

Emma was sobbing. He tried to hurry. She must be terrified, it was her nightmare come to life, the fear that Gridley would destroy her. Every inch he crawled was agony, his head splintering with the movement. What a terrible job he'd done protecting her.

Devore and Gridley were making crass jokes. Devore's hands were clamped around hers, keeping her still. Ren's vision cleared. He saw Gridley handle himself, his other hand between Emma's legs.

That was when Ren leapt. With a roar, he used the momentum of his body to knock Gridley to the side. He got an arm around Gridley's neck but Gridley wasn't ready to go easily. He wrestled, trying to break the chokehold. Mud covered them both, making any grasp slippery.

Gridley got away once, scrambling through the mud on all fours, but Ren reached out blindly for his ankle and pulled him back down. Gridley yelled for Devore to do something. Ren yelled for Emma to run. He was fuelled by anger, powered by vengeance for Emma, for Merrimore, for Sugarland. He would kill Gridley if he had the chance and damn the consequences.

But Emma wouldn't run. He heard Emma's voice. 'Get away from them!' It took a moment to register her meaning. Out of the corner of his eye, he saw Emma level the pistol at Devore. Ren felt his strength begin to fail, adrenaline notwithstanding. He had to end this soon or Gridley would end him.

A shot rang out and Devore crumpled, grabbing his leg, swearing. The noise was enough for Gridley to disengage, half crawling, half running to Devore's side. Ren staggered to his feet, stumbling to Emma.

Gridley roared, 'You bitch, you've shot him!' He lunged at Emma, but a voice brought him up short.

'Emma didn't shoot him. *I did.* It's about time, too.'

Ren looked beyond Gridley. Kitt Sherard strode forward, water streaming from his hair as he pushed Gridley out of the way with a hard, careless shove. 'I've got another pistol, Ren. Anything you want to shoot?' Kitt handed the butt end of a pistol to him. 'I heard Gridleys are in season.'

'Miss Ward, if I may?' Kitt took the shaking pistol Emma held and trained it on Gridley and Devore, not that Devore was much threat, Ren noted, following suit with the other gun. Kitt's shot had incapacitated him. 'Shall we shoot them now, Ren, and put them out of their misery or should we make them wait for justice?'

'You can't prove anything,' Gridley snarled. 'Your word is nothing, Sherard, not against mine. You're nothing but a pirate fancied up on money.'

'Then perhaps we'll just shoot you,' Ren put in, gesturing with the pistol. He wouldn't mind doing it if it meant he could lie down with Emma and assure himself she was all right.

'You never know what kind of proof might turn up. There was talk in town,' Kitt said slowly. 'If I were you, I'd get on my horse, ride home and consider how lucky I feel: lucky enough to stay and stand trial, or lucky enough to find a boat out of here.'

That did it. Ren watched grimly as Gridley got Devore up on a horse and the two men left, shouting threats and obscenities at Sherard, who just laughed and fired a warning shot over the top of the retreating horses to speed them on their way. After they were gone, Kitt laid down his gun and looked around. 'What a mess. Fire, mud, rain—an absolute tropical disaster.'

Ren was more worried about Emma than the aftermath of the fire and rain. 'Kitt, all this can wait, get us home.' Beside him, Emma swayed on her feet. Ren moved to catch her, sweeping her up in his arms, but unsteady on his own feet. He would have fallen if Kitt hadn't caught his elbow.

Kitt shot him a grim look. 'There's no guarantee there's any home there.'

'Better to find out now.' Ren gave a grunt and hoisted Emma up on to the seat of the gig. He would drive and Kitt would ride beside them. He was not looking forward to the effects the road would have on his head. But he was looking forward even less to extending that journey five miles back into Bridgetown if the house was gone.

'I did bring help,' Kitt told him as they set out. 'I ran into some of the workers on the road and organised them. If the house is still there, there will be assistance.

'Did you really hear rumours in town? How did you know to come?' Talking took Ren's mind off his own pain.

'I went to the hotel, hoping to catch you before you left. I had some papers for you to sign with the quartermaster. The clerk at the desk told me you'd gone. That was when someone in the lobby mentioned in not such nice tones that there was a bit of surprise waiting for you. I set out immediately. By then, the smoke was clearly visible. I knew you were in trouble.'

'I don't know what we would have done without you.' Ren paused. 'I never saw Devore, never heard him. One moment I was surveying the fire, the next moment I was out.' Beside him, Emma's head flopped on to his shoulder. She felt warm. Ren reached a hand out to her forehead. 'Kitt, she's hot.' Anxiety laced his voice. His mind filled with the horrid images. The mud, the rain, that bastard Gridley forcing her down into the mire until she'd been soaked with it. He could do nothing but tuck a blanket more firmly around and get her home, if there was one.

It hadn't seemed that far to the still from the house, but now the drive back seemed interminable. They turned the last corner and Ren held his breath. They needed a miracle right about now. Kitt cantered up ahead. 'Can you see it?' Ren called out.

Kitt turned in the saddle, a smile on his face. 'It's still there. The wind changed in time.'

At the house, Ren insisted on carrying Emma upstairs while Kitt called out orders for two baths. Hattie, Emma's maid, was back as were a handful of the footmen and the cook. Everyone was eager to have something to do in the face of the disaster, especially when there was so much that couldn't be done. One quick glance out windows confirmed just how close the fire had come. Another five hundred yards would have cost them the house.

He laid Emma down on the bed, mud and all. 'Ren,' she murmured. She tried to sit up. 'Ren, the house?'

'We're there now. The house will be all right.' He pushed a hank of wet hair out of her face. 'Lie back and let us take care of you. Hattie's here, I'm here, there's a bath coming.'

'Ren, I'm hot.'

'I'll take care of that, too. A bath will work wonders.' He placed a soft kiss on her forehead as her eyes closed again.

Hattie bustled into the room with towels and

disapproval, shooing him out. 'I'll take care of her from here. It's not right you seeing her without her clothes on and you need a bath, too. Mr Kitt has it all ready for you in your rooms.'

'I'm going to marry her,' Ren protested. He didn't want to leave her, didn't want to make the long trek back to his rooms. The *garçonnière* seemed farther away than ever.

Hattie smiled patiently at him. 'Of course you are. But not today, so off with you. You can see her once you're both cleaned up.'

Ren took one last look at Emma, so pale, so limp on the bed, so unlike her usual self. 'I'll be back. Soon.' He'd have his bath and then he'd move his things into the room across the hall. He was done living in the *garçonnière*.

'Everything will be fine.' Hattie assured him.

When Ren returned, much later than he would have preferred, everything was *not* fine. Emma was asleep, cheeks flushed, skin hot to the touch. There was no doubt of a fever now. Hattie and another maid were bent over her, working busily with cool rags and urging her to sip tea.

'It's willowbark tea. It'll bring the fever down,' Hattie said over her shoulder, barely sparing him a look.

Ren nodded, feeling helpless. 'What can I do?'

'You can keep yourself well,' Hattie said tersely. 'There's going to be plenty that needs doing and Miss Emma can't do it. I don't want her worrying about this place when she needs to be worrying about herself and getting through this.'

As if on cue, Kitt quietly appeared in the doorway. He, too, had cleaned up and was dressed in a spare shirt and trousers of Ren's. 'She's right, Ren. Come with me. There's nothing you can do in here. But there are plenty of ways you can be useful to Emma out here.'

Ren reluctantly had to admit Kitt was right. The best way he could help Emma was to help Sugarland. They used the rest of the daylight to survey the damage. The fields were charred. The home farm would need to be entirely rebuilt, the vegetable gardens lost. Ren pushed a hand through his hair at the end of their tour. The house was intact, the still was safe, but Sugarland was no longer self-sufficient. All their food supplies would have to be brought in from Bridgetown at great expense. There'd be plenty of work, but that meant wages and that meant feeding mouths, more expenses. 'The totals are a bit staggering, a bit alarming.' Ren shook his

head, but there was no question of not rebuild-
ing. He'd simply have to find a way.

Kitt nodded. 'I can advance you funds if you
need it. I have a nice bit set aside.'

'All right. We might need that.' Ren smiled
gratefully at his friend.

'We?' Kitt elbowed him.

'She's going to marry me. I asked her this
morning.' The morning seemed ages ago, full
of sunshine and promise. Now the estate was in
ruins and Emma lay sick upstairs. 'I promised
her she'd be safe with me. That promise didn't
last very long.'

'What happened today wasn't your fault, but
I think you could finish Gridley for good if you
wanted to.'

Ren nodded absently. 'I was thinking the same
thing. This island isn't big enough for the both
of us. Emma and I can't stay if he's here. Emma
would never be safe and I don't think Gridley is
in his right mind.' He cocked his head at Kitt.
'I'd like to put him on trial for arson.'

Kitt grinned. 'I think we could do that and
more. I asked around like you wanted. The magistrate is definitely not in Gridley's pocket. They
had a run-in a few years back. We can get a fair
trial. I can find the man from the hotel. If you

can find anything in Merrimore's papers about Gridley, that would help prove there's motivation.'

'I already have.' Ren told him about the journal. 'There's likely to be more.'

Kitt rocked back on his heels, considering. 'I know you'd like to do this legally, Ren, and we could see it done, but it wouldn't hurt to push Gridley a bit, scare him. I think he'd flee if he feared your righteous anger. Devore might even go with him. The others will not be a problem, those two are the ringleaders.'

There was merit to that. Gridley would not tolerate being ruined and Ren had no qualms about putting the choice, as it were, to Gridley. He would build his case, present it to Gridley and Gridley could decide how he wanted to deal with it. Goodness knew he'd have plenty of time on his hands while he sat beside Emma because he wasn't leaving her tonight. He was going to put her world back together. He'd promised, come hell or high water.

Chapter Twenty-Four

Hell came first. The fever would not abate. It was supposed to be a quick case of getting warm after a chill, but by the next day the fever had grown worse, not better. Willowbark tea and cold rags had little effect. Ren sat with her when she was awake, feeding her spoonful after spoonful of tea and broth, talking about the estate, offering every reassurance that all would be well. But she was listless and said very little.

'You should think about the wedding.' Ren tried a last attempt to engage her. 'What kind of dress do you want? What sort of flowers? We can marry as soon as you're up and about. This time next month, we could be husband and wife.' He wanted that more than anything, more than he wanted to see Sugarland reclaimed from ash, more than he wanted Arthur Gridley to pay for what he'd done. He wanted it with an intensity that surprised even him, which only magnified his frustration over his inability to control the fever.

Emma rolled her head on her pillow, 'No, Ren. You can't marry me, not now.' Her voice was hoarse and tired, but it was the most response he'd had from her in a day, just not the response he was hoping for. 'Gridley will never leave us alone.' The words came out one by one, her throat struggling to work. 'I will not risk you. He will come for you again until he succeeds.'

Ren gripped her hand, so hot, in his own. 'I will take care of Gridley and Devore and the rest if need be. They will no longer define the scope of your happiness.' He was sick of them, sick of what they'd done to her long before he'd arrived.

'Ren, I won't allow it. I release you from your promises.' Her voice was soft now as her energy faded. Her eyes closed and she slipped her hand from his. Her eyes fought their way open one more time. 'Ren.' Her voice was so quiet he barely heard.

He bent close with a smile that betrayed none of his concern. It was almost as if she was vanishing before his eyes. 'What is it, Em?'

'I love you.'

'I love you, too.' He kissed her forehead, unsure if she'd heard him. It occurred to him he had not said the words before, not to her, not to any woman, and he'd not uttered them reflexively in response to her own. Suddenly it mattered very much that she had heard him, that she knew she was the first and only woman who'd claimed that calibre of affection from him. He meant those words to the core of his being.

'Emma?' He shook her by the shoulders gently in an attempt to rouse her. No answer, no response, not even a physical resistance of her body against being shaken. 'Em? Answer me.' *I release you from your promises, I can't allow it, I can't risk you, I love you.* Her words echoed in his mind. She couldn't force him to accept those dictates, couldn't control him. But she could… No. A cold wave of fear swept him, the reality of what she meant to do becoming clear. She meant to set him free by slipping away, simply letting go and letting the fever take her.

'Em, no! You stay with me, do you hear?' Ren was vaguely aware he was yelling. Hattie was in the room, Kitt on her heels. 'We're losing her. We need more rags, more tea, more everything!' Ren roared. His gaze landed on Kitt. 'Get the guns. We're going to Gridley's. This ends today.'

It would all end today one way or another. Emma wouldn't last, wouldn't let herself last unless she had a reason, unless she knew Gridley couldn't hurt them any more.

Ren cast a last glance at Emma. 'We'll be back in a few hours, Hattie. Don't, um, let her go anywhere.'

It took only minutes to be underway, horses thundering down the drive to the main road, he and Kitt armed with a brace of pistols each. To his credit, Kitt didn't ask any questions. Ren wasn't sure he had answers, only that he *knew* Emma's fate lay tied up with Gridley's. He was not going to let her die while Gridley lived. *This* was what Cousin Merrimore had called him here for, to free Emma from Gridley's cycle of evil by whatever methods possible.

They reached Gridley's in record time, pistols out as they took the front steps, their horses left at the ready. Servants fell back at the sight of their weapons out. 'Where's Gridley?' Ren barked, stepping towards a servant he remembered from the dinner party.

The man hesitated. Ren cocked the pistol.

'He's in his office, second door on the left,' the man stammered.

'Nothing buys loyalty like a loaded pistol,' Kitt muttered under his breath.

'Whatever it takes,' Ren responded.

'Remind me never to get on your bad side.'

'Sirs! Sirs!' the man called out to them from behind. 'He's not alone. The others are with him. They're having a meeting.'

Ren shot Kitt a wry glance. 'How's that for gunpoint diplomacy?'

'I'd say Gridley's employees don't like him very much.' Kitt chuckled. 'How do you want to take them?'

'By surprise,' Ren said grimly. Surprise would be their great equaliser. Devore would fight if he could. Devore would be incapacitated from Kitt's wound. He might not even be there. Gridley would fight. The others he wasn't sure about. 'There'll be five, no more than that.' He remembered what Emma had told him. 'They'll be selfish bastards, every last one of them. Perhaps they'll turn on each other in order to save their own hides.'

Kitt nodded. 'I'll get the door and you fly right on in.' With that, Kitt raised one long leg and gave the door a thunderous kick. The door fell in, coming off its hinges with a crash. Ren ran through, his pistol training on Elias Blakely.

Elias was the weakest link, the one most likely to cower before a show of force, especially if that threat was aimed at his personal health. 'Was it you who set the fire?' He knew good and well it wasn't, but if Elias thought he was implicated in any way, he'd go on the defensive.

'No, of course not.' Blakely's body was against the back of his chair as far as he could squeeze it, his palms up as if he could ward off Ren's pistol. 'It was the others, not me. I didn't want anything to do with it.'

'Then you knew of it?' Ren growled, not giving Blakely any quarter. He saw fear register in Blakely's eyes. The man recognised too late his mistake. In an attempt to defend himself, he'd panicked and had implicated himself as an accomplice.

Ren's gun swivelled about the room. 'How about you, Cunningham? Did you set the fire? Blakely says you did, he said "the others". Is "others" you or would you like to rat out your friends as well?'

'That is quite enough!' Gridley roared in outrage. He reached beneath his desk, Ren pivoted, but Kitt was already there, his pistol sighting Gridley.

'Quite enough what?' Ren said coolly. 'Quite enough tattling from your so-called friends? Are you afraid they'll confess it was strictly you and Devore who set the fire, you and Devore who attempted to rape Emma Ward while her plantation burned. You and Devore who planned to kill me if Emma didn't comply with your unholy wishes.' The very words fired his blood, his anger surging. If it had been his pistol on Gridley, the man would have been dead by now.

Cunningham looked repulsed. 'You said no more murders, Arthur. I told you it was too risky.'

Ren moved his gun to Cunningham. 'No more murders? Explain. You have thirty seconds.' He knew what was coming, but a public confession would make Kitt a bona fide witness now, a third party outside of himself and Emma.

Cunningham shot a look at Gridley and looked back at Ren. 'Merrimore. The man was on his way out anyway. He only had a couple of days at most. Gridley thought the will had been changed to grant him ownership of Sugarland. He didn't want to risk the old man changing it back before he passed.'

'You will never be safe here again, Cunningham.' Gridley was positively livid, half rising out of his seat before he remembered Kitt's pistol levelled at his chest.

'Neither will you,' Ren reminded him. 'Emma is ill, ill unto death because of you. If I do one thing for her, it will be to rid this island of you and the others like you. Murder, arson, assault, attempted murder—the list grows long, Gridley, and we have witnesses, too. I am sure the court will deal favourably with those who assist the case.' Ren eyed the other three in the room.

Gridley paled, slowly realising his defences were being eroded. But he wasn't done fighting yet. 'Elias prefers men, the younger the better, don't you, Elias? I don't think you'll like that coming out in a court of law. It would certainly discredit your testimony. And you, Miles.' Miles had yet to say anything, but Gridley was determined to bring them all down. 'You've been wanting to sell your plantation for over a year. I'd say this was a conflict of interest. Perhaps Dryden has offered to buy your place in exchange for a little perjury on the stand.'

'That's not true!' Miles spluttered.

Gridley shrugged. 'Who decides what true is? Even a shadow of doubt would complicate things enough to condemn your testimony. As for you, Cunningham, I'll tell them all you were an accomplice, that you knew everything and you condoned it for the sake of forming the sugar cartel. You'll say anything to save your own hide.'

'Do you want to risk it?' Ren put in, trying hard to keep his senses focused, trying hard not to give in to the anger raging through him. He couldn't afford to let his mind wander, couldn't afford to think about Emma slipping away in a misguided effort to protect him.

'I sure as hell won't sit here and let you shoot me over that little whore of Merrimore's,' Gridley ground out, his eyes lit with a mad light.

'Then leave,' Kitt said. 'I have a boat at your disposal, *all* of your disposals. You have twelve hours to be on it. It will take you anywhere you want to go on the condition you don't come back here. There will be no charges pressed if you go quietly.'

'I wouldn't recommend England, however.' Ren looked each of them in the eyes, seeing them weigh their options. 'I have sent letters to influential friends and family about the nature of your characters. You will not be received.'

'You've ruined us!' Cunningham yelled. Ren

couldn't tell if the comment was directed at himself or at Gridley.

'You've ruined yourselves by targeting an innocent woman and bullying her into compliance. If she dies, I will come after you, wherever you are, and I will not offer second chances then.'

'Shall I start shooting, Ren?' Kitt asked. 'They seem a little hesitant to make their choice. I've already taken out Devore's knee. Perhaps this time I'll shoot for a shoulder. Would you like that, Miles? Or perhaps someone is tired of their testicles.'

Miles cringed. 'I'll go. I was going anyway. But what about the plantation? You can't expect me to give it up, it's all the wealth I have.'

'I do expect it. You were party to evil for personal gain,' Ren said simply. 'Walk out with what you can carry and consider yourself lucky. I won't let the plantation go to waste. I seem to recall being told there wasn't enough land in Barbados for the free peoples to start their own farming. Perhaps now there will be, at least enough to make a beginning.'

'You would not turn this land over to those slaves!' Gridley exclaimed.

'I would. They're free, Gridley, and they have been for two years now, not that anyone in your employ would recognise that. Your treatment is abominable.'

Gridley had been pushed too far. With a mighty lunge, he threw over the desk, sending paperweights and inkwells flying. He leapt for Ren, a knife flashing in his hand. Ren darted to the side, barely missing the slice of the secreted blade. The bastard must have had it up his sleeve. Gridley came at him again. In close quarters, it was hard to get his gun aimed. Ren would have to take the shot anyway. It was Gridley or him and Gridley was a fighting with a fiend's madness.

Gridley ran at him, Ren levelled his gun, a shot firing before he could get one off. Gridley crumpled with a cry, his eyes sightless before he hit the ground. Had he fired anyway? Ren gave his gun a quick check for powder marks, for smoke, but there was nothing. He glanced at Kitt, following Kitt's gaze to Amherst Cunningham.

'I always carry my special friend,' Amherst said calmly, putting the small gun, the type a gambler expecting trouble would carry, back in his coat pocket as if this was an everyday occurrence. 'I'll take the offer of a boat, Sherard. I trust all debts are paid? I'll be at the docks at midnight.'

Ren gave the man a curt nod as he exited the room with a *sangfroid* that sent a chill down Ren's spine, the other two following sullenly. Dash it, Emma had been more right than she'd known when she'd said these men checked in their morals at the dock.

Ren nudged Gridley's still form with the toe of his boot. 'I've asked you for so much already, Kitt. Can you look after things here? I want to get back to Emma, I want her to know it's over.'

It was over. There was only peace, only calm in this place. Emma was floating. It felt good and cool. There was no worrying, no fighting, nothing to fight against. There was nothing at all. It was empty.

That bothered her. Something should be here, surely? A sense of wrongness pricked at the perfection, at the calm. *Ren.* Ren should be here. No, she was giving him up. Why? Her mind was fuzzy. The emptiness became more menacing than peaceful, dragging on her memories, dulling them before she could retrieve them. She was forgetting something very important, something she didn't want to forget.

She struggled to retrieve that memory. That was it…Ren loved her. Ren was going to marry her, but she couldn't…why? Because Gridley would kill him, because Gridley would not rest until she was his. Because she loved Ren too much to have him die for her…so she was going to die for him. Was that what she was doing here in this peaceful place? Was this part of dying?

There was only one flaw to her plan. There would be no Ren, if she died. She'd miss so much: his arms, his touch, the way he kissed her neck, nibbled at her ears, the way he enticed her to wickedness like swimming naked in their underground lake. She'd miss his gentler side, too, the side that walked in the surf and spoke of his father and his family with unmistakable love. She would miss his sense of right. A passionate man, a *good* man, loved her. Not many women could say that. It would be something to take with her to the other side, that and the knowledge that she'd freed him.

'Emma.' Her name. Someone was calling her name. Not just someone, *him*. Ren. 'Emma.' The call came again. She hadn't imagined it. How nice to hear his voice one more time. Strong fingers closed around her hand. She would have his touch once more. It was more than she could have hoped for. She was indeed blessed to have him here at the end.

'Emma!' His voice was more insistent now, less pleasant. His words tore through the quiet peace. 'Emma, Gridley's gone. Dead. Cunningham shot him. He can't hurt you again, can't hurt me again. We are safe. I know what you mean to do, Emma. You don't have to die for me. Come back, my love, it's over.'

Emma curled her fingers around his and began the journey back towards the sound of his voice, back towards the litany of his dreams as he spelled them out for her: a home, children, a family. Things she'd given up on long ago. There might not be something to fight against, but now there was something to fight for and that was so much better.

When her eyes opened, it was to see Ren lying beside her, stretched out on his side, his fingers intertwined with hers. She had known they would be. Her body, her mind, had been aware of his presence long before she could acknowledge it. He was smiling that devastating smile, the one that showed off his dimple, the very one that had nearly undone her the first day they'd met.

'Hello, sleepyhead,' Ren drawled.

'Are you ready?' She smiled drowsily at him.

'Ready for what?' Ren's eyes danced.

'To start our life together.' Now that her decision was made, she didn't want to wait a moment longer to start her happy-ever-after. She understood what Ren had meant the night he'd told her he wanted to cherish her.

'As soon as you can get out of bed.' Ren kissed her gently. She felt tears start behind her eyes. She'd almost given this up, almost given him up.

Emma laughed. 'Out of bed? I thought the best part of forever happened *in* bed?'

'Minx.' Ren laughed with her. His smiled faded. 'Em, don't leave me again, promise? I don't want to be that scared ever.'

She looked down at their hands, locked together, her voice starting to shake with emotion. There was so much she should tell him about how she felt, about how much he meant, but all that came out was, 'Thank you, Ren.' He would know all that was encompassed in those simple words because he knew her body and soul. And he loved her anyway. What more could a girl ask for?

Epilogue

~~~~~~~~~~~~~~~~~~~~~~~~~~

What more could a man ask for? Ren Dryden could think of nothing as he waited for his bride at the altar of St Michael's of All Angels. Kitt Sherard stood beside him, hair pulled back and dressed in a respectable jacket and trousers, not so respectably flirting with the pretty girl in the front row.

The church was full, although there were few people Ren knew personally sitting in the pews. But there were many who knew him at least by reputation. They'd come to his wedding to pay tribute to his efforts and Emma's. Thanks to their efforts, the abandoned plantations had been broken into smaller farms and given to the freedmen who had worked them for the former owners. People who had given up hope of farming their own land had a chance again and those people, black and white, had come to witness his celebration.

The doors at the back of the church opened and Ren's eyes were riveted on the sight of Emma coming down the aisle. The sunlight behind her shone on the filmy gauze of her veil and caught the seed pearls trimming her dress. She'd opted to wear white, an extravagant colour choice and hardly practical, but she'd insisted. White symbolised a new beginning, a slate wiped clean and no one knew the importance of that more than she.

Ren didn't care. She'd look beautiful in any colour. As it was, the effect was striking against the foil of her dark hair. Every step she took brought his future closer to him, a future he'd only dared to dream about. When she was close enough, Ren reached out a hand for her, drawing her close and lifting her veil. He mouthed the words, 'I love you', and watched her eyes sparkle with tears.

The ceremony started. There were prayers and hymns, vows and rings, official and meaningful in their own way, a public pledge that mirrored the private one he and Emma had made earlier in front of the witness that mattered most. They'd come early and walked in the churchyard, taking time to visit Cousin Merrimore's grave and leave a flower offering, feeling the old man's presence wash over them in blessing as they stood before his headstone, hands entwined in silence as they were now.

The bishop was nearly done. Only one last instruction remained. 'Ah,' Ren whispered as he bent to carry out the bridal kiss. 'The Caribbean, land of risk, rum and most unexpectedly, romance.'

Emma smiled up at him, her eyes sparkling. 'Especially the romance.'

* * * * *

MILLS & BOON®

Why shop at millsandboon.co.uk?

Each year, thousands of romance readers find their perfect read at millsandboon.co.uk. That's because we're passionate about bringing you the very best romantic fiction. Here are some of the advantages of shopping at www.millsandboon.co.uk:

* **Get new books first**—you'll be able to buy your favourite books one month before they hit the shops

* **Get exclusive discounts**—you'll also be able to buy our specially created monthly collections, with up to 50% off the RRP

* **Find your favourite authors**—latest news, interviews and new releases for all your favourite authors and series on our website, plus ideas for what to try next

* **Join in**—once you've bought your favourite books, don't forget to register with us to rate, review and join in the discussions

Visit **www.millsandboon.co.uk**
for all this and more today!